KU-020-278

THE STAINLESS STEEL RAT JOINS THE CIRCUS

CANCELLED

Also by Harry Harrison
in Victor Gollancz/Millennium

The Stainless Steel Rat
The Stainless Steel Rat's Revenge
The Stainless Steel Rat Goes to Hell

Bill the Galactic Hero
Bill the Galactic Hero on the Planet of Robot Slaves
Bill the Galactic Hero on the Planet of Bottled Brains
(with Robert Sheckley)
Bill the Galactic Hero on the Planet of Tasteless Pleasure
(with David Bischoff)
Bill the Galactic Hero on the Planet of Zombie Vampires
(with Jack C. Haldeman II)
Bill the Galactic Hero on the Planet of the Hippies From Hell
(with David Bischoff)
Bill the Galactic Hero: The Final Incoherent Adventure
(with David Harris)

HARRY HARRISON

THE STAINLESS STEEL RAT JOINS THE CIRCUS

WEST LOTHIAN
COUNCIL
LIBRARY SERVICES

VICTOR GOLLANCZ
LONDON

Copyright © Harry Harrison 1999
All rights reserved

The right of Harry Harrison to be identified as
the author of this work has been
asserted by him in accordance with the
Copyright, Designs and Patents Act 1988.

First published in Great Britain in 1999 by
Victor Gollancz
An imprint of Orion Books Ltd
Orion House, 5 Upper St Martin's Lane, London WC2H 9EA

To receive information on the Millennium list, e-mail us at:
smy@orionbooks.co.uk

A CIP catalogue record for this book is available
from the British Library

ISBN 0 575 68663

Printed and bound in Great Britain by
Clays Ltd, St Ives plc

THE STAINLESS STEEL RAT JOINS THE CIRCUS

CHAPTER 1

"I'M EXHAUSTED," ANGELINA SAID. "ALL this hammering away on a hot computer keyboard."

"Productive hammering, my love," I said, pushing away my own keyboard, yawning and stretching until my joints cracked. "In a little under two hours we have made more than two hundred thousand credits through insider dealing in the stock exchange. Some might believe it illegal—but very profitable. I prefer to see it as a public service. To keep the money circulating, to lower the level of unemployment . . ."

"Not now, Jim. I am too tired to listen."

"But not too tired to listen to this. Right now we need a complete change. What do you say to a picnic in a leafy dell in Sharwood Forest? With champagne."

"A lovely idea, but the shopping . . ."

"Has been already done. I have a complete picnic, basket and all, in the stasis freezer. Everything from caviar to Roc's eggs. We have but to sling it into the hoverfloat, along with plenty of bubbly drink, and let joy begin."

And so it did. While Angelina slipped into something picnicky, I slipped the picnic hamper into the hoverfloat—humming happily as I did so for we had been working too hard of late. We must escape the daily grind. A change of scenery. In the nearby forest, which was one of the few green spots on the painfully boring planet of Usti nad Labam. The landscape was all dark satanic techno-factories run by computer nerds. It was a pleasure to rob them. Using the most advanced hacking techniques I had slipped some software into the operating system of a prominent broker. With this I could slow their input of information by varying lengths of time. With this advance knowledge I could buy before a price rise—then sell at the higher price. Neat.

A favor to them really, because when the scam was eventually discovered, I truly believe that the resultant news stories and jolly police chases would give them something to think about for a change. Instead of the incessant RAM, ROM, PROM. In our own way Angelina and I were benefactors, bringing joy into otherwise boring lives. The price was a small one for them. Infinitesimal. Angelina joined me and we were up, up and away.

The engine roared forcefully, the air rushed by swiftly, and we held hands compassionately as our transport of delight soared skyward.

"Wonderful," Angelina breathed.

"Merda," I growled as a police warning bleeped and blinked on the console. There it was—a police cruiser swooping towards us. I stamped hard on the power.

"Please don't," Angelina said, placing a gentle hand on my arm. "Let us not spoil the day with a sizzling chase. Could we just stop, smile at the police? Not you, me. All you have to do is pay the fine. I will charm the police, you pay their fine, and we will then go on."

It made sense. There was no point in spoiling our day out before it really started. I sighed dramatically and, with great reluctance, eased off.

Our speed dropped.

The police cruiser fired its nose guns at us.

Things happened very quickly after that.

I hit overdrive and pulled back hard into an inside loop.

The police missed: I didn't. I blew the cruiser's tail off. Then I banked hard to avoid the hosing slugs from his wingman. As the police vehicle swooped by I saw that it had no windows. Therefore no occupants.

"Robot policemen!" I chortled. "Therefore we don't have to hold back and spare their lives. Because they have no lives! To the junkyard with the lot!"

After that it was Old Home Week in the diGriz partnership. I climbed—then did a 5G dive to get away from the flock of police cruisers that had appeared all too suddenly. Hit the reverse drive when they were all on my tail. Angelina worked the armament and defenses as they zipped by and managed to get three of them. Even on the most peaceful planet I go not unarmed into the sky; our peaceful hoverfloat was a lot more deadly than it looked.

But this chase was beginning to turn nasty. We were vastly outnumbered and outgunned. "And running out of ammo," Angelina said, echoing my own thoughts.

"Change of venue!" I shouted, dropping towards the green forest below. "Grab the survival kit and get ready for a bumpy landing."

I screeched low over a rock-tipped ridge, dived into the valley beyond—and braked to a hover under the trees below. Angelina had the door open as we juddered to a stop, the kit thrown out, and was diving right out behind it when I hit the two-second-delay button. I was cutting it a little too close: the doorframe hit my bootheel as I went out. I changed the dive into a roll, hit the ground hard on my shoulders and thudded to a stop, all of the air knocked out of me.

"My hero," my dear wife said, patting my cheek and kissing my forehead. "Now let's move it."

We did. Grabbing up the kit, she gracefully, and I haltingly, dived into the protection of the shrubbery.

Meanwhile above the trees the battle roared as our faithful hoverfloat defended itself with all the robotic skill at its command. Alas, the fracas ended suddenly with a tremendous explosion.

"End of champagne and caviar," Angelina said, her voice so cold I felt my body temperature drop.

"I'll not contribute to the Policeman's Ball this year." I grimaced.

She laughed warmly and squeezed my hand. And the old, cold deadly Angelina slipped away.

"Let's make tracks," I said. "Before they discover that they were fighting the robot pilot."

"Let us not," she said. "This is a nice big tree that we are under. It will shield us from visual observation, perhaps infrared imaging as well. If they suspect that we were not in the hoverfloat they could backtrack and look for us."

"Your logic is impeccable," I said, rooting through the survival kit. Guns, grenades, all the necessities of life. "And to carry that logic a bit further—why were the police trying to shoot us up?"

"I haven't the foggiest. As far as the authorities know we are simple tourists who dabble in the market. Sometimes losing . . ."

"Most times winning!"

"What do you have there?" she asked as I pulled a silver form out from behind a belt of ammunition.

"Jolly Barman Instant Cocktails. I bought a couple of these on sale." I pulled the tab and two plastic beakers dropped into my hand. There was a hissing sound and the can turned cold in my hand; moisture condensed on it. I handed Angelina a beaker, poured it full of sparkling liquid. The gray scraps in the bottoms of the mugs were instantly reconstituted by the liquid to pieces of fruit. I poured another drink for myself and we sipped appreciatively.

"Not too bad." I smacked my lips and cudgeled my brain. "Those police were out to blast us—not arrest us. Are we missing something?"

"Obviously. I think that we should get out of the forest now and see what we can find out about this mystery attack."

"We can't exactly call the police and ask them why they were gunning for us—can we?"

"We can't. Therefore I will think of something more subtle. Call our son James and have him do a computer search of our problem. After all—he is in the computer business here and should know how to get information."

"An excellent idea. We can also have him come pick us up since it is a long walk home."

We finished the drinks and I shouldered the survival kit. There was no sound of aircraft now, just some distant birdcalls and the hum of insects. We moved through the trees, staying undercover, distancing ourselves from the action with the police fleet. We listened closely but there was no sound of any engines behind or above us. I smiled. Then I frowned when I heard the grumble of a motor up ahead.

"Perhaps that is a sturdy forester, practicing his weald-wise trade," I said hopefully.

"Would that it were. Because whatever it is out there is coming closer. If they are looking for us, then I am forced to believe that all of this activity and attention is far too murderous for a simple traffic bust."

"Unhappily, I agree. They have made no attempt to communicate with us—just came in blasting."

I looked on gloomily as she opened the survival kit and took out an immense handgun. "But let us not make it easy for them."

We didn't. The armored police cruiser had its tracks blow off as it appeared. It kept firing at us even though it couldn't move. We dived in close, so close it could not depress its guns to get at us. I jumped to the top of the tread, flipped open the top hatch and dropped a couple of sleep capsules. Then I looked carefully inside.

"Highly interesting." I rejoined Angelina on the ground. "Nobody home. Which means, like the cruisers that chased us, this thing is also robot operated and remotely controlled."

"By whom?"

"By our new enemies, whoever they are."

Distant engines sounded from behind the trees and we slipped away in the opposite direction, deeper into the forest. Which did not do much good in the end because there were now sounds of machines from ahead.

"They have trackers on us—so there is no point in wearying ourselves by running about. We'll stay here and make a stand. Get as many of these robot machines as we can."

"I thought that there were laws of robotics—about not killing or injuring humans."

"It looks like those laws were repealed. Lock and load—here they come again!"

I would have felt a certain compunction about killing a policeman, but I really did enjoy blasting police robots into tiny bits of junk. But it proved to be a no-win battle. Wherever we turned they were there ahead of us. Our ammunition dwindled as their numbers increased.

"My last grenade," Angelina said as she blasted a hovertank.

"My last shot," I said, taking out a robocycle. "It has been nice knowing you."

"Nonsense, Jim. You are not giving up, you never do, never will."

"You know that—but they don't." I stepped out into the clearing and waved my handkerchief, raised my palms in the air as I faced the circle of robot police. "Peace, pax, surrender. OK?"

"No OK," an armored robot said. It had sergeant's stripes welded to its arm, and a sneering tone to its metallic voice.

It raised a glowing muzzled flamethrower.

I blew it away with a shot from my crotch cannon.

Was this the end? Were we to be ground into the soil of this sordid planet at the galaxy's edge?

The tanks and robots and all the other military gear surrounded us, rumbled forward, weapons quivering with metallic malice. Angelina had her hand in mine. I contemplated one last attack, throwing myself onto our attackers in the vain hope that she might escape. Then, even as I tensed my muscles for a suicidal attack, a voice sounded out from among the trees.

"You really are very good," the dapper man said condescendingly as he stepped into the glade. Full evening dress, black cloak held by a diamond brooch, diamond-capped cane. This was too much. I heard a primitive, unsummoned growl grumble from the back of my throat as I fired what really was the very last shot from my crotch cannon.

It exploded with a glare of flame, a blast of noise.

Just in front of him. Spending all of its energy harmlessly against the force screen emanating from his walking stick.

"Temper, temper," he breathed, covering a yawn with the back of his hand. He waved the ebony cane in a slight arc and all of the weaponry grumbled back into the forest and vanished from sight.

"You are not the police," Angelina said.

"Anything but, Mrs. diGriz. Those were my minions who took you on. My employees, so to speak. Their ranks are now well decimated I must add."

"Tough," I said. "Call your insurance company. Remember—you started it."

"I did indeed, and am well satisfied by the outcome. I have heard from many sources that you were the best man—and best lady of course—in your chosen profession. I found that hard to believe. But now I do. Most impressive. So impressive that I am prepared to offer you a little assignment."

"I am not for hire. Who are you?"

"Oh, I think you are. Imperetrix Von Kaiser-Czarski. You may call me Kaizi."

"Good-by, Kaizi," I sneered, taking Angelina's hand and turning away.

"One million credits a day. Plus expenses."

"Two million," I said, turning back, all sneering spent.

"Done. We will both sign this." A gold-embellished contract on finest vellum unrolled from his walking stick and he passed it over to me. Angelina leaned over my shoulder and we read it together.

"Any problems?" Kaizi asked.

"None," I answered. "We undertake to undertake an assignment at the agreed fee, payment to be deposited daily to my account. Fine. But what is it that you want us to do?"

Kaizi sighed and touched his stick again. It opened up into a comfortable-looking folding seat and he settled into it.

"To begin with, you must realize my position, understand exactly who I am. You have never heard of me because I prefer it that way. If only to avoid the people with their hands out, eagerly seeking some of my money. I am, to put it simply, the richest man in the galaxy." He smiled slightly as he spoke. Undoubtedly thinking of all the money he had.

"I am probably the oldest man as well. The last time I worked out the figures, I think it was forty thousand years, give or take a millennium or two. As I am sure you realize, one's memory begins to glitch a bit as the centuries roll by. I was a scientist, rather I *think* that I was a scientist. Or perhaps I hired a scientist. In any case I developed the first longevity drug. That much I am sure of. Which I, of course, kept to myself. And have been improving it ever since. How old do you think I look?"

He raised his chin and turned his head. No wattles there. No wrinkles about his eyes, no touch of gray to his temple.

"Forty, I would say," Angelina said.

"Centuries?"

"Years."

"You are very kind. Well, as the millennia rolled by I amassed more money, more property. I could have easily assured my fortune by simply investing and letting the compound interest roll in. But that would have been very boring, and boredom is what I loathe the most. I have always sought excitement to lessen the burden of my years. In the process of growing rich I have bought, and now own, entire star systems. To add diversity to my portfolio I am presently in the process of acquiring a spiral galaxy; one never knows when one might need one. There are some black holes among my recent acquisitions. But I think I shall divest myself of them. Boring. Seen one black hole and you have seen them all.''

He took the kerchief from his breast pocket, touched it lightly to his lips, returned it. One atom short of a molecule, I thought. I caught Angelina's eye and saw that she thought the same.

''But now I have a very troublesome problem that needs to be solved. I look for your aid in that quest.''

''Three million a day,'' I said promptly, avarice beating down suspicion.

''Done,'' he said, stifling a yawn at the same time. ''My problem is that I am systematically being robbed. Someone—or some group—has been getting into my bank accounts. Right across the galaxy. Clearing them out. And if it so happens that I happen to own the bank—The Widows and Orphans 1st Interstellar Bank—why then the entire branch of the bank is cleaned out as well. This makes for bad customer relationships. From millions of clients with their billions of credits. As you might understand this is quite embarrassing for one in my position. You, gentleman Jim diGriz, must utilize all of your stainless steel talents to stop these thefts and to discover who is perpetrating them.

As I opened my mouth to speak he raised his cane and sighed. ''Yes, I know, don't bother to say it, four million a day and let us leave it there. I find business so boring.''

''You will have to give me complete details of all the previous thefts,'' I said. ''And a list of banks where you have accounts, as well as banks that you own.''

''That has already been done. You will find all of the information in your computer's memory banks.''

''You are pretty sure of yourself.''

''I am.''

''And you work pretty fast.''

''I have to—and at the price I am paying you, why you

better do so as well. I want results yesterday. However I will settle for information instantly. Might I offer you a lift—so you can get right to work?"

"You will have to," Angelina said coldly. "After what you did to our hoverfloat. And our picnic basket."

"The value of your craft has already been credited to your highly secret, known to no one, account in the Banco di Napoli. And as some recompense for hardship I do hope that you will be my guests at dinner tonight at the Earthlight Room. Just tell the maître d' to bill Kaizi's account. You will dine as you have never dined before."

A black and silent HoverRolls dropped down into the clearing: the door opened.

"After you, Mrs. diGriz. Or, might I be so bold, Angelina?"

"Buster," she said, swaying ever so gracefully up the stairs, "for what you are paying my husband you can call me anything you want."

CHAPTER 2

SO FAR KAIZI HAD KEPT his word. The promised money had been deposited to my account in the Banco di Napoli. Despite the fact that I was sure that this cache of money was unknown to anyone. Kaizi must really know about banks and banking. This could not be ignored. I made a mental note to find a new and more secure bank now that Kaizi knew about this one. And an even newer and more secure way of transferring all my funds from my present bank. I was sure that if Kaizi knew how to put credits into my account—he might very well be able to siphon them out as well.

I shuddered when I turned on my computer. There was so much information about Kaizi's banks and bank accounts jammed into the machine's memory that bits and bytes were falling out of the memory banks; pixels were dropping off the screen.

"You will need lots more computer memory than you have now," Angelina said, frowning at the electronic debris.

"I feel that I need lots more computer as well. Since we will be accessing far more data than this. Don't I recall our good son James telling me far more about supercomputers he was designing than I really cared to know?"

"I'm surprised that you remember that much. You fell sound asleep."

"Food and drink no doubt responsible for that."

"I doubt it. You mumbled something about concepts the mind cannot stomach as you dozed off."

"I apologize! I'll eat humble pie! But, yes, you are right. I clearly remember passing through a computer-enthusiast phase in my mouth. But those days are long gone. All I want to know now about computer hardware now is where the switch is that turns the thing on."

"James will take care of our computer problems," she said with the firm knowledge of our son's talent that only a mother could have.

But she was right. If it had not been for the hard work of James, and his twin brother Bolivar, our recent adventures in parallel-galaxy trotting could very well have ended in disaster. When Angelina had gone to Heaven it had been my turn to go to Hell. Or something very much like it. It took us a long time to sort out our time and space difficulties with a multicharactered individual who was causing immense problems in a number of places. We could never have been able to do it without the boys' help. But, unlike the failures that we occasionally experience when we clash with the evils of the universe, this time all had ended very well indeed. In fact the whole affair had been consummated in matrimonial bliss. The twins had both been in love with the same woman, Sybil, the top agent in the Special Corps. As intelligent as she was beautiful, she had made the fatal decision that had turned the possibility of sibling rivalry into the enduring knot of marriage. Double marriage that is.

One of the more interesting side effects of Professor Coypu's universe-hopping machine was the doubling of one of its passage portals. That is if one person went through it, he or she came back doubled. Two people that really were the same person, or had been the same person. A bit confusing to understand, but very effective if two men were in love with the same woman—and she loved them both as well. Firm of mind, Sybil had passed through the portal and Sybil and Sybill had turned. They had tossed a coin to see who got the extra *l*. This had all ended in a very festive marriage indeed. We were most happy to see Sybil joyously married to James, while Sybill was happily ensconced in Bolivar's arms. It had been a very neat solution to what could have been a rather serious problem.

''We must talk to James,'' Angelina said. ''Have him sort this computer problem out.''

''We must indeed,'' I said, reaching for the phone.

It was not pure chance that had brought us to this dreary planet. When James had discovered that Sybil shared his passion for nanotechnology, they had moved here to utilize all of the planet's technological know-how. We had reports, from time to time, about their progress. Everything seemed to be working as planned and the money, instead of flowing out steadily, had begun to trickle in.

So it seemed almost natural to consider Usti nad Labam when we were looking for a site for our money-raising operation.

''It would be quite logical,'' Angelina had said, ''to visit the newlyweds at the same time as we begin our new financial operation. There seems to be a good deal of money in circulation on this planet.''

''And little else,'' I had said, flipping through the sales brochure churned out by the planet's tourist board. ''A very dull planet if you read between the lines. Holiday camps where gambling is not allowed. At least drink isn't banned—but I am sure that they are thinking about it.''

''Jim diGriz—you are beginning to sound like an old grouch. We are going there to visit our son and daughter-in-law. And we will make a lot of money. And leave if it is as boring as you think and blast off to a planet of pleasure.''

So we had gone. And it was nowhere near as bad as I had thought. Since gambling was illegal, there proved to be a good bit of clandestine gambling. I had studied magic since I was a stripling and had been a pretty fair cardician, as the professionals call it. That is someone who specializes in card manipulation. Very handy on stage—and equally useful in playing poker. When the stock market became boring I joined some payday card games and always managed to win more than I lost.

Angelina had greatly enjoyed, as did I, visiting James and his wife. This was always an excuse for a party and my gambling proceeds turned into joyful celebrations at the best restaurants.

As good as this was, the rest of this world left a lot to be desired. The planet must have evolved from a supernova because the ground was rich in heavy metals for doping computer chips. Not to mention vast fields of the purest silicon for making the chips themselves. The computer manufacturers had thronged to Silicon Gulch. Followed by the software nerds and all the other people who lived off technological industry.

We had come for a quick visit, then stayed on when we discovered that the local and badly organized stock exchange could be a cash cow. Perhaps we had stayed too long. Kaizi's arrival had raised our morale—and the promise that it would lead to our exodus from this none too attractive world.

"I'm going to call them now," Angelina said, and called out the number to our telephone.

"I am connecting you now," the phone said. It was as good as its word and a moment later I could hear the phone ringing at the other end.

"Nanotechtrics, how may I help you?" the computer-generated smarmy voice said.

"I want to talk to the boss," I called out.

"Whom shall I tell her is calling?"

"Good girl," Angelina said, always an enthusiast for female equality.

"Not her, him, James, his father . . ."

"Grrrk," the computer said as it was interrupted. *"Good to hear from you, Dad. Long time no talk."*

"Too long. All work and no play. But work first. I need a supercomputer for some research we are undertaking, one that's not as big as a house and needs an electric cable as thick as your arm to supply the juice."

"*You have just described our Nanotechtric-68X. I'll get one to you at once.*"

"Everlasting thanks," I said and disconnected. The door-annunciator bleeped.

"I'll get it," Angelina said, then—"James, what a pleasant surprise, come in."

When my son says *at once* he really means it. "When you phoned I was in my chopper—and I had a 68X with me. I was just a hop away."

He brought in a battered leather suitcase, set it down and then it was kisses and handshakes all around. I eyed the suitcase suspiciously.

"Planning a trip?" I asked.

"Our latest model, the 68X." He swung it up onto the table and pressed the latch. A screen flipped up and the keyboard popped out. I looked at it dubiously and he laughed. "This is just about our first working model. We breadboarded it to fit into this old suitcase. Streamlining and whizbang décor will all come later. For field testing this can't be beat." He patted it affectionately. "It works in a massively parallel mode. It uses distributive resources that reach out to memory spread across high-speed networks, which makes its speed not only unmeasurable—but even hard to just estimate. Its high-end massively parallel systems are really in the several teraflop range."

My eyes crossed: he had lost me. "Teraflop? Fall to earth?"

"Not quite. One teraflop equals exactly one trillion floating-point calculations per second. So you can see that this little baby is really in the big league. One thing that helps as well is the fact that all the memory is nanobased. We have invented and patented a molecular nanomemory where rows of molecules are flipped one way or the other to record data. I will demonstrate. Do you have a database I can copy?''

''Far too much in one of them. In the computer, filed under KAIZI.''

He hummed to himself as he connected the two computers and hit a button. There was a quick crackling sound and the hairs on the back of my neck lifted up. James peered at the screen and smiled.

''Done,'' he said. ''And less than one-hundredth of one percent of the memory in this computer has been used. Now what do you want done with it?''

I told him about our encounter in the forest and Kaizi's problems. He nodded understandingly and his fingers skipped over the keys. He smiled when I mentioned the daily transfer to my bank account, shook his head when I mentioned how easily my employer had found this same account.

''We will have to do something about that. Find a secure place for your hard-earned income.'' He leaned back and cracked his knuckles while the screen before him flared and crackled. ''I've started a search program, really a lot of search programs running at the same time in a neural network. But—zowie!— we sure have a lot of material to search for. What I have done is I have tapped into the interstellar web. We are now recording every detail of every occurrence of any kind, in any city where a robbery took place. All of the details of activity before and after the time that one of the banks was robbed. Then comparisons of all the data will be made. Such as, let us say, a spacer with the same name left every one of these cities exactly one day after each of the robberies . . .''

''We have them! Find that spacer and we find the thieves!''

''Easier said than done. And that was just an imaginary example. I think the real tracks are going be a lot harder to find. But let us get all the facts first, then try to relate them. I'll leave the program running since it will take some time to produce any results. In the meantime why don't you open a bottle of champers so we can celebrate your new job—and the first real test of my 68X."

Even as he spoke Angelina brought a tray with bottle and glasses and we drank the toast. A moment later Sybil arrived, which made the party all the merrier. But James was still working while he sipped.

"Dad," he asked, "what do you know about banks?"

"That is where the money is!" I said happily.

"I mean more than that. What do you know about fiduciary bonds, roll-over percentages, PEPS, short-term interest-bearing investments, treasury bills and bank certificates of deposit?"

"Happily nothing. It is the money in the hand that counts."

"Agreed. But since we have been running our own business I have dipped my toe into the golden water of finance and find it most lucrative. But I am a mere amateur. We will need someone with expert knowledge of the banking system if we stand any chance at all of finding the perpetrators of this crime."

"I think that Bolivar is the right man for the job," Sybil said, for she had been listening to us when Angelina had gone for a fresh bottle of bubbly. My eyebrows raised.

"But he is out among the stars," I reminded her. "Indulging in his profound enthusiasm for lunar geology. And giving him all aid in his projects is Sybill who, I understand, shares his enthusiasm for life on the frontier."

"She does, but a little of it goes a long way. We have stayed in close touch and I can sense her feelings, since they are the same as mine. She has not said so in that many words, but living in a space suit for days on end does not do much for one's hairdo. Not to mention personal hygiene. We have been talking of alternative possibilities that might necessitate a little break from the joys of airlessness and free fall. She, as I do, of course, has a keen interest in art history, archaeology, and, interestingly enough, the banking profession. Between working spells as an agent for the Special Corps I have always indulged myself in a fiduciary hobby. Some investing here, a little bit of takeover bidding and asset stripping there. Just for fun, as you might imagine. But my bank balance is a pretty solid one. Such a coincidence, your new interest in the banking profession.''

''I have always been interested,'' I said humbly. She laughed.

''I don't have quite the *same* interest. I mean, after all, if no one made deposits how could you make all of those withdrawals that you specialize in?''

''Point made—I stand corrected.''

''Perhaps it is more than a coincidence, and coming events cast their shadow before them. But the very last time that Sybill and I talked it was about how much she misses the old give and take of the stock exchange. And—dare I say it?—a life that at times is more attractive than lunar exploration. If only for a short while. I am sure that if Bolivar thought about it, that he would enjoy the joys of banking as well. And I know that Sybill would be more than happy to help him with her specialized knowledge.''

''But are you sure that he will like it?'' I asked.

''Of course he will,'' Sybil and Angelina said at the same time. I am sure that Sybill was in agreement as well. Yes, of course he would. At three to one odds he didn't stand a chance otherwise.

''I will arrange it,'' Sybil said. ''There is a branch of the Banco Cuerpo Especial on a very hospitable planet called Elysium. It is a little known fact that this bank is owned, run and operated by the Special Corps. If we are all in agreement we could shake the dust of Usti nad Labam from our shoes and go there. It will be a real family reunion. The computer search will continue and I will help Sybill with Bolivar's new career.''

''Poor man,'' James said, then raised his glass to shield himself from the sizzling glances aimed his way.

When we finally contacted Bolivar and Sybill with a conference telepresence call he looked gloomier and gloomier at his unavoidable fate. He could only wriggle on the hook.

"I'm getting real close to a breakthrough on gravimetric tectonics and photon interaction."

"Sounds fascinating," Angelina said. "You must tell us all about it when we get together on Elysium."

"It won't take too long because you should pick up everything you need to know about banking in a few weeks," Sybill said, obviously feeling some pity for her husband. "And don't forget that banks are where the money is."

"True," he said, looking more cheerful. "I will need a good bit more financing to finish my research." And cheerfuller still. "It's been a long time since we were all together. Some fun in the sun!"

"And food that's not dehydrated," Sybill said, adding a grace note of enthusiasm. "We will have a ball."

And thus did my first day of honest employment end. When I awoke next morning I discovered that my Angelina had been up long before me, travel plans had been made, tickets booked, bags packed, computer fully charged, the cab at the door. I checked to see that Kaizi's daily deposit had been made—and we were on our way.

We had a good time, I must admit a very good time. Sybil and Sybill were so happy to be reunited that we all basked in the warmth of their emotion. Bolivar actually began to enjoy his work in the bank; he was assistant manager by now and still climbing the ladder of success, looking forward to applying his new knowledge for our mutual benefit. And Elysium really was a pleasure planet and we enjoyed partaking thereof. It had a delightful climate at the equator, where the bank was located, and we, of course, settled in most easily. Countless small islands were set in a warm sea. I snorkeled and scuba dived happily among the varied life-forms, getting back the muscle tone that slipped away so easily these days.

But I still worked hard at my new employment every day. That is I checked to see if my daily wage had been deposited. And patted the computer, which bleeped and kept beavering away. The search and computations would have been long finished except that there was difficulty getting data from distant planets.

"Don't let it worry you," James said. "I have search programs working in all the site cities. Enjoy yourself—and I'll let you know as soon as the gongs ring."

I needed no encouragement. Although I enjoyed the scuba diving, even more gratifying was the rugged continent near Elysium's northern pole. Here were jagged mountains and endless snow. A skier's paradise. My muscle tone actually hummed with life now. Angelina and I enjoyed every moment of our extended holiday.

Yet still best of all was waking in the morning and checking my balance in the bank. Which was growing at the rate of four million a day. Bolivar had arranged for each day's deposit to be transferred, by a theoretically untraceable route, to a distant and highly secret bank. But all holidays must end. We hung up our skies and hopped on the first flight when Bolivar sent word that the search was finally coming up with the data that we needed. We joined together in the morning for a friendly family meal.

"Now this is the kind of work I like," I said, going out onto the balcony away from the other diners and lighting an after-breakfast cigar. Just as a bell rang in the computer, a red light blinked on—and a puff of smoke came out of a vent in the top.

James looked up from his plate when he heard the ping and put his silverware down. "Results at last. It sure took long enough."

"Three weeks," I said. "That is not too long."

"It is for this machine. At the minimum it has performed thirty-two to the one hundred eleventh teraflop operations since it started. Now let us see the result."

He sat and typed in a command. Scowled, typed faster. Eventually leaned back and sighed, touched a button. The printer clicked and extruded a sheet of paper.

"The answer," he said, waving it towards us.

"Which is?" Angelina asked.

"A little perturbing. Of all the events, movements, goings and comings, crimes and punishments, accidents and activities, births and deaths, everything that occurred on all of the planets on the dates of the bank robberies, out of all these possibilities there is only one thing that they have in common."

"Tell!" I commanded and all present at the table nodded in agreement.

"I'll tell. The circus was in town."

"James—you are not playing games with us." There was a cold tone in Angelina's voice.

"Never, my dear mother. This is the truth, the whole truth, and nothing but the truth."

"The same circus each time?" I asked.

"No. I thought that at first myself. There were a number of different circuses involved."

"But they had something in common?" I asked.

"The knife of your cold logic cuts deep, Dad. It appears that all of them employed, on the day of the robbery, the same circus act."

The room was so silent as we listened that you could have heard a syllable dropped.

"Present on the planet at each theft was a man, an individual by the name of Puissanto, billed as the Strongest Man in the Galaxy."

"Do you know where he is now?"

"No. He is resting. But I do know where he will be in about a month's time. He will be heading the bill when Bolshoi's Big Top comes to town."

"And where is town?"

"On a distant planet I have never heard of, out in the wrong part of the galaxy, with the unattractive name of Fetorr. The city has the equally unattractive name of Fetorrscoria."

"Our next stop," I said, climbing to my feet and leaving the cigar to die in the ashtray. "Start packing."

''Brilliant,'' Angelina said, the scorn in her voice signifying the direct opposite.

''Of course,'' I said, sitting back down. ''What would we do when we got there? Well, I know what we have to do. We all have to settle down quietly while I put Plan A into effect.''

''Which is?'' Angelina asked, now as confused as the rest.

''I join the circus. We are certainly not going to learn anything by sitting in the audience. While I am doing that we put the rest of the operation on hold. James and Sybil, do I hear the sibilant hiss of your nanotechnology business calling to you?''

''You do, Dad. This planet has been a lot of fun—but even the best vacation must end. You will be going to work now and I feel that we should do the same. But—even while it is back to work—we will keep the communications link open and will be with you instantly if you need us.''

''Grateful thanks. Bolivar—does the rough outback of the stars call you?''

''Not too loudly yet. Now that I am involved in banking I find it very interesting. I want to learn as much as I can, then make a little money to prove I know my business. And I want to know enough about the business so I can come to your aid with my know-how when you need it. Time enough after that for Sybill and me to get back to outer space.''

''To work then!''

This time when I jumped to my feet I stayed there.

CHAPTER 3

"AND JUST WHAT TALENTS DO you plan to present to this circus that will entice them to employ you? Acrobatics?" Angelina asked.

"Not quite—although I could if I tried."

"I am sure that you could. Despite . . ."

"Despite my advanced years?" I said in a cracked and ancient voice. Then leapt into the air and clicked my heels together five times before I landed. She applauded enthusiastically.

"I think I will do something less strenuous." I took a five-credit coin from my pocket and let it roll from finger to finger across the back of my hand. "Magic. I have always been a keen amateur. And as a cardician—even more than that."

"Cardician? I thought they just called it cheating at cards?"

"That is the technical term magicians use when referring to this particular skill. I will demonstrate."

I took a sealed deck of cards from the shelf and tore off the wrapper. Fanned them out, reassembled them, shuffled them enthusiastically and fanned them out again on the table, backs up.

"Now choose a card, any card, that's it. Look at it. Right."

I whipped up the cards and fanned them out again. "Put it back into the deck."

When she had done all this I gave the deck many good shuffles, then fanned them out—this time face up. "Will you kindly point to your chosen card."

She looked at the cards closely—then carefully looked again and shook her head.

"It's not there."

"Are you positive?"

"Of course I am."

"Was your chosen card the King of Spades?"

"It was! How did you know that?"

"Because I see that card in the pocket of your skirt."

I reached in and took out the card and handed it to her.

She gasped. "That's my card. You really do magic—and have been hiding it from me all these years. And I thought you only cheated at cards."

I bowed and accepted her praise. "Magic had to look like magic. But it is hard work. First there is misdirection, where I see to it that you look only where I want you to. Then there is forcing—"

"You didn't force me to do anything."

"A technical term, meaning I did this trick in such a way that you took the card I wanted you to take. Then I watched as you put the card back into the deck. And marked the card by inserting my little finger next to it. Which you could not see because I made sure that I only showed you the back of the deck. Then I removed and palmed the card before I shuffled the deck. It was in my hand when I placed it into your pocket."

"I never saw it."

"You were never intended to. Then I removed the card from your pocket. Magic! End of the trick. But to be a stage magician I will have to be able to do a lot more than manipulate cards. I must now abandon my amateur status to become an even keener professional."

"A sound idea," she said. "You have certainly worked

magic in the past, cleaning out banks.'' Then she smiled and clapped her hands with happiness. ''And I shall be your beautiful assistant! All women dream of a career on the stage. Think of all the lovely costumes I will wear.''

''I am thinking—and think very much of the idea. And I also think that it is time to get some more information on my new vocation.''

Unhappily, it was not easy to come by. Magicians, down through the centuries, have been a close-mouthed lot. Passing their secrets on all too reluctantly, keeping the details of their trade very close to the chest. Despite the billions of entries in the databases I searched, I could find very little real information. Just card tricks and vanishing rabbits and things like that. I had the strong feeling that Bolshoi's Big Top would sneer at my act if that was all that I could do.

''Nothing,'' I growled as I shouted at the computer to turn itself off. ''Maybe it is the acrobat-way after all.''

''Do not despair,'' Angelina said, pouring me a glass of alcoholic despair-destroyer. I sipped at it and smiled thanks in her direction.

''You are right. Worry not and put the old brain cells to work. If magic were that easy we would be up to our thighs in magicians. We are not. But there are magical acts on the gogglebox all of the time. I've watched them in awe. How do they do it? Or rather how did they ever learn to do it? Not from books and computer programs—I've checked that out. But they do learn. How?''

''You mean *who*, don't you?''

''I do, I do!'' I chortled as I sprang to my feet, finger raised in the air. ''They learn from each other. Every sorcerer must have an apprentice. That is what I must be.''

I turned to the familiar suitcase form of the Nanotechtric-68X. ''Awake, good computer,'' I commanded.

''But speak and I obey, oh master.''

Angelina raised one lovely eyebrow. ''You have been teaching this thing to be your electronic slave?''

''Why not? Anything to keep the old ego happy.'' I turned back to the suitcase. ''Magicians, good magicians—galaxy famous magicians. Track them down and prepare a list of them.''

The printout was humming away even before I had finished speaking. There were only six entries on the page. A very exclusive fraternity indeed. I spent a good hour preparing an irresistible sales pitch, listing my varied and convincing talents, and applying for the position of apprentice sorcerer. With the added inducement that I was prepared to pay vast sums for my education. When my missives were dispatched into the electronic void I finished my drink and cocked my head as I heard a distant digestive rumble.

''Lunchtime,'' I rumbled in echo. ''Let us dine at some exclusive and hideously expensive restaurant while my applications are being processed. And return to find out who my mentor will be.''

Dine we did, well and expensively, and were just signaling for the bill when Sybill appeared. Yes, it had to be Sybill because Sybil, her other self, had returned with James to Usti nad Labam to work with him on their mutual computer project.

''Food—or drink?'' I said.

''Thank you, no. Well, maybe a small bite and a drop of wine. Thank you.'' She sipped and smiled. ''I just grabbed a few minutes to talk while Bolivar attends a board meeting for our newly established private bank, Credit Dew. There are some investments we have been toying with.''

''Investments? Perhaps I should consider something like that myself, with all the credits from Kaizi just lying around.''

''That's just what Bolivar said. And he wasn't too sure that your secret secret account was all that secret. So he transferred all your money here so he could watch it closely.''

''How kind!''

''He also used it to finance the establishment of Credit Dew.''

A little too kind, I thought. But kept the thought to myself. I am sure that he knew what he was doing.

"A little more wine." I said and tipped a bit into each of our glasses. We all drank.

"But you didn't come here to talk about banking," Angelina said.

"You're right. I have been thinking about Jim's new career while Bolivar is busy making money. Through my Special Corps contacts I did a little more investigating of the circus. I did a little checking on the acts myself and have found one that was of great interest. Gar Goyle's Freak Show. Intergalactic monstrosities."

"Doesn't sound too attractive," Angelina said. "I thought that sort of thing was illegal."

"It is—that is why I made some even more discreet inquiries through the Special Corps. It is all very legal—and interesting . . ."

This caught my attention. "Interesting—in what way?"

"I'm afraid you will have to find out for yourself. This is all I could uncover now. Plus the fact that Special Corps thinks that Gar Goyle can be trusted. If I find out anything else I'll let you know. How are your magical studies going?"

"We will know as soon as I get answers to some inquiries. I feel that I am on the cusp of an entirely new career."

"Best of luck." She looked at her watch, touched the napkin to her lips. "Bolivar's meeting should be done by now. I must fly. Bye."

Then she was away in a burst of enthusiasm. We finished our luncheon and returned, sated, to our rooms. Eager to find the response to my queries.

Which was exactly nothing. Nor was it any better a day later. My letters had vanished into the interstellar void. Like magic. Then the message-received bell pinged and, with sudden joy, I lifted the sheet from the tray.

Glanced at it and cursed fluently in Esperanto as I crumpled it and hurled it to the floor.

"Fiegulo! Bastardego! Ekskrementkapo!"

"I gather you are not too happy at the result?" Angelina said.

When I answered her I had to speak through grated teeth. "I have never been so insulted in my life. Not only rejected but sneered at, put down, derided, despised . . ."

"And all of the rest. Well the study of magic is obviously a very secretive thing. So what do you do next?"

"Find another answer," I said as I paced gloomily about the room. Which is not an easy thing to do. Nor is pacing angrily. Nor raging fatuously. "Not a single famous magician will take me."

"Then why don't you try the not-so-famous?"

"Not so good. I need only the best."

"Maybe the best are dead. If they were really good they should be able to speak to you from beyond the grave."

"No jokes! This is a serious matter . . ."

Then I stopped in my tracks as the idea popped to the surface. "Not alive, not dead . . . but . . . *retired!*"

My faithful suitcase had but to be commanded. There were only two names on the new list, the first one light-years away right across the galaxy. But then, with quavering finger, I pointed out the address of the second name.

"Retired and living in Happy Hectares, a retirement home for actors. Sounds very nice."

"But do you see where Happy Hectares is?"

"Of course. Here on Elysium. And why not? This is a pleasure planet serving a number of star systems. Shall I call Rent-a-Rover and get us some transportation?"

"By all means. I look forward intently to meeting the Great Grissini. While you do that I'll get a printout of his career highlights."

Some hours later we rolled through the entrance of Happy Hectares, under a curling archway that had HOME OF THE STARS spelled out in twinkling lightbulbs. We passed resplendent gardens with elderly types strolling the paths, or sitting in shaded pergolas. Robot gardeners worked away in the flower beds; butlerbots circulated with trays of tea and little sandwiches and cakes. And some with chilled glasses. Angelina saw the direction of my gaze and shook her head.

"Too early for you to get tucked into the sauce, Jim. First we find your magician."

The elegantly gowned and carefully coiffed lady at the front desk was kindness itself.

"The Great Grissini, of course. Let me find out where he is right now." She punched the keys; and I tried to remember where I had seen her before. Angelina was far quicker off the mark then I was.

"Why you must be Hedy Lastarr. I so enjoyed seeing you in *Planet of Passion.*"

"How *nice* of you to remember," Hedy cooed, patting the curls of her stylishly gray hair. "Not many people remember the old threedees these days."

"They are missing a lot. Far better than the current rubbish."

"I could not agree more. Ahh, here we are. The Great Grissini is in the west garden—just follow the attendant. And don't forget our tax-free status."

She pointed delicately at a collection box on the desk before her that was labeled with HELPING THE NEEDY IS A REAL GOOD DEEDY in ornate curled lettering. I stuffed credits through the slot in the top until she beamed with pleasure. We followed the blue-painted robot out into the gardens.

"He is the one you seek," the robot said, pointing to a man under an umbrella, then rolling away.

The Great Grissini was not looking that great today. He was very thin, pale and bony, with his toupee not too well secured. He looked up suspiciously when we approached. I remembered the reaction—and lack of reaction—of the magicians I had tried to contact. I did not want to repeat my mistakes. They were surely a prickly lot. A strong sales pitch was very much in order now. I had boned up on his biography while

Angelina drove, so I could be a little more subtle in my approach.

"Might I ask if I am speaking to Pasquale Grissini—known throughout the galaxy as the Great Grissini?"

The grunted response could have meant anything. I tried to smile warmly while I introduced myself and Angelina. He broke in before I was done.

"You want a drink?"

"Why, yes, of course. Kind of you to ask."

His next grunt was a more enthusiastic one as he pressed a button on the table before him. When he took his thumb away I saw that the button was inscribed with a symbolic cocktail glass. Things were indeed looking up.

A boxish wheeled robot rolled over. It had arms at the front end beside a male mannequin's head. "May I be of service?" the thing said. "The special today is Zubenelgenubian Iced Tea. One hundred and fifty proof."

"I'll take a double," Grissini said, leaning forward; the first sign of animation I had seen. We ordered the specials as well. Something hummed in the thing's interior. Then a hatch sprang open and the iced drinks were there on a tray. Behind a transparent door.

"That will be twenty-two credits," the robot said. "Cash only." Then it opened its mouth wide, revealing a money slot where its tongue should be. I looked out of the corners of my eyes at Grissini who was as a marble statue. My round, obviously. I stuffed in coins until a horn sounded a quick fanfare and the door slipped out of sight. Mechanical arms seized the tray and deposited it on the table before us.

"And some deep-fried seaweed pretzels," our new friend said, almost smiling. I paid with pleasure. Then, while he was getting tucked into his toxic tea, I hit the high points of his career.

"Your vanishing Boy Sprout was the hit of the circuits. Where a real live Boy Sprout climbed a rope right before the audience—then vanished in an instant. Did you know that there have been two books written about that trick? Each one said that they knew how it had been done."

"Did they?"

"No. As far as the galaxy goes your mystery is still a mystery. Living on in the memories of your grateful audiences."

"They loved it," he said, nodding but not letting this interfere with some serious sipping.

"What the public admired most, I do believe, was your disappearing porcuswine. Where right before their eyes this large and ferocious creature simply vanished. The magic-loving theatergoers of the galaxy owe a lot to the Great Grissini and will never forget him."

"Porcuswine-crap," he snapped, stirred to activity at last. "If they remembered me I would not be retired and sitting here thirstily in the sun and living off my memories." His eyes went damp for a moment. Then he drained his glass, put aside the moment of self-pity, and held the glass out for a refill. He sat silent until it arrived. A long swig put him back in control.

"Audiences don't give a damn when you start to get old—nor do producers. Plenty of new acts coming down the pike. So I got out before they threw me out. Now I'm stuck here in this pay-as-you-die dump. Room and board as promised when I signed up. My fault was that I didn't read the fine print, too smart by far in those days. Let my wiseguy lawyer take care of it for me. Didn't know until it was too late that he was senile. Signed me up here without looking at the contract. Didn't even notice that just the basics are provided. Enough food, but not too good. A bed, but not too soft. Anything else you gotta pay. Which they forgot to tell him when he signed me up here." He slurped up the last of the drink and I enthusiastically thumbed the button on the table again. There was nothing forced about my smile now. Bad news for him was good news for me.

"Make note of the date." I told him. "For this is the first

day of the rest of your comfortable life. Think of the best meals you can imagine—and they shall be yours. Think of a liquor cabinet that never runs dry.''

''Why should I think about them?'' he said, suddenly suspicious. But not too suspicious to stop himself from grabbing the drink when it arrived.

''Because they could be yours. Plus some better geriatric treatment—get rid of some of those wrinkles. All this will come true—plus the added benefit of your magical miracles once more gracing the platforms of the stars.''

''No way. Have the shakes too much to work them.''

''You won't have to do a thing on stage. But you will know that your new assistant will continue in your noble tradition.''

''Don't have an assistant. Always worked alone.''

''You have one now. Me. Interested?''

''No. My magic is my magic. Don't share it.''

''Not sharing. Continuing.'' I pushed the brimming glass closer to him. ''I shall study what you teach, and reveal nothing I learn to anyone.''

''Not even to me,'' Angelina said. ''Except of course those illusions where I assist you. It will all be so wonderful.''

She patted the back of his hand and was rewarded with a wintry smile.

''Would be nice to work again. Keep my hand in, you know.'' Then he frowned.

''No way. When I go—the secrets go. You can't bribe me.''

''I'm not trying to bribe you!'' I said loudly to cover the fact that I was trying to bribe him. ''Your magic should not die with you. Thousands yet unborn are already lusting after you.'' That didn't sound right. The booze must have been getting to me as well; these drinks were lethal.

''What my husband is trying to say,'' Angelina said, the only one still sober apparently. ''Is that he admires your work so much that he wants your retirement years to be happy ones. If you share your magic with him they certainly will be. A career for him and years of happiness for you.''

''Well—'' he said, and I knew that we had won the day.

We rented a house nearby. Every morning the limo would pick him up and bring him over. He was looking rehabilitated already. The better diet, a certain amount of booze, plus the geriatric jabs worked their wonders. Also, I think he grew in stature as he worked his miracles for us. While we waited for some stunning—and expensive—apparatus we had ordered, he drilled me in the basic skills.

''Misdirection, misdirection and misdirection. Those are the three words you must never forget. Remember—the audience wants to be fooled. While they look *here* you are working *there*.''

Here was his raised left hand which plucked a palmed coin out of thin air. *There* was a top hat, empty a moment before, now containing a white rodent, which he pulled out by its long ears. I had been completely fooled. I had never seen him take the creature from the bag hanging behind the table. Then, concealed by his body, slip the creature into the hat.

It seemed so obvious once he showed me how it was done. He saw my expression and smiled.

''Of course it is a letdown when a piece of magic is exposed. So obvious, you think, why didn't I see it? Which is why magicians never reveal their secrets. Discovering the truth behind the manipulation is like the loss of innocence. You must believe in magic—even though you know better—and convey this belief to your audience. Do this and they will love you for it. In a world without magic you must make magic. The audiences will beat a happy path to your door. Now try it like I showed you. Smoothly. That is better—but not by much.''

Angelina knocked on the door and I unlocked it.

"A delivery. A large crate from Prospero Electronics."

"Aha!" Grissini said, elated, rubbing his hands together with happiness. "Very soon now we will recreate the supreme mystery of the Vanishing Porcuswine!"

CHAPTER 4

One of the reasons we had rented this particular house was the fact that it had an immense living room. When all of the furniture had been removed and stuffed into the garage, the room became our stage. Blue curtains divided it, curtains that opened and closed at the touch of a button. Angelina and I, sitting in chairs that faced the curtain, became a happy audience. Watching while Grissini instructed the workmen as they assembled the apparatus for the Vanishing Porcuswine.

It looked simple enough. A two-sided cage made of metal slats was erected on the stage before a rear curtain, making a triangle with the curtain as one side, the slats the other two sides.

Only when the workmen had been well tipped and dismissed did Grissini turn his attention to us.

"The illusion is now ready," he said. "All we need now is a porcuswine."

"That will take a bit of doing," I said. "Couldn't we use another creature to demonstrate?"

He thought for a moment, then pointed at Angelina. "The effect is much greater, of course, with a large and threatening animal. However, for demonstration purposes, she will do. Come with me, my dear."

Grissini led her behind the rear curtains, then out through the gap in the curtains and into the cage.

"You must stand very still," he said. "Whatever happens you must not move. Do you understand?"

"Absolutely. Like a rock."

"Good. When this illusion is done correctly the porcuswine is chained and immobile. Now—we begin!"

He came back through the curtain just as he had gone in. Angelina stood demurely, hands folded before her as the Great Grissini faced his audience of one and bowed. I clapped enthusiastically.

"Ladies and gentlemen," he said, his amplified voice filling the room. "You have seen the handlers lead this dangerous porcuswine—lovely lady, sorry—into this cage. A cage made of solid steel, solid and unbreakable." He tapped his metal-tipped wand against the slats, which gave a solid and satisfactory steel ring. "You have examined the solid locks and chains which secure this great creature in place." The shackles were in place. The porcuswine, unhappily, not. "There is no possible way to escape from this cage—except by magic. Magic that will astound and amaze you. Behold!"

Invisible drums rolled thunderously and then, in a final crashing crescendo, they stopped. In that very same instant a black curtain dropped between cage and audience. It remained for a single second before Grissini seized it and whisked it away.

"Angelina!" I cried aloud.

For she was gone, the cage was empty. I sprang to my feet and started to lunge forward.

"Patience!" Grissini ordered in a voice of thunder and I stopped, sat down, only an illusion. Then why was I soaked with sweat? It took a great effort of will to sit still while the magician went behind the rear curtain once again.

And reappeared with Angelina on his arm. I could no longer remain in my chair. I rushed forward to embrace her.

"What happened?" I asked.

"I don't know. Everything just went black until Grissini

appeared and led me back here. What did you see?''

''Nothing. That is, the curtain fell for an instant—and you were gone.''

''I don't think I was. Other than being in the dark I don't believe that I moved.'' She turned to face the smiling magician. ''What happened?''

He bowed and swept his hand gracefully in the air. ''I will be most happy to tell you, since you will be part of this illusion in the future.'' His smile broadened as he stabbed his finger theatrically into the air.

''It is all done with mirrors.''

I am afraid that all we could do was gape blankly and adenoidally at this news. Yet it was true. He had us stand to the side, squarely facing the metal slats of one side of the cage.

''Now all will be revealed. Without the obscuring black curtain. Watch closely now—abracadabra!''

Instantly and silently the space between the slats became a mirror. We were looking at our shocked expressions. He laughed with pleasure.

''So simple—yet so convincing. The lengths of mirror are concealed behind the slats. Then they slide into place when I actuate them with this concealed radio control. To the audience the cage appears to be empty since they are looking at the blue side curtains reflected in the mirrors. While they gape the porcuswine is led away, the illusion is reversed, the mirrors vanish—and the cage is really empty this time. Simple and highly effective, is it not?''

''A showstopper and a winner,'' I said.

''I agree completely,'' Kaizi said, strolling in through what had been a locked door. ''You have been spending a lot of my money, Jim, and I had a natural desire to see where it was going. I have been reading your daily reports, as well as those of my agents of course. You are sure that this circus is connected with the thefts?''

''Computer programs don't lie. Every theft to every bank was logged. I ran search programs to examine the relevant dates in incredibly minute detail. News files were combed, spaceport and airport departures gone through meticulously. Some similar events did occur, but these were merely coincidences considering the amount of data that was searched and compared. Out of all this there was only a single overlap with the robberies. There were different circuses in every city when the thefts occurred. But the strongman, Puissanto, was in every one of them at the time.''

Meanwhile the Great Grissini was staring at us, baffled by what was going on.

''Time for a break,'' Angelina said, taking him gently by the arm and leading him away. ''With perhaps a small drink for your dry throat.

''The logic is sound,'' Kaizi said, sitting down in a chair and pressing smooth the hairs of his fur morning suit. ''However you have been paid a great deal of money and I would like to see some positive results. In fact, to encourage you in your investigation I am suspending your daily payments until you actually make contact with this suspect strongman.''

''You can't do that!''

''Of course I can. Clause six, paragraph eighteen of our contract.''

''I don't remember any clause that said that.'' My vision was blurred by the image of winged credits flying out into the night.

''You would if you had looked more closely at what you signed. You have a copy of the contract with you?''

''No. It's in the bank.''

''A wise precaution. It just so happens that I have a copy with me, should you wish to peruse it.''

He took a copy from his fur purse. No crisp vellum this time, but a printed copy. I read through it quickly, then raised it victoriously over my head. ''I was right! There are only seventeen paragraphs in clause six.''

''Indeed.'' Kaizi did not seem disturbed by this announcement. He leaned over and pointed to end of the seventeenth paragraph. ''And what do you think this is?''

I leaned close and blinked rapidly. ''It looks like a blob of ink.''

''Some might differ.'' He took a brass tube out of the bag and passed it over to me. ''Look at it through this optic magnifier.''

I did. ''It still looks like a blob of ink.''

''That is because the instrument is set on four times magnification. Try setting it to four hundred.''

I found the setting wheel and gave it a twist. Looked again. The blob of ink resolved into a chunk of copy; paragraph eighteen. I was hooked.

''Do not despair,'' he advised. ''Just work faster. This golden goal should act as some inspiration.''

''It does! I'm on my way. Soon. My agent has been dealing with Bolshoi's Big Top and contracts have been drawn up. I will join them shortly, in time for opening night in Fetorr.''

I spoke with firm resolution. A sales pitch to hide the fact that I had not mastered all of the illusions that I would need. Plus the fact that there wasn't a single porcuswine farm here on this pleasure planet. Still the fact remained that up until this moment Kaizi had been a good and munificent employer and I wanted to keep him happy. Even if it meant being a little parsimonious with the truth. If he could renege on making the agreed daily payments, it seemed perfectly fair for me to massage the facts a little as well.

''See that you do arrive in time for opening night at the circus. For our mutual benefit,'' he said. ''See you on opening night.'' He exited as swiftly as he had arrived and I went looking for Angelina, looking forward to one of those drinks she had talked about. She and Grissini were sitting and chatting in the atrium garden. I joined them and looked with more need than pleasure at a chilled and brimming glass that awaited me.

''Thank you,'' I said, and knocked it back in a single gulp.

Angelina's lovely eyebrows rose in a singularly questioning manner.

"Well some of us seem to have developed a sudden thirst. Trouble with Kaizi?"

"Not exactly trouble. But not exactly pleasure as well. You know those little payments he has been making daily? It seems, according our contract, which contains a paragraph that looks like a blob of ink only isn't, that he can suspend them whenever he wishes. He now wishes. He will start them again when we join the circus."

"Blob of ink?" Angelina asked, puzzled.

"Only to the naked eye. Under magnification it becomes the dreaded paragraph."

"Then what we have been discussing before you came is most relevant. The Great Grissini and I have been talking about deadlines. Made more imperative now by the appearance of our employer."

"Everything cannot be done in time," Grissini said. Gulped from his glass and sighed. "You catch on quickly, but not quickly enough." I lowered my eyes and tried to look humble before my maestro. "I will see that you have enough illusions and tricks for a performance. But you will not be able to do the Vanishing Boy Sprout . . ."

"But I must! Your most famous turn. Why can't we do it?"

"Mainly because we don't have an eight-year-old Boy Sprout," Angelina said with chill logic. "I have looked into it and little boys are hard to find. Also against the law."

"My great blessing was that the Grissinis are a large family," he said. "I could always find a small cousin or nephew to aid me. Alas, all grown now and scattered to the far corners of the galaxy."

"Couldn't it be done without a boy?" I asked peevishly.

"Never! That is the strength of the illusion. The boy has been planted in the audience so he can volunteer. I always save this illusion for the last, the closing and most appreciated act of magic. To begin I shake out my great cape. A pigeon flies up, two rabbits hop away. The audience claps and applauds. I then raise my hands and there is a loud fanfare and a roll of thunder. The audience is instantly silent. I speak to them. This is the moment you have all been waiting for. Is there a Boy Sprout in the audience? In uniform? There are always a few. Show yourselves I say, and they spring to their feet. Come forward I cry. The first one here will join me in this next act of magic—and will receive twenty credits as well. They cry out and struggle to reach the stage first. But my assistant is seated in the first row, close to the aisle. He springs to his feet, pushing himself forwards. In doing so he brushes against people in his hurry, even stepping on their toes. Assuring all present that he really is a corporeal little boy. He assists me by bringing over a basket, sets it down before me. I take a length of rope and throw it into the basket. The boy waits patiently as the most eerie music begins. I make magical passes over the basket and the end of the rope appears, unsupported, and rises writhing into the air. The boy is just as impressed by this as is the audience. I wave him over and he passes behind me to approach the basket. The music grows louder still. Take the rope I command him and he draws back, afraid. I make a magical pass and his eyes roll back, his body stiffens. His will is now under my control. Now he does exactly what I order him to do. I wave my hand and he seizes the rope, then begins to climb it.''

I nodded, enthralled by the illusion, actually seeing the boy climb, as impressed as the unseen audiences.

''And then—'' he said dramatically, ''—the boy reaches the top of the rope. The music ends with a mighty crash of the brasses, and I wave my hand. As I do this the boy is gone, vanished, and the rope falls limply back into the basket. I turn the basket over and the rope falls out. Nothing more. I bow and the curtain closes.''

''Marvelous,'' Angelina said.

''How does it work?'' I asked.

"Since you won't be doing it, you don't have to know."

And no amount of cajoling would get him to change his mind.

"I will not tell you. However I will reveal to you the illusion of the levitating lady. The apparatus arrived this morning and I will go to install it." He rose, then turned to Angelina. "Did you purchase the black dress I mentioned?"

"I did."

"Capital! If you would be so kind as to don it now, we will proceed."

I was left alone. Grissini was working, Angelina was dressing, I was drinking. Just enough to mellow me after Kaizi's grim financial machinations. I had really begun to enjoy my morning calls to the bank.

"Do you like it?" Angelina said.

"Divine!" And it was—floor-length, black and velvety, fascinatingly low-cut above, flaring out when she turned.

"It will do," the Great Grissini said from the doorway. "Let us begin. I must instruct Angelina in her role." He looked at his watch. "Jim, you will join us in exactly a half an hour."

"Good as done," I said, looking at my own watch, then at the bottle. Well, maybe a small one while I marked the passage of time.

I was feeling remarkably mellow when I entered our home theater and took my seat. Dark curtains were drawn at the back of the stage. Which was empty save for three large cubes. Music welled up at Grissini's entrance and the maestro himself came on stage. He bowed to the audience and I clapped like fury.

"Thank you, ladies and gentlemen, thank you. You must now prepare yourself for a magical thrill that will amaze, entrance and mystify you. Let us begin."

He walked over to the white cubes and tapped them with his wand; good, solid wood. Then he ran his fingers along his wand—and it vanished. Reaching down he turned the cubes, one by one, to face the audience, showing that they were four-sided and open at both ends. Black outside, white inside and on the edges. His wand reappeared in his hand and he ran it through the opening of each one.

"Empty as you see. Simple, four-sided constructions, empty as you can see. I will now place them—so."

The wand vanished again to free his hands. He picked up the first box and walked over and placed it in the center of the stage. Then placed the others on each side of the first to make a platform. The wand reappeared to be tapped on their solid surfaces, passed through their open ends. This done he turned and bowed.

"Now, ladies and gentlemen and honored guests, I ask you to welcome my assistant, the lovely Angelina, who will assist me in this display of magic."

I clapped as loudly as I could, as any audience certainly would as my Angelina made her entrance. Slowly and seductively, smiling warmly and waving to the enthusiastic crowd of one.

Soft music welled up as Grissini took her hand and led her forward to bow. Then back to the row of cubes. Slowly and carefully, she sat down on the center cube, then swung her legs up and lay down on the cubes. She smiled at the audience, her right hand supporting her chin, her full black skirt draped over the white edge of the cubes. Grissini was making magical passes over her in time with the music and his wand vanished yet again.

Then he bent over and pulled the center cube out from under her.

I gasped in awe, as any good audience would gasp, because she still lay there, unbending and straight as a die even though the center of her body was no longer supported.

Then I gasped even louder as he slowly pulled the supporting cube out from under her elbow so that she was floating in midair.

Floating totally in midair when he pulled away the third and last support. She smiled and waved at me when Grissini looked away. I applauded until my hands hurt. The music crescendoed as he held up a large metal hoop, bounced it on the floor to prove its solidity—then slowly slipped it over her head. Moved it down the entire length of her body. Even around her feet to show that that she was truly suspended invisibly in midair. My hands were numb with unceasing applause.

The ring moved back the length of her body and was thrown, clanging, into the wings. Now the sprightly music accompanied the magician as, one by one, he slipped the white cubes back under her floating body. Then helped her down to join him in a bow. She came forward: I jumped to my feet to embrace her.

"My magical wife!" I cried aloud. "Didn't the wires hurt?"

"No wires. You saw the ring go the entire length of my body."

"I did—and I didn't understand it. Real magic?"

"Let us rather say real illusion."

Grissini exited—towards the atrium I noticed; magic can be exhausting. Or perhaps he did not want to be there when his magic secrets were revealed.

"I still don't understand how it is done. Something about the cubes maybe?"

"No. They are exactly what they seem to be. Solid wood. Placed in a row you will remember. Then I made my entrance, you will remember."

"Unforgettable!"

"But distracting. Grissini walked across the stage to greet me and the spot stayed on him as he moved. Distraction. That is when the magic happened—not later when he took the boxes away."

"Of course! Many magic tricks occur well before the trick is seen to be happening. The audience was looking at you and him. And not looking at the boxes. That *was* when the illusion occurred."

I went to look at the spot where the boxes had been placed

close to the black curtains at the rear of the stage. The illusion was so good that I was a foot away before I saw it.

A thin black platform, floating in midair, that had supported Angelina.

"But that is magic as well! That can't just float there."

I looked closely at it, under it, then ran my hands along it.

To find the strong black steel beam that protruded from the curtains. Undoubtedly supported by a strong frame hidden by the curtains. Understanding struck.

"Of course! That platform wasn't there when he walked around the stage, then put the boxes into place. Only when he went to greet you and the spotlight followed him. In the darkness, radio-controlled undoubtedly, the beam came forward and slid the platform into place atop the boxes. Invisible from the audience because it was black like the tops of the boxes. But the ring—it went the length of your body, even past your shoes—"

"And back," she reminded. "The loop was big enough for the back of the loop to stop when it reached the supporting bar. Big enough for the front of the ring to go past my feet and even behind me."

"Of course! It had to come back the way it came on because the bar was stopping it from going all the way. What a wondrous effect!"

We went to join Grissini and to congratulate him. He shrugged it off as his accepted due. And shook an admonitory finger.

"You have little time left and very much more to learn."

He was right, of course. I had only a week to go.

I worked even harder. Drank nothing and slept only a few hours a night. And I practiced. By this time I was adroit at producing large birds from apparent thin air, and could draw hundreds of flags from an empty tube. I practiced with the floating apparatus, which Angelina greatly enjoyed, until I had the illusion under perfect control.

I could even read written questions from the audience by

pressing the papers with their questions to my forehead.

I was most happy when I learned to do this. It had always impressed me on stage. And the illusion was so simple. I read the name of the first questioner and he responded from the audience. After answering his written question, I opened it and read his name aloud again. Discarded the paper and took another one. Which I read aloud as the audience gasped.

But the first question had been a plant, the man in the audience my accomplice. When I glanced at his question to verify it—it was not his question at all. But the first real question. Memorized and read out while the second real question was on my forehead. I was one question ahead all of the time. Illusion! Misdirection!

The week was over, our bags packed, tickets bought. It was time to go—and begin earning money again. It hurt to spend my own money as I had been doing since Kaizi produced his microscopic contract.

We all shook hands and the Great Grissini was not looking that great.

"It was nice to be working again," he said, then sighed heavily.

"I will be ever grateful for your aid. Sorry it had to end so quickly." I turned away, trying not to see the pathos in his eyes.

"Take care of yourself," Angelina said. He grimaced.

"It will be Happy Hectares that will be doing the caring," he said. No pleasure in his voice.

I got ready to plant the prepared spear—but I could not.

"Look," I said. "It was a privilege to work with you, to bring some happiness into your life. And it is going to continue, I promise that."

"What do you mean?"

"The bank. They'll send you a check every week. Enough to buy better food and decent drink and all the little pleasures of life that make it worth living."

He was shocked at the thought. Then his eyes narrowed. "What's the catch? Why you doing this?"

"Because he is a nice man," Angelina said.

"Not that nice," I said. "I had not planned to be so uncommonly generous. Let us say I have had a change of heart."

"Jim—what in the world are you talking about?" She looked puzzled.

"I just couldn't go through with it. You see, I was going to arrange for the payments to continue, but only in exchange for . . . the secret of the Vanishing Boy Sprout. But I have to look at myself in the mirror every day. And the one crime I have suddenly realized that I have never committed is blackmail. I'm a little too old to start that kind of thing now. So enjoy your retirement. And think of me every night when you celebrate the cocktail hour." I whistled to our luggage and tiny motors hummed as they followed after us.

"I don't believe it!" he called after us.

"Believe it," Angelina said. "Tough-as-nails diGriz is really an old sweetie at heart."

"I'll blush if you keep that up," I said as I kissed her on the cheek. I had reached the cab when the door opened behind us.

"I'll tell you," he said. "My decision."

"Our spacer won't wait," Angelina said.

"This won't take a minute. You should have picked up on it when I said the boy walked behind me. Out of sight of the audience for a moment. Misdirection."

"Something happened then!" I shouted happily. "But what?" I muttered gloomily.

"He stopped. Concealed by my cape. That's why I always close with this illusion. When it is over the curtain comes down. He runs into the wings before the curtain comes up again and I take my bows."

"But—if he doesn't climb the rope—who does?"

"An image. That was not a rope that rose from the basket—it was the image of a rope. At the precise moment that the boy walked behind me I actuated the holograph projector to continue with the recording. The rope apparently rising in the air before me is just a holographic image of a rope. Remember—the real boy stopped and is hidden by my cape. Now the holographic image of the boy walks out from behind me so that it is his image that appears to climb the image of the rope—''

''And disappears as only an image can. The image of the rope falls back into the basket and only the real rope remains.''

''The curtain closes,'' Angelina laughed, ''and the crowd leaves, happily pleased. As we do, maestro. You are really great, the Great Grissini.''

We left him bowing—he left us laughing. It really was a great performance.

CHAPTER 5

ONCE WE WERE ABOARD THE spacer that would take us to Fetorrscoria, the euphoria of the Great Grissini's last great performance quickly wore away. One major problem still faced us. Angelina must have seen my scowl and she tried to jolly me out of it. It was no good. Thoughts of a porcuswine danced in my head. How could I make one of those fine creatures disappear—if I didn't have one in the first place?

"What do you say to a glass of champagne in the Star Bar before lunch?" I growled throatily and she patted my arm. "Yes, dear."

Before we could leave the cabin the message bell pinged and the comscreen lit up. "No doubt vital information about the next lifeboat drill," I sneered as I grimaced—which is not easy to do—at my image in the mirror as I combed my hair.

"Not quite," Angelina said, going over to read it. "It's from James. He's found a porcuswine for us! Full details follow. He has arranged for us to be met as soon as we clear customs. By a man named Igor who has a truck. He knows where we have to go. He closes with best wishes and good luck." She pressed the print button and a copy of the message rolled out of the machine. "He has arranged our entire schedule."

"That's our boy!" I elated fondly. "And I'll take you up on the champagne offer."

The Star Bar was just that. The ceiling was a vast crystal dome, beyond which the stars burnt down upon us from the blackness of interstellar space. Perhaps. I greatly doubted if a hole had been cut in the spacer's hull just to let us see out. It was an illusion and a very good one. We sipped and smacked and plotted. I scribbled notes on the message from James.

"If this spacer is on time, and it has to be due to the laws of celestial mechanics, we land on Fetorr just one day before we are due at the circus. The porcuswine ranch is about five hundred clicks from the spaceport. Then two hundred more to Fetorrscoria. We are cutting it very close."

"We are. But we have no other choice."

"Agreed. So we worry about it after we land." I put the message into my pocket, drained my glass and pushed the bottle away. "I must make the most of this trip and practice every moment. Without booze to awake tremors in my hand."

"But a drink at bedtime?"

"Of course. I don't plan to become a teetotaler."

Thus the days passed quickly. I practiced until my fingers were supple as snakes. Angelina had been very busy shopping in the days before we left. I had been vaguely aware of this at the time, but too tied up with my magic to take any real notice. I was practicing a very complex card manipulation when she emerged from the bedroom.

"Do you like it?" she said. I turned around.

"Zowie!" I enthused and playing cards went in all directions. It was a shocking scarlet one-piece creation, cut high on the thighs, low on the bust and skintight everywhere. I rushed to embrace her but a friendly little fist to the jaw stopped me dead.

"You don't think that it is, well, too revealing for a woman of my age?"

"Your age is the right age," I enthused. "You are gorgeous and desirable and every male past puberty in the audience will be watching you, not me. I can hear the orgone sizzling already.''

''The emerald tiara is not too much?''

''Fine. It matches the thingumbobby at your waist.''

''I'm not sure,'' she said, pirouetting prettily before the mirror. ''Maybe the green one . . .''

''You have more outfits like this?''

''Of course.''

''Make my day! Let's have a fashion show.''

I scrabbled up the cards and put them away. Pulled up an armchair, lit a cigar, then poured a small glass of white wine. She had an outfit for every illusion. Green to match the rusty red of her hopeful porcuswine partner to be. Black and red when she passed me the playing cards. Midnight black when she floated in midair. And thus did a pleasant time ensue before the dinner gong bonged.

The rest of the voyage passed this way. While I honed my magical talents she finalized her costumes. We ate well, slept well—and other than a glass or two of wine with meals the only booze I enjoyed was my evening libation.

Our schedule was going to be tight when we arrived at our destination. I had to take more positive action rather than just wearing running shoes and elbowing past the rest of the passengers. This involved a little financial meeting with the chief purser. A smarmy type given to much dry hand-wiping and white-toothed grinning.

''And how may I be of service to you, sir?''

''You can advise me about my luggage. If we pack our bags the night before we arrive—would you be able to take them then?''

''It will be my great pleasure.''

''So if you have them the night before there is no reason why they cannot be unloaded first?'' I slipped him fifty credits as I said this.

''As good as done, sir—you have my word on that.''

''And some additional information, if you please. Who

would you suggest that I should talk to, to insure that my wife and I are first to leave this admirable vessel?''

''Myself, sir! Disembarking is at my discretion.'' Another banknote vanished.

''I imagine that you make this run very often. Do you have any suggestions about easing our way through customs?''

''It is funny that you should say that, sir. My cousin is a customs agent at the spaceport and—''

Much lighter in pocket, but much more relaxed about our arrival, I returned to our cabin to pack.

Through all this not-too-subtle bribery we were first off the spacer when she landed. First through customs, courtesy of the purser's cousin, where our untouched and unsearched luggage awaited us. Waiting there was a burly type in soiled and wrinkled coveralls who held a sign that read MISTUR DEGRIZZ. I signaled to him and he approached.

''You deGrizz?''

''Me diGriz. Who you?''

''Igor. Come.''

I whistled and our luggage followed us, as we followed him out of the terminal into the dusty, fume-filled street outside. Angelina sniffed.

''I don't like this place—nor do I like our monosyllabic friend, Igor.''

''I'm afraid it's that kind of a planet. Mining and heavy manufacturing for the most part. Did you detect a certain tone of desperation in James's last memo?''

''I did. Let us see what kind of transportation he has provided. Uggh!''

Uggh, indeed. The truck was a great, scratched, filthy cubical thing with wheels on all four corners. It had once been painted pink, surely a mistake, and on its side, under a layer of dirt, a message could be read.

IGOR VAN SERVICE—GO ANYWHERE

I hoped that this was true. Igor opened a hatch and pitched our luggage in. Then climbed a ladder to the cab above. The engine rumbled to life and belched a fetid black cloud over us. Through watery eyes I saw his hand appear in the open door where it made a single gesture of invitation before vanishing from sight. We climbed after him, settled onto the scratched and patched seat, stared out of the filthy front window as gears ground somewhere below us. The thing lurched and vibrated, then rumbled forward onto the road.

"Do you know where we are going?" Trying not to let my lip curl at the depressing scenery moving by outside.

"Ungh," Igor said, or something like that.

"We are going to Lortby, right? To the Rashers and Quills Porcuswine Farm there."

After another long period of waiting, this simple query elicited a reluctant and monosyllabic sound of agreement. Eventually something that passed for speech followed.

"Get dirt, pay more."

I suppose that this could be translated as, "If you allow an animal to track filth into my vehicle of any kind, the already preposterously high fee will be even higher." I grunted in return and that was the end of conversation as he knew it.

Factories, smoke stacks and grim walls reluctantly gave way to scrubby countryside of some sort. Mostly swamp. The shoulders of the road made a handy dumpsite, so rubbish of all kinds marked our none-too-swift passage. Angelina and I tried a desultory conversation that soon died away. We bumped and jiggled around on the seat, looking out glazedly at the worn landscape. Some hours, or centuries, later we turned off the main road and down a rutted farm track past a sign that read. RASHERS AND QUILLS, decorated with a not-too-bad illustration of a porcuswine rampant. The legend below informed us that ALL TRESPASSERS WILL BE SHOT.

Thus assured of a friendly reception I slid down from the vehicle when we stopped. Stretched and groaned, then headed for the only door in the large building that faced onto the yard.

A bell tinkled when I opened the door, and the man behind the desk looked up; same build and demeanor as Igor. I was going to say "Good morning" but quickly changed it to "Ugh," which he ugghed right back.

"Need porcuswine," I said.

"Carcass or quartered?"

"Alive not dead. In one piece."

This stopped him and his forehead lined with the unaccustomed effort of thought which finally produced speech.

"No sell alive."

"Now you do." I rolled a hundred-credit coin across the desk which he snatched up.

"Against law."

"Law just changed." Another coin followed the first. With a great effort a smile slowly appeared on his granite features; he stumbled to his feet and headed for the door. Angelina was waiting outside with fire in her eye.

"One more minute with Igor and I would have killed him. I could see the mute passion building in those bloodshot eyes. We needed a driver. So instead of zonking him here I am. Have you arranged everything?"

"I sincerely hope so!" I said with faked bonhomie. "This other brilliant conversationalist is taking us to the porcuswine. Shall we follow him?" With the thought of visiting these fine creatures my good spirits did return. "We must never forget that they have traveled with mankind to the stars. Providing protection—as well as nourishment. A cross between the deadly and spiny porcupine and the mighty swine, they are a beauty to behold. Ahh!" I said as we entered the building and were face-to-face with a gigantic boar. Angelina's nostrils widened; she did not completely share my enthusiasm for the creatures.

This was indeed the swine of my dreams! His reddish quills rose when he saw us, tiny eyes glittered with anger. A drop of saliva rolled down one tusk and dripped to the floor. "Sooey," I intoned softly, "Sooey, sooey—good swine."

And I reached between the bars and scratched him between the ears. He rattled his quills and grunted with happiness. Porcuswine can't reach this spot and just love to be scratched.

Angelina had seen me do this before, but the swinemeister bulged his eyes and looked as though he was suffering a coronary.

"Watch out! He's a killer!"

"I am sure of it. But only for those who deserve killing. To the rest of mankind the porcuswine is loyal, protective—yea, even reverent. Good swine," I said, admiring the immense form. Loath to leave, but I had to. Fine as this boar was, he was too big for our theatrical act. "Need smaller one."

We went deeper into the swinery, passed wary-eyed mothers with piglets, more and more of these lovely creatures. We turned a corner and I gasped and halted. There in the pen before me was the most endearing yearling I had ever seen. Tiny eyes sparkled with good cheer, delicate quills all-arustle. She trotted over on tiny hoofs when I called, burbled with happiness when I scratched the right spot.

A deal was struck, more credits changed hands, a piece of rope was produced. She took to the leash at once, trotted delicately ahead of us as we returned to our vehicle.

"A swine of delight," I said. "We shall call her Gloriana."

"Who was that?" Angelina asked, instantly suspicious. "One of your early girlfriends?"

"Never! It is a name from legend, mythology. Gloriana, the goddess of the barnyard, often depicted with a piglet on her lap—"

"You are making this up!"

"Never!"

"If I didn't know you better, Jim diGriz, I would think that you were a closet bestialist with your mad adoration of these creatures."

"When I was a small lad they were my only friends."

"Well you are a big lad now, so you can keep your friendship priorities in order. Let us make tracks to the circus."

I let down the ramp in the rear of our transport and Gloriana trotted in happily. There was a little window that looked in from the cab, so I could keep an eye on her. But she was very self-possessed and instantly went to sleep.

I will add nothing about our trip to Fetorrscoria. Some things are best quickly forgotten, dropped out of the memory cells, to shrink and vanish. Our spirits leapt, or at least stirred feebly, when we entered the city limits of Fetorrscoria.

It was well after dark by the time we pulled up before the large building that was our destination. Igor dropped our luggage into the gutter, then scowled down at Gloriana as she trotted past.

"Pig poo in back. Twenty credits more."

I looked in back and shook my head. "No poo, no pay." I passed him the agreed amount. He counted it slowly, then shoved it into his pocket. Then his brow furrowed in unaccustomed thought. Memory surfaced sluggishly.

"I see poo. Pay!"

"I no see poo, you no see pay."

"You pay!" He waved a granite fist in my direction and lurched forward. Angelina smiled.

"My turn, if you please."

I had no time to answer before an extended foot caught him in the ankle. As he fell past, her joined hands thudded into the back of his neck. He hit the road with a satisfying thud.

As he stumbled to his feet muttering foul oaths I pointed at his truck and said, "Go. Before it gets a lot worse."

I almost hoped he would try something. He had offended my Angelina and I do not take that lightly.

I wasn't the only one who felt that way. There was a blur of ruddy quills as Gloriana shot forward. He shrieked and bounced about on one foot, clutching the ankle where a sharp tusk had made its impact. Still muttering he climbed up to the cab. The now empty vehicle vanished into the night, Igor's pockets heavy with my coin. Gloriana snuffed with pleasure as her nose rustled through a trash bin beside the door. I pressed the button under the sign reading COLOSSEO STAGE ENTRANCE. The door rattled and opened and a bewhiskered face appeared.

"Whatcha want?"

"Is this the present home of Bolshoi's Big Top?"

"Yeah."

"Then swing the portal wide, my good man. You have the pleasure of addressing none other than the Mighty Marvell!"

"You're late."

"Never too late for the entranced audience that will very soon await the Mighty Marvell with bated breath. Guide us to our dressing rooms, my friend."

He led us into the depths of the Colosseo. I followed with Angelina on my arm, Gloriana trotting at our side, the luggage coming up behind. My new and illustrious career was about to begin.

"You're late," another voice said. I turned.

"Cerberus at your portal said exactly the same thing. And you are . . ."

"Harley Davidson. We've been in touch." He stepped into the dressing room and we shook hands. He was a tall, dark-haired man looking quite dapper in his ringmaster's garb. From shiny black boots to even shinier top hat he radiated showmanship.

"I hope that you are as good as your reviews," he said.

I hoped so too since they were all well-planted fakes.

"Even better!" I tried to exude charm and emit positive vibes.

"Last magic act we had the guy was too drunk to go on most nights."

"I assure you that I am a lifetime teetotaler. May I introduce my wife, Angelina?"

Like a true showman he took her hand and kissed it.

"And this is Gloriana."

He looked quizzically at her, but did not kiss her. "I like animals in an act. Gives them style. Do you know the Great Grissini? He had some routines like yours."

"Know him! He is my mentor. Taught me all that I know."

"That's good to hear. A quality act. There are a couple of hours yet before the first curtain. Take a rest. You look bushed. The call boy will give you plenty of time."

"Is there a restaurant nearby?" Angelina asked. "It has been a long time between meals."

"None that I would recommend. But there is a list of take-aways by your phone. They aren't too bad . . ."

"You have been avoiding me, Harley. We must have a talk."

The deep voice rumbled like a volcano as the man stepped into the room. He was my height, but must surely have been twice as wide. His head was shaved bald, his trailing mustache long and black. I expected his clothes to split when he moved because his muscles rose and knotted like tree trunks; his forearm was thicker than my thigh. I recognized him from his pictures. The man we had come countless light-years to see.

"Well met I say!" I said. "You can only be the galaxy-famous Puissanto. It is indeed a great pleasure to meet you. I am the Mighty Marvell." I stepped forward and held out my hand in greeting. He extended only two fingers and I could barely get my hand around them. I squeezed hard but they were as unyielding and inflexible as rods of steel. His little red eyes blinked and his forehead furrowed in thought.

"You heard of me?"

"In the farthest star systems they sing your praises."

The slightest of smiles came and went, accepting my blatant flattery as revealed truth. The scowl was back when he turned to Davidson.

"How come the guards won't let me out of the building?"

"Because you are barred from the city, that's why. And every credit of the bribes that I laid around, to keep you out of jail, is coming out of your salary."

"Nothing to do here all day."

"Nothing for you to do in the city."

"It didn't happen like they said."

"Of course it did! Do you know how many witnesses I had to bribe to back up your lies? And it has happened to you too often before this, as you know very well."

"They mugged me."

"What? Twenty-eight steelworkers mug one bald-headed joker? Three in hospital, all unconscious when the police came."

"Just having fun . . ."

"For the last time. One more occasion like this last one and you are out of here and looking for a new circus."

Harley had nerve—and guts enough for three—standing up to this monster like he did. For a moment I thought it would be murder and destruction right before our eyes. Puissanto tensed his muscles, his biceps rose up, veins writhing under the skin like snakes. Then he muttered something better unheard, turned and stalked away.

"This happen often?" I asked as the tension drained away.

"Too often. He gets his walking papers when this booking is done. I have enough trouble with the hippogriffs." He looked gloomily down at Gloriana. "And this one better be house-trained."

Then he was gone and Angelina closed the door behind him, sat down and said *"Whoosh."*

"And I second that."

She smiled. "Welcome to show business," she said.

CHAPTER 6

IT WAS SURE GOING TO be a hot time on the old town tonight. I found this out when I passed the security station for the Colosseo, which was close to our dressing room. The rows of screens caught my eye; I stopped and looked in. On the screens I could see that floodlights illuminated the plaza before the entrance doors. There was a lot of action there and good things were beginning to happen. Chauffeurs opened doors and saluted. Well-dressed couples emerged from vehicles of all kinds. Transportation that flew, rolled on wheels—or tracks—and in one case an ungainly contraption that actually hopped. There was respectable money out there: I should have realized that. So far all that we had seen of Fetorr was the dirty underbelly of this industrial world. Mines, smelters, factories, grime. But all of this meant serious credit accounts for the lucky few on top. Good old Capitalism red in tooth and fang; little for the many at the bottom, plenty for the few at the top.

All thought of economic ambiguities vanished when I returned to our dressing room, where Angelina was examining herself in the full-length mirror.

"The green outfit!" I cried aloud. "Perfect, gorgeous, incredible—I must kiss this goddess of charm."

An upraised palm halted me in my passionate plunge.

"Later. I've been half an hour getting this theatrical makeup on and I am not going to let you smear it now."

"Can I smear it later?"

A very negative sniff was about all I deserved for this not-too-snappy rejoinder. I realized now that her eye shadow was shadowier than usual. Her eyebrows arched high, black and intense; ruddy patches glowed on each cheek. "Get your makeup on now, Jim, just as I showed you."

"I will, I will." Seating myself at the mirror, I rubbed on a layer of foundation. A motion caught my eye, and I saw the imaged form of Gloriana settling into her basket.

"Has she been any trouble?" I asked.

"Quite the opposite. Very good-tempered, until some drunken lout tried to get in through the door. She's faster than I am. Had his trouser legs in shreds in an instant and him yiping back down the corridor. As a small reward she had a cheese sandwich with black truffles, and a bowl of milk, and is now having a rest. I wore the green outfit because it goes so well with red quills."

We had time to wait, because our gig ended the program, the last one before the first interval. But enthusiasm gripped us so much that we went up to the stage and looked out through the peephole in the main curtain. The seats and boxes were filling up; looked like a full house. Then we had to step aside as Puissanto's heavy gear was dragged into place. His was the opening act.

"Get into the wings," Harley Davidson ordered us, just as the band blared out a brassy fanfare. He pushed through the curtains and was greeted by enthusiastic clapping.

"Ladies and gentlemen, and peons—welcome to Bolshoi's Big Top." This provoked even more ecstatic applause, particularly from the workers in the highest balcony, separated from their betters by strong wire mesh. The ringmaster waited until the clapping had stopped.

"The finest acts in the galaxy are now yours to enjoy. Put your cares behind you and allow yourself to enjoy the finest entertainment that the galaxy can provide. Tonight you will be amazed by the mysterious magic of the Mighty Marvell. You will marvel at the multivaried life-forms of Gar Goyle and his astonishing troop of monstrosities. They are matched in outstanding attraction only by the sinuous beauty of Belissima and her Bouncing Ballerinas.''

This drew not only applause, but shrill whistles from the upper reaches of the audience.

''To open this evening's performance of the daring, the dynamic and the death-defying, I give you the man of titanium, the strongest man in this galaxy and any other galaxy, the unstoppable, the unforgettable, the unbelievable—Puissanto!''

The ringmaster stepped aside as the curtains opened and there was the strongman, oiled and sleek, bulging of muscles and undoubtedly reeking of testosterone. Where Angelina and I stood in the wings we had a fine view of his act—and fine it undoubtedly was.

''High-carbon steel,'' Ringmaster Davidson said, as Puissanto clanged a finger-thick, meter-long bar of steel on the anvil before him. He then held it by the ends, knelt and placed it across his knee. There were oohs and aahs from the audience as he tensed his muscles, his shirt splitting open with the effort, and bent the steel across his thigh. Everyone liked that—liked it better when he opened his mouth and chomped down hard on the steel.

And bit it in two.

''You will notice before you—'' the ringmaster said when the shouting died down, ''—that the jolly brickworkers who have just come on stage will now be plying their trade while Puissanto continues to amuse you.''

Silence from the gentry in the audience below, but hearty oaths and shouted insults and advice to their comrades on stage from the workers above. Puissanto continued with his feats of strength while the workers on the stage sloshed cement on bricks, slammed them into place, and began to build a wall. It was as high as their heads when another fanfare blared and the ringmaster stepped forward.

"Solid brick and mortar—you saw it built. A strong brick wall, or at least it will be when the mortar has set. But we will not wait for that. The machine you now see coming forward, used only in the most hazardous conditions, will set this wall before your very eyes."

There were screams and gasps as a tongue of flame flared out. The machine's operator, wearing a protective suit, played the flame up and down the wall. When it was fried to his satisfaction two heavies carrying sledgehammers came forward and, accompanied by the anvil chorus from the orchestra, swung the sledges and tried to bring down the wall. It remained intact.

The laborers left, taking the machine and their tools with them; the ringmaster bowed his way out as well. The theater darkened and the spotlights picked out the solid figure of the strongman as he stalked forward to look at the wall. There was not a sound from the audience as he tapped it with his fist—and smiled. Now it was just wall and man, lit up against a background of darkness.

He walked the width of the stage, turned back and stood poised. Snare drums rattled with excitement, growing louder in a rising crescendo of noise—crashed into silence.

Puissanto lowered his head, braced his arms—then ran swiftly at the wall. Bending double as he ran. Lowering his head.

At full speed crashing his bald skull into the brick wall.

Which shuddered, cracked—and fell to pieces.

Pandemonium all around as he wiped brick dust from his skull and bowed to the cheering crowd.

The audience loved him, and were still cheering and clapping after three curtain calls. He was going to have to do something more before they would quit. So he did. None of his familiar props this time.

"Puissanto hears you and understands your enthusiasm,"

the ringmaster said. "Therefore, for your continuing pleasure, he will perform a little encore."

Instead of returning behind the curtains, the strongman now went down the steps from the stage and into the audience. He shook a few hands—or rather let them try to shake his fingers, smiled happily while lovely women kissed him. Then he went back to the first row and bowed.

And while he was bowing he reached out and seized two seats, one in each hand, where they were bolted to the floor.

Then, with one concentrated contraction of his muscles he wrenched them from their moorings and held them on high.

Louder cheering if possible, and laughter at the man and woman in the seats, holding on to the chair arms and trying to smile. The curtains opened to a blare of trumpets. Holding the seated couple over his head Puissanto climbed back to the stage, turned and bowed to the audience.

Then proceeded to juggle the pair like giant dumbbells!

Up into the air they went in brief arcs. To be seized by those giant hands as they dropped. Grabbed and thrown aloft once more. Five times he performed this act of strength and coordination before he lowered them safely to the stage at last. The girl kissed him, the audience went wild. Harley Davidson, who was standing close by me, shouted aloud across the stage. But so wild was the audience that I was the only one who could hear him.

"You'll pay for those chairs, Puissanto! I'll take it out of your pay."

Stagehands removed the chairs while the strongman bowed one last bow and left.

When the shouting died down the music changed to a lugubrious funeral march, accompanied by shrill screams and manic laughter. All the house lights dimmed and died while the frenzied screaming grew louder. A single blue spot came on and there in its glow was a handsome tuxedo-garbed man who bowed to the audience and said, in a voice filled with menace, "Welcome—welcome to Gar Goyle's Interstellar Freak Show."

He stepped aside and a four-armed, green-skinned man took his place and bowed low. He was wearing a tartan kilt and sporran. He took a small white skull—with tiny horns—from his sporran and tossed it into the air. Then another until the air was filled with flying skulls, juggled in complex patterns by his four hands. It was most impressive and greatly enjoyed. Particularly when he launched the skulls, one by one, into the audience. The audience fought to catch them then, after examining them, ate them. Because they were made of candy.

"Greetings dear friends, greetings. I am here this evening to bring you a gaggle of ghastliness, a hemorrhage of horror, a dribble of disgust. Gathered from all corners of the galaxy for your edification and repulsion are the freaks of nature heretofore concealed from the eyes of the public. The misborn misfits, the monstrous mutations that you may heard about, perhaps dreamed about. But if you dreamed, ladies and gentlemen, your dreams were nightmares. Terrorizing riders of the night—like Snailman!"

The curtains snapped open and a harsh, bright spotlight burned down on the creature on the stage. There were gasps and cries from the audience. With good reason. He was bent and twisted, half-emerged from a spiked shell, recoiling into it away from the clamor of the audience. Then he sought to escape, crawling slowly across the stage leaving a trail of slime behind him. He came towards me, eyes bulging wildly, and I recoiled. Not human, a pseudoflesh robot I kept telling myself. Yet I was relieved when he turned and crawled in the opposite direction. Whoever had designed this creature had a very warped mind.

Next the audience cheered the bird girl, with stunted wings for arms, a horny bill instead of a mouth. Enjoyed it when she fluttered a few feet into the air.

There were more like this. The audience loved it; which told me a lot about the inhabitants of Fetorr. I found that a little repulsion went a long way. Still, I hoped that it would never stop. For every minute that passed drew me one minute closer to my stage debut. Could I appeal to this audience? It was too late to put a little blood and slime into my routines. It would have to be magic, pure and simple.

I was barely aware of the acts that followed as I fussed with my props and shuffled cards from hand to hand. Angelina came up, leading Gloriana on a golden chain, and cocked her head when she looked at me.

"How do you feel? Your color is awful."

"First-night tremors. Do you realize this is the very first time we have performed the act in public? Despite all those pages of fake reviews."

"Jim diGriz—this is not like you. You have faced down large guns, small generals, giant animals, grasping tax men. You have never hesitated. Stop sweating, pull yourself together, drink a bit of this." She produced a flask of medicinal brandy. "And remember the motto of show business."

"It will be alright on the night," we intoned together and I took a good slug from the flask.

Then we were ready to go on, listening to the ringmaster's masterly introduction of fake facts.

". . . dived from a thousand-meter-high tower into a small bathtub of water—and survived! Handcuffed, chained and locked into a steel safe and dropped into the ocean, struggled for hours to escape—and escape he did!"

Had I been mad to write this kind of nonsense for the fake reviews? My sins were coming back to haunt me.

". . . so without further ado I bring you that master of magic, the supremo of sorcery, the wizard of witchcraft—the Mighty Marvell!"

Act cool and you are cool, Jim, I kept telling myself. Cool, cool. I walked to center stage and bowed—and almost lost it. Because just in front of me, in the center of the front row, was my son Bolivar, clapping like crazy. But he was supposed to be light-years away.

I couldn't speak. Luckily I did not have to. I turned and extended my arm, waved Angelina to make her entrance. Which she did most handsomely. Applause thundered. Either they loved porcuswine on golden chains—or they appreciated the fair Angelina as much as I did.

I could not say how the act went since I was possessed by a chill numbness as I performed. At least I didn't drop anything. And they oohed at the right places and laughed when I expected them to. Angelina handed me the props at the right time, screamed when I put her into the box and cut her in half, collected the slips of paper for the mind-reading act. Floated mysteriously in midair. Then suddenly she was before me, leading Gloriana and I knew we were ready for the vanishing act that closed our performance.

"Look on and admire," I called out. "Beauty and the beast. In the flesh and alive—for now. I beg you to be silent, because if anything goes wrong, one slip, one instant of inattention, and the results could be incredibly disastrous. There now, they enter the cage. Now the glorious Angelina will lock the ferocious porcuswine to the floor with heavy locks and chains. They are now in place. Are you ready? Yes you are. Now, the magic word, *Monosodiumglutamate!*"

The canopy dropped down, rose an instant later and they were gone. The audience roared with appreciation when they saw that the cage was empty. Woman and swine had vanished. The curtains closed and I stepped out for a few last bows. Bolivar threw a bouquet of flowers which I neatly fielded. With a small movement of my thumb I indicated backstage and he nodded.

He was in the dressing room before me, pecking the air next to his mother's cheek so he wouldn't smear her makeup. She made a neat curtsy when I presented her with the flowers.

"From Bolivar," I said.

"And from James, Sybil and Sybill. I promised to call them

as soon as the act was over. It was really great. And that's a powerhouse porcuswine you have there.'' Gloriana snuffled agreement and let her back be scratched.

''Is it permitted to ask what you are doing here?'' I asked.

''Working in a bank, of course. As soon as we knew that you were coming to this planet, James had his search engine digging deeper and deeper, building a data bank on Fetorr like you wouldn't believe. There are forty banks in this city alone.''

''I believe it. Where there's crud there's credits.''

''The bank here with the greatest reserves is the Bankrott-Geistesabwesed. Did you ever hear of it?''

''No. Should I? It is not a name that exactly trips off the tongue.''

''We did some digging, and it wasn't easy, and eventually discovered that it belongs to an old friend of yours. One Imperetrix Von Kaiser-Czarski.''

''Not Kaizi?''

''None other. The Widows and Orphans 1st Interstellar Bank, the one he told you about, is owned by him as well. For some reason, best known to him, this one is supposed to be secret. So I sent him a message, telling him that we were helping with your investigation. Told him that I could help him a lot more if I were a teller in the branch of the Widows and Orphans bank here, to sort of be on the spot if anything happened. I thought he might have a certain influence that might get me appointed here.''

''Did you get the job?'' Angelina asked, always interested in her son's career.

''Not quite. He liked my new banking expertise so much that he made me manager instead.''

''My son the bank manager!'' Angelina said and smiled.

''Then that is something else we can celebrate tonight,'' I said just as a phone rang. He slipped it out of his pocket, listened, then hung up.

"Anything important?"

He nodded, a little grimly I thought.

"That was the night manager of the bank on the line. It seems that, just a few minutes ago, the bank was robbed."

CHAPTER 7

"I MUST GET BACK TO the bank," Bolivar said, starting towards the door.

"I must go with you," I said, hopping about on one foot while I tried to pull my dress trousers off.

"We must all stop and think first," Angelina said, most practically. "The bank has been robbed. By this time security men and the police will have sealed off the crime scene. So there is no need for us to rush about in circles flapping our wings."

Bolivar had his hand on the doorknob—but did not open it. "Good thinking," he said. He let go of the knob, turned and sat down.

"You are the bright torch of wisdom in the dark night of stupidity," I said. Sitting down and taking off my shoes; which made the process of removing my trousers that much easier. "While I change out of my show clothes, perhaps Bolivar would be kind enough to book us a room at the nearest and most elegant hotel, with transportation provided therewith. We came here too late to do it ourselves."

"Good as done." He tapped into his phone. "Done. The Royal Suite at the Waldorf-Castoria awaits you and the limo is waiting."

"Tell them that I'll need an hour to change and pack," Angelina said, slipping behind the screen. "And make sure that there is first-class accommodation for Gloriana. I'm sure that she is tired after tonight's performance." A petite porcine snore from the direction of her basket underlined the assumption.

Intelligence was beginning to slip back into my overexcited cerebellum. I pointed at the leather suitcase. "We'll take the supercomputer with us. It might come up with an answer or two."

"You will call me and let me know what happened at the bank?" Angelina said.

"As soon as we know ourselves," I said and blew her a kiss as we left.

Since the night's performance had not yet ended, there were plenty of floatcabs in the rank outside. We climbed into the first one, Bolivar gave the driver instructions, then turned on the machine that was built into the partition before us.

"What is that?" I asked. He pointed to the label.

SURVEILLANCE DETECTOR UNIT

"Industrial espionage is big business on this planet. This thing monitors for bugs in the cab, generates white noise to stop detection from outside."

"How do you know that it is not bugged itself?"

"Because I test it with this." He unclipped a small device from his belt and held it out. It bleeped and flashed a green light. "A surveillance detector detector. The bank issues them and tests them daily with . . ."

"I know—a surveillance detector detector detector. Continuing down this road leads only to madness. Because every morning, before it is used, the banks surveillance detector detector detector detector must be tested by . . ."

"Best not to think about that kind of thing Dad. Better to think about what we should do about this robbery."

Bolivar leaned over and pressed the actuator on the cab's

detector. It instantly flashed a red light and spoke in a metallically reedy voice.

"Eavesdropping device under seat cushion to the left."

Bolivar dug down behind the cushion and pulled out a few coins.

"False alarm?" I asked.

"I doubt it."

He looked at them quizzically—then opened the window and threw them out. The detector buzzed once, flashed a green light, then turned itself off. "One of those coins had to be a transmitter."

"Why should someone want to plant that thing to spy on us?"

"Probably not after us at all. Whoever they are, they may have wanted to observe someone who was attending the performance. So they bugged every cab there."

"Expensive way to work."

"Plenty of money available for that sort of thing. So—now that we have privacy—isn't it time to think about what action we should take about this robbery? We need a game plan."

"You are absolutely right," I said with great authority. Then slumped into the seat. "Only we don't have one."

"We do. For the first time since the thefts began we are on the spot when the robbery occurred. We gather all the evidence—and I mean all, then feed it into your supercomputer and see what it comes up with."

I patted the thing's leathery hide. "Good as done."

Only it wasn't. There were plenty of flashing lights ahead, ranks of policemen, great lengths of tape bearing the legend POLICE LINE DO NOT CROSS. Our cab slowed and stopped at the barrier. As we emerged a burly minion of the law strode up.

"Leave. No one permitted."

"Stay," Bolivar said, producing his wallet. "I am manager of that bank and I am going in."

The policeman frowned down at the ornate jewel-encrusted badge and reached for his phone. His superior was of little help so we clanked up the chain of command until we reached a gold-braided copper with enough authority to let us by.

"Who are you?" he snarled at Bolivar.

"I am Bolivar diGriz, the manager of this bank. And you are? . . ."

Gold-braid glared first. "Captain Kidonda of the Serious Crime Squad. They called me at the theater. I tell you, I don't like my evening ruined like this."

"I couldn't agree more. It is not doing much for my evening either."

We stopped in front of the bank and stared at the great hole in the outer wall. Someone other than a widow or an orphan had made a massive withdrawal.

"Impressive," Bolivar said, looking at the opening. "There used to be a cash machine there."

Gold-braid nodded. "Eyewitnesses say they pulled it out with a skyhook. One tug and it was up and away. Every policeman on duty is looking for it now."

"What about the bank?" Bolivar asked.

"No alarms went off—other than the ones on the cash machine."

The captain's phone beeped and he snarled into it. "What?" He listened, then nodded. "Yes, do that. The lab technicians as well." He hung up and turned to us.

"The cash machine had been found, abandoned. And empty. Do you know how much cash was in it?"

"The records will be in the bank. Let us go and see." Bolivar leaned over and looked into the glowing eye of a retinascope. It beeped twice. When he put his palm on a metal plate beside the front entrance it burred slightly and unlocked the door. The three of us went in.

Low night-lights illuminated the interior; security cameras moved in slow arcs. Street light poured in through the immense hole in the bank's wall; chunks of debris fanned out across the floor.

Our presence was detected and gentle music began to play.

Serious financial music with an arpeggio of profit, while a compound-interest melody played in counterpoint we crossed to the massive bank vault and Bolivar leaned over to look at the indicators.

"At least we have no problems with the vault here. This is sealed tight. It has a time lock that cannot be altered from the outside. It will only open in the morning after the staff arrives."

Was the vault waiting to hear these words? As soon as he had spoken the ceiling lights came on and the big wheel in the center of the door began to turn.

"Good morning, customers," the vault said. The wheel clicked to a stop, then the thick steel locking bars withdrew from their sockets.

"You said it couldn't be opened?" Captain Kidonda was not pleased.

Before Bolivar could answer him the massive portal swung wide and we could clearly see inside through the barred gate.

The floor was strewn with empty safe-deposit boxes.

At that instant the alarms sounded deafeningly and all of the security lights began an eye-stabbing flashing. The captain was shouting into his phone, then waved forward the jumble of policemen that was coming through the door.

"Get a squad around to the back of the bank." He turned to Bolivar. "Is there a rear entrance to the bank?"

Bolivar nodded. "There is a a small pedestrian entrance, as well as a garage entrance for armored van deliveries."

"Got it. I want this building surrounded so tight that a gnat can't get out. The perpetrators are probably still in the bank. Move it!"

They moved. Then he ordered up a heavily armed squad. "Shoot anything that as much as twitches," he said.

"I assume that does not include us," Bolivar said. The captain ignored this levity. "Take us to the rear entrances," he ordered.

Bolivar obliged. I trailed behind, anxious to see what was happening, but at the same time not wanting to draw their attention to me. Bolivar unlocked the doors as we went. Through offices and storerooms to a final door.

"This opens into the garage area," he said.

"Unlock it—then step aside." He waved a command and an armed and armored zap squad moved forward. "When I open this, get in there. Don't take any chances. Fire first."

They nodded grim agreement, stood poised.

The door flew open and they charged through it. Firing into the darkness as they ran. Bolivar reached in and turned the lights on.

Layers of gunsmoke drifted in the air. The room was empty.

"Open the outer door," the captain ordered.

Bolivar threw the switch. Motors whirred and gears ground as the heavy armored door sank down into the ground. We waited tensely, guns ready. There were people outside.

Another row of policemen, also aiming guns.

"Don't fire!" Bolivar shouted at the trigger-happy cops. "We're all on the same side!"

Fingers twitched, then relaxed. Safety switchs were turned on.

"Can you explain how this happened?" Captain Kidonda said, turning on Bolivar.

"Certainly not. I was at the theater as well."

"But you know what happened?"

"I know exactly as much as you do. The money machine was pulled out of the wall. And somehow, someway, person or persons unknown entered the vault and removed all of its contents."

"How?"

"How should I know?"

"You should know because that is your job." The captain was losing his temper. "And I am beginning to think that this was an inside job. Planned by someone who knew exactly how to open the vault. Then took himself off to the circus for an alibi."

"I don't need an alibi!" Bolivar said heatedly. "I did not

do it, had nothing to do with it. Can't you get that fact through your thick skull?''

''Insulting a police officer in the course of his duty!'' the captain roared. ''That is a criminal act! Arrest this man!'' he shouted and burly rozzers leaped forward to seize my son.

''You can't do that!'' I shouted, swinging the computer like a weapon as I started forward. The captain got in my way.

''Not only can I do that—but I can throw you in the pokey beside him if I hear another word from you!''

''Forget it, Dad. It's all some kind of mistake.''

''*Your* mistake!'' the police oaf said grimly. ''A new manager from offplanet is *most* suspicious.'' He hesitated a moment, listening to the telephone in his ear. ''Right. The commissioner agrees with me. I have orders to bring you in.'' He jerked a fat thumb in my direction. ''You get out of here or you are also going to be in *big* trouble.''

His breath was redolent of the last three or four meals he had had, his voice gravelly with disdain. I glanced over his shoulder at Bolivar—who gave me a quick wink. I understood. Don't get involved now. Don't make a scene. Get out of here—then think of more subtle ways of solving the current problem. Other than running off at the mouth. His was a mighty informative wink.

I cringed. ''Dear, sir,'' I whined. ''You must forgive me, carried away by these terrible events, you are of course right. Justice will be served. While I crawl back to my miserable hovel and berate myself deeply at my mistake.''

I bowed and hunched and shuffled backwards away from the scene. Gold-braid was about to say something when Bolivar pulled free of one policeman and planted a solid punch on the other. There was much avid cursing and struggling that covered my exit. I crossed the police lines and waved down a cab that was slowly cruising by as the driver ogled the scene.

''Pull over.'' I said. ''Start the meter, stay here, we are waiting for someone.''

He was happy to oblige. Enjoying the arrival of the siren-screaming van that backed up to the front of the bank. There was a quick glance of people getting in the rear door, then it pulled away.

"Follow that vehicle," I said.

"No way! Them's security police and they are bad news."

"Only to the guilty. I am a newspaper reporter on assignment and here is my identification."

I passed over a golden fifty-credit coin that he took with some hesitation. "Okay. But I'm not getting close."

The traffic was light enough to follow from a distance. We could clearly see the police van drive through an open door in an immense dark and ugly building. The driver hit the brakes and we screeched to a stop.

"Out, out!" he squeaked. I opened the door but took my time about leaving.

"What building is that?"

A moan and a gasp was my answer. Finally he choked out the words. "That's . . . Slawter House . . . headquarters of the Fiscal Constabulary. Also known as the Roach Motel. They go in—but they don't come out." I closed the door and gave him some more money.

"That's great. This will make a fine story and my editor will be pleased. Now take me to the Waldorf-Castoria where my employer awaits my arrival." A chill passed over me since it was Angelina who was waiting. I knew in advance what her reaction would be when I arrived. The cab was fleet, the distance short, her wrath understandable.

"You let them imprison our son?" Angelina said with venom in her voice and murder in her eye.

"I was ready to take them out—but Bolivar said no. He winked at me."

"He has an old head on a young body. Probably saved your life—taking on the entire police force at your age. What's next?"

"We get him out of there. The course of events has taken a very ominous turn. There are too many coincidences and I don't believe in that. But I do believe in active malice. I am sure that our role in this affair has been rumbled. First, we are here in this city when the robberies occur. And it is a totally different kind of crime from the previous ones. Always before there has been no alarm—but the banks have been found cleaned out in the morning. Now we have a cash machine plucked out with noise and jumble. That has never happened before. Then, when we are inside the bank, the vault is apparently robbed just before our eyes. No good. We get Bolivar out now. But we have to have a good alibi for the time when all this is happening."

"You have arranged that?"

"I will. Or rather you will. Call down for great amounts of food and drink. We are going to have a party."

While she did this I dug our apparatus out of the bags, stuffed needed items into my pockets. A portable radio filled with functions never imagined by its manufacturer. A camera that took good pictures—but picture taking was probably the simplest of its functions, only the smallest fraction of its abilities. I had just finished changing into dark clothes when I heard the door announcer. I was sitting on the couch with a lit cigar when the trolleys rolled in.

"Eat drink and be merry!" I announced, tipping freely and breaking open a bottle of bubbly. But as soon as the door closed I jumped to my feet and produced the webber from my pocket. "We go," I said. "Garbed in black and ready for action."

"And you have some subtle plan to save our boy?" Angelina said as she pulled on her slacks.

"Not that subtle since we have little time and less knowledge of where he is being held. So we just blast our way in."

"Good. Let us do it."

I went out onto our balcony and slapped the webber to the wall beside it, where it adhered with an unbreakable molecular grip. Seizing the handle on the thing I swung out into the darkness. "Join me," I said, and Angelina took my waiting hand. A touch of the button and the liquid web was expelled from the spinneret; it congealed instantly. We went smoothly down just as a spider would on a web.

I swung right on past the balcony on the floor below us, since there were lights on in the room. The window on the floor below was dark, so we landed there. I concealed the webber against the wall, turned, and opened the sliding door with a quick twitch of my lockpick. Down four flights to the basement, thankfully without being seen. Then out through a sealed and alarmed emergency door. Which unsealed at my touch, alarm silenced as well.

"I like that little blue sports car," Angelina said.

"I do too. But I think we need something bigger and more sober. That one."

A large, black saloon which opened to my touch, started instantly, bore us away into the night. "I'll park around the back of the building," I said. "We will go in through the front. Move fast, play it by ear, not stopping, get Bolivar and get out."

"Sounds good—and could be fun as well. I realize that we have been leading what could be called a dull existence of late."

"You can't go in here," the guard at the front entrance said as we walked up. He was raising his weapon when I reached out and cracked the deepsleep capsule under his nose. He dropped. Dropped his memory too, since I had incorporated a bit of an amnesia drug in the formula. We pulled on gas masks before entering the building. Fairly quiet at this time of night, even quieter when the blackout spray and deepsleep took effect. Uniformed bodies thudded to the floor on all sides. We stepped around them to get at the uniformed bully who was slumped behind the reception desk. He woke and gurgled briefly when I injected him, drooped again when the next needle hit.

"I am your master," I whispered into his ear.

"Yes, master."

"You will obey me."

"But speak and I obey."

"Where is the prisoner who was brought here earlier? The one involved in the bank robbery."

"Interrogation room six."

"Take us there."

He did. Most docilely. The few people we met slept comfortably in the corridors. We stopped at the signaled door, our guide joined the others in slumberland; somewhere in the distance an alarm sounded.

"They've finally rumbled us," Angelina said.

"Took them long enough. Ready?"

She nodded. Her features unseen behind the mask—but I knew that she was smiling as she opened the door and threw in the capsules.

They were all unconscious, even Bolivar who hung limply from a rack of some kind. There was blood on his face and hands. As Angelina went to get him down she managed to plant a foot in each of the men around him.

"Thanks," Bolivar said simply when he opened his eyes. "Bunch of sadists this lot."

Was it by accident that Angelina managed to walk on their faces as we left?

The alarms were louder now, with the sound of running feet in the distance, hoarse shouts and the occasional sound of gunfire. They were obviously panicked and firing in the dark. We stayed away from the growing clamor and instead worked our way to the rear of the building where we descended to the ground floor.

"This should be the outside wall," I said dubiously.

"That *better* be the outside wall," Angelina said positively. "Now get us out of here."

Not sure of the thickness of the wall I planted a treble charge. Even around the corner of the corridor we were stunned and deafened by the explosion. We staggered through the debris and out of the immense opening into the night. Not too far from our car. We were well gone before anyone else appeared. Returned the stolen vehicle to the spot where we had found it parked, then made our way back to the balcony and our room, reversing our escape route.

"I am going to clean Bolivar up and change," Angelina said. "While you order up more drink for our party."

"Now it really is a party," I said. "So we can celebrate a bit—before we figure out what the next step will be. I have the strong sensation that our invisible enemies have been one step ahead of us ever since we arrived on this planet. Let us then do something to even the score."

CHAPTER 8

I POURED THE CONTENTS OF two bottles of good booze—what a waste—down the drain. And ordered more. The party must go on. A newly patched up Bolivar wandered about the suite, detector in one hand, a barbecued porcuswine rib in the other, checking the detectors. Gloriana had wandered out to see what the excitement was about, squealed woefully when she sniffed her departed relative, and had retired again to her bed. Angelina, attired in a nifty tigerstriped negligee, was repairing the damage inflicted on her fingernails by the night's events.

"As a reward for your medical ministrations I would say that another cool glass of bubbly would be in order," I offered.

"Very much in order." She took it and sipped. I knocked back a double dram of Old Kidney Killer, then took some more—with ice this time. Nibbled a canapé or two and let myself relax. But could not.

"What do we do about Bolivar?" I asked, phrasing aloud the question that was prominent in everyone's mind. "This hotel room is not the safest place for him to be."

"Nor this city—nor this entire planet," Angelina said with some venom. "I am uneasy about everything—because everything seems to be falling apart in a most unpleasant way. I am beginning to wish that we had never met Kaizi. Or let ourselves by hypnotized by all the money he offered.''

I was very much in agreement—but felt that I had to at least attempt to be cheerful.''

''It is going to work out—and we will be rich. But first, as you said, what do we do about Bolivar?''

''I'll be just fine,'' he said. At the very same moment the door chime chimed to contradict his words. ''But I think that I'll be finer if I step into the other room.''

''The police are a very thorough bunch on this backwoods planet,'' I said. ''So I think that you will be finer still—if you step out onto the balcony instead of the bedroom and hang out about there. I smell trouble.''

My prognostic sniffer was indeed right. Three large and burleys filled the hall outside when I opened the door.

''This is a private party and you are not invited,'' I said and closed the door. Or rather tried to, but a large shoe stopped me.

''National Security Police,'' the lead goon said, flashing an ornate badge with a hologram of a striking snake. ''We are coming in.''

''Without permission or a search warrant?''

''None needed. Not on Fetorr. In the name of justice we have the right enter any premises that we deem suspect.''

''We are having a bit of a party here—what is suspect about that?''

''*You* are,'' he snarled, pushing me in the chest. Normally I would have dropped him for this, but now I was just playing for time. I moved back hesitantly and he smiled. ''You were in the presence of a known criminal early this evening.''

''That's no crime!''

''It is if I say it is. Out of the way.''

They rushed in and I had to step aside or be trampled. Angelina sipped her wine and did not grace them for an instant by acknowledging their rude presence.

"Where is Bolivar diGriz?" the one who spoke asked in a nasty and suspicious way. Perhaps the others couldn't talk.

"Who are you?"

"Inspector Mwavuli. Where is he?" He looked around. "Search this place."

"Where is who? Bolivar? He is in jail—where your fellow officers took him."

"He is not. He escaped."

"That's nice to hear. Drink?"

There was none of that "not on duty" nonsense on Fetorr. He poured a glassful of hooch and knocked it back without taking his eyes off me. His co-conspirators returned from their search of the premises and answered his raised eyebrows with negative grunts.

"Don't leave this city," he ordered. Then they left.

"Charming," Angelina said as she double-locked the hall door, put on the safety chain and propped a chair under the handle.

Bolivar came in from the balcony and touched his finger to his lips. He made a careful search of the suite with his detector and returned with a handful of bugs. They were disguised as coins, soap cakes, picture hangers—and even one roach. He flipped them off the balcony then poured himself a glass of red wine.

"Bolivar—you are going to join the circus," Angelina said.

"My lifetime ambition!'

"Don't be cheeky. I mean it, seriously."

"Of course you do. But I was also thinking of the little matter of reaching the Colosseo. I'm sure that all the police have my photo by now and are on the lookout. The streets are not safe."

"For a young man, yes. But for a young women they are as safe as they possibly could be on this despicable planet. Prepare yourself for a temporary sex change. I pity the thug that tries to get smart with this particular young lady. Shave your legs while I get you some clothes."

The sky was getting light by the time our son was dressed to Angelina's satisfaction.

"What do you think?" she asked.

"Bolivera has never looked better!"

Nor had he. Neatly turned out, long skirt and svelte bosom. Good makeup and a not too wiggy-looking wig. Angelina nodded approval as well.

"Now get a few hours sleep—and don't wrinkle the dress! You will leave by the main entrance. And do try to mince a bit when you walk. Like this."

When he was mincing fine we all retired, very much in need of some rest.

I managed a few hours sleep and awoke feeling a bit better. After a picker-upper pill I felt better still. As I did, first thing every morning, I checked my bank account. The expected four million from Kaizi had not come through. But there was a message.

NOT TOO GOOD, JIM. TRY HARDER.

It was late morning before we left. Angelina and I went out first, me with the computer and her leading Gloriana. Bolivera slipping out of our suite as soon as we signaled him that the hallway was clear. He waited for the second elevator since we were sure to be followed. We were. We ignored the tails and hailed a cab to take us to the circus.

"No animals," the driver said, looking suspiciously down at Gloriana.

"This is not an animal," I said as I slipped him a more than generous tip. "It is our daughter who has a piggish spell cast upon her. We are on our way to a witch who had promised, for a price, to restore her to her normal form."

He bulged his eyes at the story. But the money spoke louder than the fairy tale and we followed our sprightly swine into the cab. There was no way of testing the detector so we spoke of nothing important until we were in our dressing room. I swept the room for bugs with my own detector.

"Clean," I said folding the instrument and putting it away.

"Good. Now we must leave a note for Bolivar telling him to wait for us here. Then we must go out and find his dressing room—so we can talk to Gar Goyle. I am sure that he will be happy to help us."

"Why?"

"You will see."

I did not press the matter. I recognized the tone of voice. I would be informed at the right time—and not any earlier. Gloriana squealed lightly when we started to leave, then trotted happily after us when we called out to her. Then grunted enthusiastically when we opened the door to Goyle's dressing room. It had a very barnyardy smell to it. Or zoo. I had smelled it when the act was on stage. An artificial pong to add realism to the act.

The tuxedoed man from the act was sitting at a desk writing something; he did not look up when we came in. Was he Gar Goyle? Or was he the four-armed man who had introduced the acts? He was there now, wearing his kilt and sporran, sitting across the desk from tuxedo, speaking on the phone. I looked around. The rest of the large room was dimly lit: there was just light enough to see the cages. With things in them.

And what things! Some had been in the act. Yet there were lots more. A two-headed carnivore of some kind was pacing its cage: it hissed and bared immense fangs when I looked at it. And there was Mr. Bones—I recognized him from the posters—taking a nap on the couch. He was at least two meters tall, but no thicker through than my arm.

"What do you want?" a voice asked. I turned to see that Gar Goyle was still scribbling away at the desk.

"We wish to speak to you, Mr. Goyle."

"About what?"

Only then did I realize that it was the four-armed man who

was talking. "Just general chitchat about the circus, you know. How do you like the weather?"

I continued to ramble on as I walked about the room with my bug detector. I found six of them, five writhing bug bugs and only a single coin this time. I stepped on them all just to make sure. Crushing them with my heel until the detector flashed green.

"We have heard a lot about you," Angelina said, menacingly.

"From the Special Corps," I whispered.

He sat expressionless and silent, shifting only when Gloriana came over and sat by his feet. Then she leaned over and bit him in the arm.

"Naughty swine!" Angelina snapped. "Let go of that man at once."

Only then did the man look down and nod. "She can tell flesh from plastic, you see. A fine nose like all porcuswine."

Then he reached up with his upper set of arms and plunged his hands in the flesh of his neck and ripped down. Angelina gasped as the skin parted. He pulled the opening wide and a man wearing a kilt stepped out: he only had two arms.

"Why do you mention the Special Corps?" I looked from him to the man still writing at the desk. "Don't worry about him. He is a pseudoflesh robot, like all of the others. The audience watches him and never notices that I am controlling the act."

"Misdirection!" I said happily.

"Of course. Now please answer my question."

"Mr. Goyle we have reason to believe . . ."

"Call me Gar."

"Gar, of course. You will have heard of the Special Corps, the mythical group that fights crime and seeks justice throughout the galaxy."

"Of course. Everyone has heard of it even though it does not exist. But let me ask you a question. If this mythical Corps had a mythical laboratory and research program—what mythical scientist might be head of it?''

I touched my detector again; still green. ''Professor Coypu,'' I said as quietly as I could.

Gar sighed and slipped out of the rest of the four-armed flesh man. Gloriana let go of the arm and lay down. The pseudoman at the desk stopped writing and fell over sideways onto the floor. Gar took his chair. ''I had a brief message from Professor Coypu. He has been of great aid to me in developing my troupe. He said that I should help you if you asked.''

''Are you in the Special Corps?'' Angelina asked.

''I was. Retired. I worked in the forensic lab. Very boring once you got used to it. As the saying goes—see one corpse and you have seen them all. But I did get inspiration from the work, used it in developing my act. So you see, I do have a far more interesting job now.''

''This act.''

''A cover. I am . . .'' He waved us close, looked around fearfully, then whispered, the word barely audible. *''Guu.''*

''Goo?'' Angelina said, and he fearfully waved her to silence.

''The Galactic Union Union,'' he whispered. ''You must have heard of us?''

''Vaguely. Aren't you union organizers?''

''We are. We go boldly forth to organize unions were none have been permitted to exist before.''

''Like here on Fetorr?''

''You have it in one, comrade. And I must say that if a planet was ever ripe for organizing this one sure is.''

''It could also do with a little more free free enterprise, a good bashing for the police bullies, and the introduction of some pollution controls,'' I said.

''That about sums it up. But keep it quiet for now. Meanwhile—what can I do for you?''

''Help us hide our son Bolivar.''

''Is this the same Bolivar diGriz that cleaned out the bank

yesterday, killing a number of women and children when he escaped from the police?''

''The same. Minus the women and children of course. Plus the fact that he did not rob the bank.''

''Of course.'' He rubbed his jaw and looked around the room. ''Do you think he would mind being Megalith Man? He's having trouble with feedback controls, see.''

There was a stirring in the darkness and a gray creature stumbled forward. Angelina gasped and I had to struggle not to do the same. A rotund bulging forehead almost covered its eyes. Prognathous jaw, clawed fingers and suchlike combined to produce a really disgusting simulacrum of a human being. Gar smiled and nodded.

''Good, isn't he? One of my best creations.'' The creature groaned, rolled its eyes up—and crashed to the floor. ''Your son will be safe in there.''

''He certainly will,'' Angelina sniffed. ''And knowing him I am sure that he will probably enjoy it very much as well.''

''When he arrives we will get in touch with you,'' I said. ''Thanks.''

''No thanks. The Corps takes care of its own.

I had locked our dressing-room door when we left—and it was still locked. Obviously this hadn't slowed down the once-again male Bolivar who was now staring at the computer screen.

''Your disguise obviously worked,'' Angelina said. ''I'll pack those clothes away.'' He nodded abstractedly as he typed a quick command into the machine.

''Interesting,'' he said. I made quizzical noises.

''I have been using the search engine on your employer.''

''Kaizi? Have you found anything of interest?''

''A good deal. For one thing—he doesn't exist.''

''He must! We have met him!''

''I don't mean the physical form, he was there all right. I mean the story about Imperetrix Von Kaiser-Czarski, the richest man in the galaxy. I can find no trace of him.''

"Those banks he owns—all over the galaxy . . ."

"Are not owned by him. They are held by corporations who in turn are owned by other corporations. I have traced back through a number of owners and they all appear to be different. No trace of Kaizi. It looks like everything that he has told you is a lie."

My head was beginning to hurt. I sat down heavily and checked off the facts on my fingertips. "Firstly—he must be very rich or he would not be paying us four million credits a day. Except for yesterday of course. I checked. Not only didn't he deposit the money—he left a very insulting note."

"Of course he paid you. You had to think that he was whom he said he was. The large sums involved made his story plausible. Think how suspicious you would have been if had offered, say, a hundred credits a day."

"I would have kicked him out! But let us stick with what we know. Secondly, we know that all those banks on all those planets were robbed—that's a matter of public record."

"They were indeed. It is the secondary information about those planets that I am concerned about."

"Such as?"

"The circus performances, what acts were playing on what dates, that kind of thing."

The coin was slowly dropping into the slot.

"Of course! When you examine a database there is no way of telling if the events ever really happened as they are listed—or if they are figments of imagination that a skilled hacker had planted. And there is no way of determining facts from planted facts on a distant planet without getting right into the records themselves, to see if they had been altered. Which, of course, cannot be done from light-years away."

"My thinking exactly. Which is why I have been snooping around in the databases here on Fetorr. Without much success. There are security locks on almost everything except train timetables. Lots of electronic doors were slammed in my screen."

"They don't like snooping."

"I was sure of that before I started. So I routed all my queries though a number of other systems. I didn't want them getting back to this computer."

Even before he had finished speaking the words there was a hammering on the dressing-room door.

"Open up in there! You have thirty seconds to comply before we break this door down."

"Who is there," Angelina said.

"Computer Crime Corps. Do not attempt to resist. You are guilty of illegal computer use and the searching of restricted files."

CHAPTER 9

THE POLICE, OF ALL KINDS, were entirely too efficient here on Fetorr. I looked around desperately. There were no windows in the room and but the single door. There was only the screen, which offered privacy when changing costumes, which might provide even a feeble chance to hide our son.

"Bolivar—behind the screen!" I hissed. He was across the room in an instant: the door shuddered and creaked as it was pounded. "Stop hammering—I'm coming!" I shouted.

Angelina was moving too. She closed the computer and put it on the floor, then pulled the armchair in front of the screen, sat down on it. Holding tight to Gloriana's chain as the disturbed porcuswine champed and raked the floor, her quills all aquiver. I went and unlocked the door and threw it wide. "Did you knock?" I asked sweetly.

He was immensely fat with hanging jowls and giant belly. He pointed an accusatory finger at me and said, "You have been using an illegal computer on these premises."

"Never!"

"Search this room carefully, Hafifu," he ordered. His partner, who was about as skinny as his commander was fat, scuttled into the room. He looked around slowly, beady eyes glinting, thin nose twitching like a rat's. He looked at the computer, then looked away. Undoubtedly mistaking the computer for a leather suitcase.

"I don't see no computer here," he said in a thin and reedy voice.

"Then look behind that screen," the fat cop blurbled. "You saw the readings. There is a computer in this room someplace. Our detectors never lie."

Hafifu obeyed the command and walked over and started to look behind the screen. Screamed and retreated as flashing tusks savaged his trouser legs, not to mention his ankles. Instant decision was needed—and saving Bolivar was far important than saving the computer.

"Step back!" I ordered. "That is a savage watchpig trained to kill anyone foolish enough to approach its owner. In any case—the computer is over there. It is built into that suitcase."

Hafifu circled wide of his porcine persecutor and grabbed up the computer. He opened it, pulled out the keyboard, turned it on and typed furiously. "This is indeed the criminal instrument," he squeaked.

"What criminal? I was just searching the public records. Is that against the law?"

"Yes!" Fatty said with great enthusiasm. "That is because there are no public records here on Fetorr—everything on record is private. I am confiscating this machine." Hafifu was out the door with it before I could raise a word of protest. "As well as fining you five hundred credits for attempting to illegally access the private public records."

"You can't do that!"

"I certainly can. With power vested in me by the state I can make on-the-spot fines, as specified by the statues. If you have reason to believe this confiscation is doubtful in any way you may ask for a trial."

"A trial, right!"

"That will require a two-thousand-credit deposit for the trial chamber, plus a five-hundred-credit fee for the judge."

I opened my mouth to protest. Shut it when I realized I was being stupid. "Do you take checks?"

"Yes—but there is a fine equal to double the amount of the check if it bounces."

Angelina let out a bit of chain as I scribbled the check. I didn't have a Fetorr bank account. I wrote a check for five hundred Galactic Credits. I remembered that they were on a par with the Fetorr Credit. Gloriana grunted ferociously and hurled herself forwards. Fats lurched towards the doorway, grabbed the check in passing and was gone. I locked the door behind him.

"Very efficient," Bolivar said, emerging from behind the screen. "We are going to need a new computer."

"We probably will, eventually," I said. "But they seem to be as much use as doorstops on Fetorr. For the time being we will just have use our own brains—which were around long before the electronic ones were invented."

"And writing as well," Angelina said, taking a pad and stylo from the drawer of her dressing table. "Let us first list what we know—and then what we must find out."

"Right," I said as I paced the floor and cudgeled my slightly fuzzy brain. "There is the ongoing mystery about our employer, which is not germane at the present moment in time. Who or what he is can wait . . ."

"As long he keeps depositing payments daily," Angelina said with great practicality.

"Very true. And we can forget all the other banks on the other planets that were robbed as well. They may not have any relevance to this investigation, since the facts that apparently linked them together were probably fabricated."

"Why?" Bolivar asked.

"That is the question we must answer. The easy answer is that Kaizi wanted us to come to this planet. Ostensibly to investigate the bank thefts. Though I am beginning to doubt that story as well. Why he did it in this roundabout way is not important now. We are here and on the job."

"And theoretically investigating Puissanto," Angelina said. "Which, as I dimly remember, was the reason we came here in the first place. Shouldn't we take a closer look at him?"

"We should—but things have been rolling downhill at a furious rate," Bolivar said. "What with a bank being robbed almost as soon as we got here. And me being fingered as the criminal."

I shook my head. "I think that was pretty accidental. The thieves had no way of knowing you would be here when they planned their heist."

"I agree," Angelina said. "Kaizi went to a lot of effort to get us here at this time. Bolivar's arrival certainly wasn't part of whatever game plan he is pursuing."

"What *is* his plan?" I asked, then answered myself. "For us to find the thieves who are emptying out his bank or banks. To do that we must first find out just how the bank was robbed. We need someone on the inside—that's why it was perfect when Bolivar was working there."

"I'm not working there any longer."

As he said this, and I considered the implications—inspiration struck.

"Yes you are. You will be restored to your former pinnacle of banking success."

"For about two seconds before the police arrive."

I rubbed my hands together with gleeful self-admiration. "They won't arrest you because they will think you are your twin brother James. Who will come here as soon as he is summoned—and incidentally will bring along a new computer."

"How will that help?" Angelina asked. "James knows nothing about banks."

"But Bolivar does!" I chortled. "He will just resume his old position. Since Kaizi owns the bank he will help us to fake the identification, retina patterns and all that."

"Congratulations," Bolivar said. "It sounds so insane that it has to work."

"I agree," Angelina said. "I'll send an interstellargram right now to tell him that his presence is strongly requested."

She unleashed Gloriana, who scratched under her collar with a rear hoof. Then the pleasant rattle of quills stopped suddenly. She was on her feet, head cocked and ears erect. I touched my finger to my lips—then pointed to the door. There was a gentle scratching there. Bolivar slipped back behind the screen as Gloriana trotted over to the door, muttering swinish oaths in the back of her throat. Something white appeared under the door and she had it in a flash.

"A sheet of paper—a message perhaps," I said. "Good swinelet, bring it to daddy."

She click-clacked across the floor and dropped it at my feet. I turned it over and read: "Burping Barney's Robot Takeaway—free and most speedy delivery."

"Sounds interesting," Bolivar said, emerging from his hiding place. "It has been a long time since breakfast."

"Featuring free beer with every order over fifteen credits. Vegetarian nutburgers, carnivore girafburgers, Styrofoam dietburgers—plenty of good stuff."

Angelina phoned in the order and the service really was fast; there was a tootling of tinny trumpets in the hall. Even before Angelina had contacted the local communication center and finished phoning in her interstellargram. The robot steam table—shaped for some obscure marketing reason like a coffin—rolled in. Accompanied by a recorded organ recital and the smell of ancient grease. I poured in five-credit coins until a bell dinged and the coffin lid flew open. The food was hot, the beer cold, and the damned coffin stayed there playing gloomy liturgical music until I stuffed more coins into the *tip* slot and kicked its wheels until it exited.

"Good," I said as I licked my fingers and watched Gloriana munch her way delicately through a spiced bananaburger.

"Too greasy," Angelina said, "as well as being bad for the waistline." Then she picked up the phone when it chimed. Listened and nodded. "Ten minutes," she said, then hung up.

"That was the front box office. A reporter from the *Fetorr Times-Picayune* wants to interview the Mighty Marvell for their *Live Today, Everyday Program*. You must remember that we show people do thrive on publicity, so I said yes." She rose and beckoned to Bolivar. "This dressing room is getting entirely too busy. Come Bolivar, let us get you over to Gar's before the press arrives."

I changed into my tail suit, and was just tying my tie when there was a discreet tapping on the door. I opened it and stared up at the large and impressive silver robot that was standing there.

"Greetings," it said in a mellow voice. "I am robreporter number thirteen, representing the *Fetorr Times-Picayune*. A friendly newschannel bringing you all the news as it breaks. Here is my identification." It extruded a green press pass from a slot in its thorax, gave me a quick glimpse, then pushed it back out of sight.

"Might I come in? Thank you." I jumped aside before it ran me down. "It is rather dark in here. I will need more light."

The transparent top of the creature's domed head flared brilliantly. A camera popped out of its chest, pointed at me. A directional satellite dish on the creature's back buzzed as it oriented itself. Then a screen just below the camera lit up and I was staring at my glazed expression; I smiled theatrically and showed my teeth, which was a bit of an improvement. Number thirteen began to speak.

"Greetings to all our viewers with the news as it happens, where it happens, why it happens, however it happens. This is Baridi Baraka, your favorite reporter on the magical scene now with none other than the Mighty Marvell."

The camera lens whirred and my image on the screen was joined by a dark-skinned man in a green suit who was apparently talking to me. Only he wasn't there. I mean in the room with me—but he was on the televised image. Which meant that he was just a computer-generated image of a reporter. They saved a lot of money this way.

"Now tell me, Mighty Marvell—what is it like to be a magician?"

"It is a laugh a minute, Baridi old friend. Something is *always* happening. Like this."

I waved my hand in the air, distraction, then raised my other hand with a bouquet of black flowers apparently plucked from thin air. And held them out to thin air. On the screen the reporter bent over and sniffed them, smiled with pleasure.

"I tell you viewers—real flowers, just like that, smell great too. You are a master of your profession, Marvell, I can see that. Do you like being a magician?"

"Like it, Baridi old buddy—I just love it. I love to travel and love to entertain crowds." The door opened and Angelina came in. I waved her over with an expansive gesture. "And even more I love my assistant, Angelina, who never minds being sawn in half every evening and a matinee on Saturday."

"Hi, Angelina," our invisible interviewer said. "Say 'Hi!' to the millions of viewers out there who are hooked on magic—and hooked on *you* as well, of course. Now, without giving away any magic secrets, just how do you get sawn in half?"

Angelina smiled deliciously, and was beginning to explain absolutely nothing in words of one syllable or less to the millions of morons who were watching daytime television, when our friendly reporter broke in. The computer-generated reporter had been nodding his head as if he had understood every word. When she had spoken for exactly thirty seconds—which was probably the attention span of his viewers—he interrupted and thanked her. Turned back to me.

"Tell our viewers, Mighty Marvel, what was the most exciting moment in your exciting career?"

"That's an easy one. It was during a performance I was giving on a distant planet named Wirtschaftlich, much given to farming and like pursuits, that there was an accident in the road outside the theater. One of the vehicles involved was a farm vehicle transporting a ravening porcuswine in must. It escaped from the battered transport and attacked the theater doorman, obviously enraged by his red uniform. The doorman fled into the theater with the great beast right behind him. I knew instantly what I had to do. I ran towards the creature, crying aloud and flapping my cloak, which has a red lining. The beast then charged me! The ending is obvious. I lifted my magic wand and, before the horrified gaze of the audience—did my vanishing porcuswine act. Would you believe the creature was gone in an instant?''

''No, I wouldn't believe it.''

''I would wring your computer-generated neck if I could get my hand on it!'' I shouted as my hands clutched at empty space. It looked better on the screen as I happily throttled him.

''Temper, darling, temper,'' Angelina said soothingly, gently pulling me away from my tormenter.

''Well, if you put it that way, ha-ha, of course I believe you. Now, Mighty Marvell—and Angelina—don't go away quite yet because I know that you have plenty more exciting anecdotes to tell about the marvels of magic to our millions of viewers. But I have been told that a big news story is breaking. Over to Patikana Peke who is, yes, now at the very scene of the crime.'' The screen flared, died, brightened again with another computerized reporter standing in front of a bank.

''Just behind me,'' the image said, ''is the Bankrott-Geistesabwesed Bank. Peaceful and prosperous. Even if its name is unpronounceable, until a short while ago and just about to open for the day when *this* happened.'' The screen widened to take in the front of the bank, now torn open. Computer-generated oohs and ahhs oohed and ahhed, along with the sound of breaking glass. ''Hard as it to believe that this bank robbery occurred right in the middle of the day, right here in lovely downtown Fetorrscoria. One moment peace and prosperity reigned. The next moment . . .'' An immense explosion echoed out, followed by more breaking glass. ''This was happening. The bank was not broken into—it was broken out of! The thieves apparently gained access to the money vault sometime last night and entered the vault. Not only did they break into the vault—but they took their armored motorcycles inside with them. Well! I'll bet you can just imagine the look on the bank manager's face when he spun the wheel and opened the vault door! Vroom! Right out of the vault they came—and right over him. If you look closely you will see him lying inside the bank and being treated for wheel marks. Over him and across the lobby and right through the plate-glass window of the bank. To instantly be lost in traffic. A city-wide police hunt is on for the thieves. Keep watching and we will bring you this incredible story as it breaks. I have a bulletin, stand by, yes. They have made good their crime. They have escaped in broad daylight, taking their loot with them. The police made contact and pursued them but, unhappily, they have now managed to make their escape into the industrial zone by leaping a high wall on a prepared ramp."

There were more quick scenes of crowds at barricades, police holding them back, confusion and alarms. Then a gray-haired uniformed officer emerged from the bank and walked towards the reporter who managed to keep on talking without flagging in the slightest.

"And there is more news—evidence has been found at the scene of the crime. Evidence that may lead the police to the thieves, to track them down and apprehend them. Tell us what you have there, captain!"

"Evidence. Found in the vault. A telltale clue we are sure."

"What is it?"

"A clue."

"Yes, you said that." Did I detect a note of electronic exasperation? "Would you please tell our millions of viewers just what kind of a clue you are holding in your hands?"

They were big hands, and the camera was jiggling around irritatingly trying to see the clue in question. "A metal clue," the policeman said. Then finally held up the object in question. "As you can see I am holding what appears to be a cutout figure made of thin metal of some kind, of a sort of rodent, a mouse maybe."

The camera panned in until the object filled the screen.

"The captain is right, yes he is, that is a metal rodent if I ever saw one. Too big to be a mouse, it must be a rat. Yes, screen viewers, you can see it now very clearly."

And, yes we could see it very clearly.

"Stop me if I am wrong viewers. But I do believe, yes it is—that must be an image of—a *stainless steel rat!*"

CHAPTER 10

I WAS VERY GLAD AT that moment that I was not on camera. I am sure that my expression was one of gaping stupidity; that of an eyeball-popping, hang-jawed moron. What was happening? I took a quick look at Angelina and saw that she was as stupefied as I was. She recovered faster; touched her hair with the back of her hand, her expression now one of abstract interest.

This was Not a Good Thing, that was for certain. Someone in the bank-busting business was having a good laugh at my expense. A stainless steel rat indeed! A clue for the police—or a warning for me? By the time the current crime report had ended I had restored my composure and managed to carry off the rest of the interview in a fairly relaxed manner. I even managed a few quick card tricks without flubbing them.

"There you are viewers—a magic end to our interview with this magic couple. Playing nightly at the Colosseo right here in lovely downtown Fetorrscoria, the home of theater, sport—and just good funery!"

The light on the robot's head paled and died. A metal plate with a piece of paper secured to it emerged from the creature's midriff: it handed me a stylo.

"Standard release form, sign her, initial here and here. And now the lady, thank you."

The paper was whisked away as a small panel clicked open in the thing's metallic hip. It reached in and took out a thin bundle of banknotes, split the bundle neatly in half and handed one sheaf to me, the other to Angelina.

"One hundred and eighty credits each, standard fee. Good-by."

It opened the door for itself and was gone. Angelina locked it carefully, then turned to me. "Any explanations?"

"None whatsoever. Except someone is after me—and I'm not being paranoid."

"What do we do about it?"

"The stainless steel rat? There is nothing we can do, is there?"

"We can leave this repellent planet."

"No!" I was suddenly quite angry. "He, they, it, she—whoever or whatever is behind these games is not going to get away with it. If we leave now we will never know what the goings-on on this planet are all about. And besides, I like earning four million a day."

She arched her eyebrows at that. "Greed goeth before a fall."

I thought about that as I stamped over to the bar and retrieved a bottle of Zubanishamali Sour Mash and a glass; two glasses. Held one out. She shook her head.

"Thank you, no. I don't how you can drink that filthy stuff. A white wine, if you please."

I opened and poured and pondered the future. We clicked glasses and drank.

"It's not the money," I announced at last. "It's my reputation—or lack of one. Someone is diddling with my life. I have to find out who it is and cause it to cease. I am being set up—worse my whole family is being set up. I do not like this. But who is doing it?"

"Kaizi," she said firmly.

"A possibility. Or it could be whatever dark power I am being paid to discover. This would not be the first time that the hunter became the hunted." I looked at my watch. "Before anything else exciting happens I am going to begin our investigation of our only suspect, Puissanto. I have plenty of time before the next performance."

Before tempting fate I went to the stage door, where its geriatric guardian was reading a holo-horror comic. Little shrill screams and demonic laughter sounded thinly when he turned the page.

"I'm looking for Puissanto. Have you seen him lately?"

"Yeah. Gone out to eat a meal. Does it four or five times a day."

"Do you have any idea when he will return?"

"An hour. Usually takes him about an hour to eat. I saw him do it once. Unbelievable."

"That's great, thanks. I'll try him later."

For a lot of obvious reasons I tried him now. His dressing-room door was locked. I knocked sharply, but there was no reply. Remembering him biting the steel bar in half, I made no attempt to enter until I had listened at the door with my electronic eavesdripper. Silence. No clatter nor sound of breathing. I then checked for alarms. Finding none I use the lockpick to make a quick entry. Closed the door behind me and stared into the darkness.

Light switch, somewhere on the wall, found it and blinked when the brilliant lights came on. There was the standard dressing table, the screen, the couch with broken springs—as well as some mighty solid-looking props. Weights, bars, an anvil, two barrels of beer, a smoked porcuswine ham hanging from the ceiling with a great bite taken out of it: just what you might expect in a strongman's room. Nothing unexpected. Some papers in the wastebasket. Receipts from a dry cleaner. One lion skin with moth holes. Man's jacket size 108 large. Not too revealing.

I went to the dressing table. No notes or pieces of paper in the drawers, one book on the table. I checked through it, held it to the light so I could see the title. *Star Bashers of the Galaxy Strangers.* Mindless and sordidly violent fiction—what else would a mindless and sordidly violent weightlifter read?

And a battered computer on the table. I switched it on. The screen flickered and then went black and displayed the flickering red message. ENTER PASSWORD it said. I turned it off and noted the make; an Eprom-80. I would dig out the specs and then, when I had a little more time, I would see if I couldn't break the secret password. Or wait until James turned up—this sort of thing was right down his hacking alley.

There was a rumble of masculine voices just outside the door.

Was Puissanto coming back? Panic struck: I could feel those steel fingers sinking into my windpipe already. Was there any place to hide? Possibly behind the giant trunk in the corner—if there was room enough to fit.

The door handle was turning!

I hit the light switch a nanosecond before the door opened a crack. Then stopped.

"... and I am deducting the cost of replacing the wheel of the lorry you tore off of." It was Harley Davidson, I recognized his voice.

"Tried run over me. Puissanto don't take hestelort from dumb driver. No way."

"It was an accident, you saw the police report, the driver never touched you."

"Wheel touch. Pull off."

"Indeed you did—and the half-axle and the differential along with it!"

"Cheap lorry, built like crap."

"Nevertheless you are paying for it."

While this intellectual conversation was going on I tiptoed across the room. There was just enough light coming in through the partially open door to find my way around anything in my way. I had to move the trunk a bit before I would fit behind it. There was a horrid grating sound when I pushed on it. Apparently not heard in the hall. I slipped behind it just as the door was flung open and the light came on.

Puissanto slammed it shut and walked across the room muttering to himself in a bass rumble. The floor squeaked, then the chair groaned as he sat down. He must have picked up the phone because I could hear the low clicking as he punched in the number. It should be ringing somewhere; he breathed hard and was still muttering.

''Talk Paka now. Get.'' He said to whoever answered the phone. More heavy breathing until Paka answered.

''Paka?'' he said. ''Is there any comprehensible reason why you failed to meet me at the appointed rendezvous? You did? Repetition will only bring retribution. Negative. Be there in fifteen minutes or our pecuniary relationship will be terminated.''

The phone slammed down, heavy footsteps crossed the room again. The light switch clicked and darkness fell. The door slammed, the key grated in the lock. I breathed out a deep and shuddering breath and crawled out from behind the trunk.

A new mystery had now presented itself. Our moronic slab of muscle could talk like a professor when he had to. Was it relevant? Of course it was. The computer had uncovered the fact that he had been present whenever the bank robberies had occurred. If his head was just bone and muscle, as he made it appear, then he was not involved in complicated and surely technological crime. But he wasn't dumb at all—which meant he could be involved. I sighed. Another mystery to add to all the others.

I waited a decent amount of time, then exited. When I opened the door to our dressing room I was preoccupied, still pondering my recent discovery. Angelina was at the dressing table.

''Do I have some interesting news for you,'' I said, throwing the door wide. ''I have just discovered that . . .''

My voice ran down as I saw that she was not alone. A beady-eyed and black-uniformed official of some kind was sitting across from her, now turning to stare coldly at me. His uniform was dead black with silver buttons, and it had interesting lapel ornaments of crossed swords over grinning skulls.

"What did you discover, darling, I'm dying to know," Angelina broke in, giving me a moment to recover.

"The house is sold out again tonight—so bonuses are in order all around. And who may I ask is your visitor?"

Swords-and-skulls spoke before she did, cold and menacing.

"I am Captain Wezekana of the Alien Interrogation Police. Let me see your identification papers."

I dug them out. They had more different kinds of police on this planet than I had ever seen before. He shuffled through my ID, held one page up to the light and squinted at it.

"If you tell me what you want perhaps I can help . . ."

"No."

About the kind of brilliant conversation one could expect from someone who wore his kind of uniform. The silence lengthened as he studied my papers in ever greater detail. If he was trying to frighten me he was succeeding.

"Did you get the porcuswine swill?" Angelina asked.

"Sorry, the shop was all out of it."

"I will try myself later. We mustn't let the dear piglet starve."

"No indeed. Perhaps I could get her a sandwich."

"An excellent idea—but no pork."

Our feeble attempt at conversation petered out in the shadow of this grim copper.

"I'll keep these papers," he said, stuffing them into his pocket.

"You can't do that!"

"Of course I can."

"What do you want them for?"

"You are under suspicion of having alien criminal identification."

"No way! And why am I under suspicion?"

"Because you are from offplanet. You have arrived recently. You are male and of a certain age. That is enough to make you a suspect."

"That's pretty broad grounds to make me a suspect."

"It is a beginning. We have six hundred and twelve suspects like you. We are narrowing that number down. Where were you when the bank robbery occurred today?"

"Sitting right where you are sitting. I was being interviewed for a television program. In fact that's how I know about the robbery. The news flash broke into my interview."

"Your alibi will be checked. Meanwhile I don't want you to leave this city."

"Of course I am not going to leave the city. I am performing in the circus here with a performance every night. Thousands of people watch me and applaud wildly."

"I will look into that alibi as well," he said coldly.

"It's not an alibi, it's the truth." I dug into my pocket. "Here. A free ticket to tonight's performance. You will personally see me there."

"I will personally see you in prison." He took the ticket and tore it in half and dropped the pieces onto the floor. "I will charge you with attempting to bribe a police officer."

He brushed his hands together as if he was disposing of something nasty. Stood and started towards the door. Any relief I felt ended when he turned back to me.

"What do you know about the Stainless Steel Rat?" he said.

Instead of screaming out loud and rushing to escape I stared at him with the same cold glare he was using on me. "What in the world are you talking about?"

"It is the alias of a criminal with a record of serious crimes on a number of planets."

"I am not interested in criminals. I am an honest theurgist

who earns a modest living as a theatrical magician.''

I was starting to tap my fingers against my leg. Keep cool! No signs of stress. Put my hands into my pockets. Pulled them out again. Something metallic tinkled to the floor. We all glanced down.

It was the lockpick I had so recently used on Puissanto's door.

''That is a lockpick!'' the captain said with cold triumph, his eyes locked with mine.

''Of course it is,'' Angelina said walking between us, bending to pick it up. The spell was broken.

''I go nowhere without it,'' I said calmly. ''Look here.''

I strolled across the room and took up the book of imaginary clippings about my totally fake career. Riffled through it, held it out to him.

''The Underwater Magical Escape. See the manacles on my hands. The locks and chains on my legs. The steel cage about me. The fact that I am about to be lowered into the water. Without that lockpick I would very quickly drown. Thank you my dear.''

I took the pick and put it back into my pocket. I could feel that basilisk gaze burning holes into the back of my skull as I turned away. Crossed to the chair and sat down.

The stare continued until he made up his mind.

''It is illegal to possess a lockpick on Fetorr. I am going to have to confiscate the one that you have.'' He put his hand out. I shied back.

''You can't do that! I will drown if I can't pick the locks in the underwater cage.''

''That is no concern of mine.'' He was all heart. When I didn't oblige him he took out a large gun from his holster and pointed it at me. ''I will not ask you a second time.''

Muttering complaints I dug the lockpick out and handed it to him. It vanished as did, happily, the gun.

''I will be back.'' He turned and left.

Angelina went to the door, waited a moment then opened

it. The hall was empty. I took out my detector and swept the room. The captain had been busy. Two coins, bugs, in the chair where he had been seated. More under the carpeting and in the wastebasket. They sparked and crunched when I stepped on them until the green light on the detector blinked.

"I don't like it," I said. "I am beginning to feel trapped, as though the powers of darkness are closing in on me."

"A little overdramatic—but very close to the truth. Let me pour you a drink."

"My angel. A large one. Thank you." It helped. I think.

"We had better cancel this tour and leave this planet," Angelina said. "Weren't you the one who always said that he who fights and shifts his freight, lives to fight another date?"

"I did—and I meant it. But that was some years ago when I was much faster on my feet. Always on the lookout for a fresh challenge. Right now this old rat is feeling a bit rusty and put-upon. And stubborn. For a lot of reasons, including some I am not sure of, I do not want to back out of this one."

"The four million credits a day. That's all you can think about—right?" I nodded reluctant agreement. "Why don't we forget about it? There is no point in being the richest prisoner in some foul Fetorr jail."

"There is a certain wisdom in what you say. But let us not quit just yet. What I started to say, before I saw your unwelcome guest, is that I have discovered something interesting about the apparently moronic Puissanto. He has the vocabulary of a college professor, when he does not know he is being overheard. Therefore when he is on stage tonight, and I can't be disturbed, I am going to take a look into his computer." I grabbed up the phone.

"I am going to dial up the local database-search and get the specs and documentation on the Eprom-80. As long as they are not a state secret."

They weren't—but that did not mean it was easy. Paranoia seemed to rule on Fetorr. I got the phone number of Eprom Ltd. And called them. And spent the usual endless period working my way through recorded voices and punching in the numbers that they gave me. At long last I talked to a human being. And instantly wished I was still talking to the robots.

"An Eprom-80? What's the serial number?"

"How do I know. The machine is not here and the number on the documentation is lost with the documentation."

"I don't know . . . "

"You don't—but I do. Can't you just give me the price and send me the specs? They aren't secret are they?"

"No—but they are copyrighted."

"Of course they are! And so what? They come with every machine you sell. Give price. I'll send money."

The repeated use of the word money finally penetrated. In the long run he took the order. By this time my ear was sore. I went and opened a bottle of Old Ear Cure and poured a long one.

It really had been that kind of a day.

CHAPTER 11

I HAD TO WORK VERY hard during the evening performance to put all the disquieting events of the day out of my head. I succeeded—but it was not easy. Still the audience liked it, so I had not done too badly. We cleaned off the makeup, changed, and caught a cab back to our hotel. The message light in the room was blinking so I touched the button for the voice mail recording.

"Hi folks—James here. I hope that all is fine with you. I've got my tickets and I'm on my way. I couldn't get a direct flight to Fetorr so I'm not sure when I will get there. But my spacer leaves in a few minutes, bound for Helior. And I'm bringing a new and much improved computer with me. I'll let you know my ETA as soon as I get it."

"The reinforcements are on their way," I said as I reached for the booze bottle. And stopped. Things were getting very complicated and I did not need to complicate them even more with a thick head. I had a small dry sherry and a cigar instead. Gloriana rattled her quills enticingly, so I reached down and scratched her behind the ears. I felt a sense of impending doom and I did not like it. Angelina must have seen my expression because she sat on the couch next to me and took my hand.

"You are looking pretty grim, dear husband. Want to tell me about it?"

I gave her a hand an appreciative squeeze and polished off the sherry.

"If I look grim it is because I feel grim. I am possessed by the feeling that events are out of my control. When, as you know, I am used to being in charge of things, being in control of my own destiny at all times. That is not happening now. Just look at the disasters and near-misses that have occurred since we arrived on this depressing planet. First Kaizi's bank is robbed and Bolivar is charged with the crime. Admittedly we did spring him from the hoosegow—but now he has to hide out in the freak show until James gets here. Then the second bank heist, on a bank we know that Kaizi secretly owns—with a planted stainless steel rat left at the scene of the crime. Next the police are investigating me and have pinched every bit of my almost-legal identification. All in all the back of my neck feels quite warm and I am sure that it is from hot breath. So I ask myself. Is all this aggro worth a measly four million credits a day?"

"And what does myself tell you?"

"It tells me to cut and run."

"Will you?"

"You betcha. There are a lot of other ways to earn money—both legal and illegal. I would feel a lot better if we pursued some of the other possibilities rather than having ourselves in hock to Kaizi."

"Shall I pack the bags?"

I shook my head no.

"Not until after tomorrow's matinee. In the midst of all this rushing about I have come up with one solid fact. Puissanto, the suspect we have come here to investigate, is not as simple as he pretends to be. I want to find out who or what he is. When he is onstage tomorrow I'll be tapping into his computer.

As soon as I know that, we get offplanet—and take Bolivar with us.''

''Two things that bother me about this. The police have your papers—and Bolivar has none at all, as well as being a refugee from the local disgusting form of justice.''

''You are speaking to the master forger himself. Not a problem. I'll get new papers done in the morning for both of us. And the second thing?''

''Do we leave James here to carry the can after we are gone?''

''No way!'' I poured another sherry, downed it in a gulp. ''With our new and accelerated schedule we may be gone before he arrives. If we forget the complicated plan of him theoretically taking his brother's place in the bank—why then there is no reason for him to come here at all. We stop him before he gets here. I am afraid that the four-million-credit-a-day job is turning into a nightmare. What did he say his first stop was?''

''Helior.''

I grabbed up the phone. ''I'm going to get a message to him to stay there until we arrive. There are enough people in the soup now without adding another one.''

''I couldn't agree more.'' A bubbly porcine snore sounded from the direction of Gloriana's basket. ''Let us emulate that dear creature and get a good night's sleep. I think we are going to need it.''

We did. And after breakfast next morning Angelina went off with a purse filled with cash to find a crooked travel agent. Or is that an oxymoron? I used some of the portable radio's hidden talents to fake up our identification documents. I had prepared the ones that we had used to reach this planet; it was easy enough to alter the standard forms to effect a safe exit. I was finishing this task when Angelina returned and waved a thick envelope in the air.

''Done. The most time-consuming part of it was fighting off all the types who found me attractive. Six of them are sleeping peacefully but one, I'm afraid, is in the hospital.''

''I am sure that he deserves to be there.''

''You don't know how right you are. A bent taxi driver took me to a bar where he assured me the local mafia hung out. He was right. The one in the hospital is the ex-bodyguard of the local capo. He was so impressed that he offered me the bodyguard's job. It is nice to be appreciated. When I assured him that I was not a police spy, and that my fondest ambition was to shake the soot of this planet off my shoes, he contacted associates who specialize in the transport business.''

''Transporting what?''

''I hesitate to think. But in the end a deal was done. There are three tickets here on the midnight hovertrain to Mtumwaport. An industrial city known for its pollution and high death rate.''

''Wonderful! And why are we visiting this holiday city?''

''Because it is right beside the industrial spaceport for that area. And we are listed as crewmembers on a steel freighter that leaves the following day.''

''Sounds a winner. Our jobs?''

''I'm an assistant cook. You and Bolivar are engine-room artificers.''

''Will we have to work our way to the stars?''

''Not after I have given the captain the second half of his bribe.''

We packed a single bag each; everything else would be left behind. Gloriana watched all this with close attention, then made an interrogatory grunt. Angelina frowned.

''Do we take her with us?'' she asked.

''When they discover that we are missing—why a couple traveling with a porcuswine would be, how should I phrase it, pretty memorable.''

''You are right, of course. But if leave her here, why her fate is pretty certain.''

It certainly was. I looked down at this endearing creature and saw in my mind's eye a vision of a side of bacon.

We will put the decision off until later,'' Angelina said.

''No—we cannot! Call a pet supply, get a dog carrier. We'll put her in that, take her with us. We cannot leave her behind.''

We reached the Colosseo early. I was dressed for my performance and waiting in the wings when Puissanto started his act. I had timed him at exactly thirty-one minutes. Now I started my stopwatch and walked quickly to his dressing room. Once I had locked myself inside I took the documentation from my pocket and turned on his computer. It was a cheap production model with a security code that was very easy to bypass. Within ten minutes I was in. I put the stopwatch where I could see it and went surfing through the files. Mostly spreadsheets and financial returns. There were some mighty large sums being processed here—but no clue how our strongman had anything to do with all this.

Ten minutes to go. I sweated as I scrolled through another directory, it was time to get out of here. I felt the cool air on my neck.

Cool air!

I spun about and there was Puissanto standing in the open doorway. Terrifying little red eyes gleaming. Closing the door behind him.

This was a nightmare come true. Locked in a room with this monster.

''Kill,'' he said simply and reached out for me.

Covered with chunky muscle, he wasn't very fast on his feet. But then again the dressing room wasn't that big. There was a single window—but it was covered by thick bars. I jumped back, sprang onto the trunk—then did a diving roll over his head when his clasping fingers reached out for me. Hit the door with my picklock ready. Had it open—

When a hand as big as a ham slammed it shut. Cruel fingers closed on my neck. Lifted me into the air, shook me like a used rag. I choked and couldn't speak since my larynx was being slowly crushed. Then he dropped me. Put a heavy foot on my chest as I gasped in air. Bite steel rods in two, I remembered. Head through a brick wall.

"I can explain . . ." I finally choked.

"Tell."

"I am not what I seem . . ."

"Police spy!" The foot pressed down and I waited for the snapping crack of broken ribs.

"Never! I'm a . . . special investigator!"

"Who pay you?"

This was no time for lies or evasions.

"A banker! A very rich banker by the name of Imperetrix Von Kaiser-Czarski . . ."

"You lie!"

The pressure increased and darkness descended. At a great distance I heard a cracked voice saying *"no no"* over and over again. Was that me?

Then the pressure ceased. A mighty hand lifted me and dropped me into the armchair. Vision slowly returned to reveal the monster sitting quietly before me. It spoke.

"The time has now arrived for you to be more truthful in your revelations, oh not so mighty Marvell. I have an undetectable detector concealed in this room. So I knew someone had been in here during my absence. Therefore I abbreviated my act today in order to see if the same mysterious invader might return."

"You suddenly talk a lot better."

"I do. And if you give me the wrong answers no one will ever hear about it from you."

The temperature in the room went down ten degrees. He smiled.

"Now that we understand each other, feel free to tell me all about your presence here."

I told him. Everything. Except of course any details of my career before being employed by Kaizi. An interstellar private eye, that's who I was. He nodded and listened, steepling his fingers before him as he took it all in. When I had finished he appeared to stop and consider what I had told him—then nodded again.

"That is a preposterous story, Jim. Thousands might not believe it—but I do. Because in my investigative capacity on this planet I have also come across traces and trails of your employer. There are a lot of crooked business practices going on this planet. As far as I can determine, with really only a superficial examination, your associate Kaizi is one of the most reprehensible. I have uncovered these facts in the course of my investigations. You see I am really a git."

"Never! I'll challenge anyone who calls you that! You are not a git."

"Not git—GIT!" he said with anger in his eyes. I shrank away. "That is a Galactic Inspector of Texas."

"A tax man!" Not in my wildest dream.

"I am. It is a profession much needed in these tax-evading societies. Without law and taxes we would have interstellar anarchy. And this planet, Fetorr, is home to some heroically greedy tax evaders. And high on my list of suspects is your employer."

I still found it hard to believe. "A tax man . . . no one would ever suspect."

"No they wouldn't. I have what might very well be called a perfect disguise. That of a simple-minded muscle-man. Bit of fun too, I must say. I was really tired of teaching at the university. Even though I had my own department of Fiduciary Intransigence. But when I began to get reports of the tax goings-on here on Fetorr I volunteered for the present assignment. My natural assets, of course."

"Natural assets?" I was beginning to feel that I was missing some vital facts.

"That is correct. You must have heard of my home planet, Trantor?"

"Sorry—there are thousands of inhabited worlds out there."

"Yes—but there is only one with the mass of Trantor. A

little over three times the standard as expressed in planetary gravity. 3Gs in fact.''

''No wonder you can do what you do!''

''I feel light as a feather on your tiny worlds. I dream that I am floating at times. But to more important things. The man you informally refer to as Kaizi is an interstellar banker of great renown. And suspicion . . .''

He broke off when there was a sharp rap on the door.

''Locked. Go away,'' he growled in his Puissanto personality.

''I want to contact the Mighty Marvell,'' a muffled voice said. ''Do you know . . .''

''No know! Go!'' he roared.

The sharp rapping came again. Puissanto picked me up by the throat so I could not speak, held me out at arm's length behind the door when he opened it.

''Umph!'' he said. ''Who you?''

''Me Megalith Man,'' a grating voice said. ''Need to find Mighty Marvell.''

I struggled and writhed and managed to squeeze out a few words.

''Let—in—it's OK . . .''

I dropped when he opened his hand. Megalith Man came in and looked down at me where I sprawled on the floor.

''Are you alright, Dad?'' he asked.

Puissanto closed the door and looked from me to Megalith Man. ''If this is your son, then you have some really crunched recessive genes in your lineage,'' he said.

''A working costume,'' Bolivar said, talking off Megalith Man's head. ''There is big trouble coming down the pike. Mom was worried when Puissanto here cut his act short. Told me to get to this dressing room—but didn't have time to tell me why because that's when the trouble started. The rest of the program has been canceled and the theater is filled with uniforms. I saw three of them going into your dressing room. The theater entrances are sealed except for one, and they are searching and checking the audience as they leave.''

''Do you have any idea why?'' Puissanto asked.

''There's no secret about it.'' He looked at me with a most unhappy expression. ''They have pictures of you. And are asking everyone if they have ever heard of the Stainless Steel Rat.''

CHAPTER 12

I KNEW THAT THE POWERS of darkness were drawing ever closer: what I had not realized was just how close they really were. The hot breath on the back of my neck was scorching. Reality crushed in: I really had called this one wrong. We should have cut and run the night before. Now, in order to make one last stab at investigating the ongoing mystery, I had endangered the entire operation. Not to mention the health and well-being of my entire family. I took a deep—and shuddering—breath.

"Right," I said with more authority than I felt. "I have to find a way to get out of here. Any suggestions?"

"Are you the Stainless Steel Rat individual that the police apparently want to apprehend?" Puissanto said.

No point in lying—particularly since the police had linked my photograph to my name. "I have that pleasure."

"That name has a very familiar ring about it. Could I have come across it in the records?"

"Which records?"

"Tax records."

"Impossible. My motto is the golden one of the confirmed capitalist. Buy cheap, sell dear—and avoid paying taxes. Legally, that is."

"The Stainless Steel Rat—it still sounds familiar. Yes! Weren't you linked at one time to the destruction of large amounts of income tax records?"

"A calumny! Never proven! I prefer to think of my career as that of one who rights wrongs. A modern version of the old myth of the benefactor named Robbing Good. My specialty involves ironing out the bumps in the income graph, redistributing resources one might say. I might also add that I have saved the galaxy on more than one occasion. Which should count for something."

"You are sure about those tax files?"

Like all tax men he would not let go easily. "I am sure—never!" I lied. There are times when the bare truth can be embarrassing. Puissanto rubbed his jaw in thought.

"We will forget the matter of the tax files for the moment. If it is not taxes—why are the police so eager to capture you?"

"They are blaming me for the recent robberies—when in fact I am here to investigate them as I told you."

"Then you are, in fact—being framed?"

"Got that in one," Bolivar said. "And it is a frame big enough to include me as well. I was manager of the first bank that was robbed. The police claimed that it was an inside job and arrested me. With some help I managed to escape."

Puissanto pondered that for a while, then reached a reluctant decision. "If you both are innocent, then it is my duty as a good citizen—and a tax inspector—to aid you in escaping from the law. I have already investigated the police forces of this planet and they are most corrupt. Completely controlled by the tax-evading industrialists. Let me give you a name and a phone number." He found a stylo, which vanished from sight in his massive fist, and wrote the information down, passed it over. "Paka is an associate of mine who will be able to help you. Call this number and identify yourself by—"

There was a sudden hammering on the door and loud voices.

"Open up in there! This is the police."

"Go away. Me sleep." Puissanto looked around the room, saw the window. "Quickly!" he whispered.

Bolivar put his Megalith Man head back on and we hurried after the strongman. He opened the window, then reached out and seized two of the iron bars. He didn't even grunt as he bent them wide.

"Out," he said, then shouted—right in my ear which almost took my head off. "Wake Puissanto up—he kill!"

If this didn't stop the police—it at least slowed them down while we climbed out of the window. He bent the bars back into shape behind us, then went to open the door. We left.

And were soaked in seconds. At least I was. Bolivar was of course nice and comfy in his pseudoflesh disguise. Lightning flashed, thunder rolled and the rain poured down. Which was all for the best since we made an interesting and surely memorable pair. Me in my formal attire, he in his repulsive guise. The few people we passed had their heads down as they hurried to shelter. We hurried as well, eager to put some distance between ourselves and our pursuers. Turning one last corner I saw the lights of a restaurant beckoning ahead.

"There," I said. "Safe haven in the storm."

"Are you sure? Poison Pete's Red Hot Take Away—Or Eat Here If You Dare. Doesn't sound that attractive."

"Then don't eat. All we want to do is use the phone. Let's go."

Perhaps Bolivar was right, I thought as the door closed behind us. The place was grubby, the two tables nicked and scratched, the drunk clutching the bottle in the corner completely unconscious. When I breathed in the sweet perfume of food I coughed. My lungs hurt.

"Welcome, hungry strangers in the night. Poison Pete say eat and drink—food so hot your feet will shrink."

Wonderful. Poison Pete was a robot with long mustachios and a frayed blanket slung over one shoulder. The creature was also wearing an immense hat with a wide brim. Representing, no doubt, some culture now lost in the depths of time.

"What you gringos want to eat? Cactus-spine soup? Chile con serape picante?"

"We want to use your phone."

"You eat here, *cabrones*, you use the phone here." Well programmed it was to screw the last credit out of the customers.

"All right—two orders of what you said." I looked at the pictured foaming mugs on the wall. "And two beers."

Now the robot restaurateur sprang into action. Slapped two overflowing mugs of beer down in front of us, filled two bowls with a lethal-looking lumpy green concoction and slid them across the counter. Then produced a portable phone which it dropped into the food.

"Thirty-five credits, real good price," it said.

I doubted that greatly. While Bolivar paid I dug the phone out of the food and dialed Paka. My fingers burned where I had wiped off the cruddy comestibles. Someone picked up the phone.

"Puissanto said I should call this number."

"If you're Marvell, I got a call from Puissanto about you."

"That's good news."

"He said it's bad news. But he also said to pick you up. Where you at?"

I told him and he found Poison Pete's in the directory. Meanwhile Bolivar—ahh, the impetuosity of youth!—had made the mistake of tasting the food. He now laid his head on the counter while I poured the mugs of beer into his mouth. The beer steamed. He had almost recovered when a rodent-looking man came in. His nose was pointed and his bristling mustache twitched as he looked around.

"You Marvell?" he asked, poking the drunk with his shoe; his yellow and ratlike teeth slipped in and out when he spoke.

"Over here," I said.

He looked me up and down—then recoiled when he saw Bolivar's repellent guise.

"We are from the same circus as Puissanto," I explained. "All good friends. Do you have transportation?"

"I got a kangaroodle. Puissanto said to take you to his office."

"I never knew that he had an office. Are you sure? Has this anything to do with GIT?"

"Quiet!" He looked around, but neither the drunk nor the robot restaurateur had taken notice of my remark. "Word must not get out about his tax investigations. Of course he's got an office. It's a secret of course, because no one is supposed to know he's here. I'm the bookkeeper. You ready?"

"Sure. Let's go."

When we went out I looked suspiciously at his machine: I had seen its like on the opening night of the circus. The passenger cabin of the kangaroodle was suspended between two immense, piston-actuated legs. We climbed the ladder mounted on the vehicle's nearest leg.

"Belt up," Paka said. "This thing really moves. Surveyors use them in rough country." He reached out and turned on the engine just as the police car braked to a stop beside us; a powerful searchlight bathed us with light. Bolivar and I scrunched down out of sight.

"Get out of there!" a growly official voice said. "And keep your hands out where I can see them."

"I didn't do nothing!" Paka squealed.

"Just get down from that thing—now."

"Do that and you are a dead man," I said with as much menace in my voice as I could summon up. I ground my knuckle into his side and he squeaked. "This is a gun with a hair trigger—and it is about to go off—if we don't leave this very instant." He stomped on the accelerator.

With a single bound the kangaroodle hurled itself into the air. Springs and pistons absorbed the shock of landing—then it was off again on another immense leap. It was comfortable enough when we were in the air, but my chin hit my collarbone each time we struck the ground. Behind us the police cruiser roared into life and came after us, siren screaming. Our transport of delight was good in heavy traffic; leaping over any vehicles in its way. But its speed on the open road could not match that of a wheeled vehicle. As the traffic lightened the police began to catch up. We were bounding through an industrial area now. With factories on both sides of the road. At the next junction buildings changed to fencing and I pointed with my free hand.

"Over that fence—jump now!"

"I can't! We'll die—I can't see what's there."

"You'll die when this gun goes off—jump!"

Squeaking with fear he twisted the controller hard. When we landed our machine pivoted neatly on one foot, ninety degrees, then flew into the air.

And landed in a ploughed field. We bounded on gracefully, leaving the police far behind.

"You wouldn't have shot me, would you?" Paka asked.

"Of course not—particularly since I don't have a gun."

He muttered rodentine curses under his breath as he drove. Or rather bounced. We eventually came to a farm road that led us back to the paved roads, and our bounding progress was smoother after this. Paka seemed to know the country well because we proceeded through side streets and back alleys, until we reached an industrial site of workshops and small businesses. We jolted to a stop next to Udongo's Financial Services. The engine stopped and we sighed down as the pistons relaxed. Paka unlocked the door and led us inside.

"If you had had a gun—would you have shot me?" he asked. The close brush with the possibility of death still shocked him.

"I'm sorry." I really was. "It was just about the only thing I could think of at the time. Those police are bad news." I looked out of the window at the kangaroodle parked close by. With a big number plate on its rump. "Can that thing be traced by its number?"

"It could—if that was the right number. Mr. Puissanto is very thorough. Purchased legally, but the plates are false. This building is rented under a dummy company."

I looked around. An office like any other, but heavy on computers and files. Bolivar took off his head and looked around as well. ''Do you have a water cooler around here?'' he asked. Memories of Poison Pete still searing his throat.

''Other room, through that door.'' Bolivar left.

''I want to use your telephone,'' I said.

''I'll have to bill you for the call.''

''Yes, of course, whatever you say.'' I dug out my wallet. Regretting breaking my lifelong rule of never associating with accountants or tax authorities. I dialed the number which rang and rang. And with every unanswered ring my body temperature dropped a degree. Why wasn't Angelina in the dressing room? In the end I dialed the box office.''

''This is the Waldorf-Castoria,'' I said in what I hope was a disguised voice. ''I have a message for one of our guests. A Mrs. diGriz—''

''Not here.''

''But where?''

''I haven't the slightest idea. I had a quick glimpse of her when she left with her friends. They drove away in a large black car.''

I was facing the window as I spoke. The rain had stopped so I could clearly see in the glow of the streetlight a long black car easing to a stop outside. I put down the phone and moved out of sight of the window, concerned.

''Are you expecting anybody?'' I asked.

''Just Puissanto. He said that he would get here as soon as the police were gone.''

I heard the car door slam—then someone knocked on the door.

''That's not Puissanto—he got keys!''

''Stall! You're here alone.'' I grabbed up Bolivar's head and slipped into the next room.

''Just a minute,'' Paka said; I heard him unlock the door. ''We're closed, it's after hours.''

''I'm sorry to hear that. I'll come in anyway.''

That voice, somehow familiar—but who?''

''You can't come in—squeak! Is that . . . a real gun?''

''I assure you that it is. May I?''

Another squeal. Paka was not having a good day with guns. Real or otherwise.

''Where is he?''

''I'm alone!''

''Paka, you are not a very efficient liar. Besides, I have had a tap on your phone for quite a while. I heard you arrange to pick up a certain individual.''

Individual? I tried to remember my conversation with Paka. Had I mentioned Bolivar? I handed Bolivar his head and put my finger to my lips, cozening him to silence. If the gunman didn't know he was here he still had a chance. He nodded his head—I waved him back, then opened the door.

''What do you want?'' I asked.

The man with the silver-plated and pearl-handled gun turned to me and smiled.

Kaizi! Imperetrix Von Kaiser-Czarski. My employer.

''You seem to have gotten yourself into a bit of trouble, Jim. You and your family. That is not like you.''

''Why the gun?'' The black opening of the barrel was trained on my midriff.

''You are a man who is wanted by the police. Perhaps it is for my own protection.''

''You are lying, Kaizi. I have a feeling that you have never told me the truth at any time.''

He smiled. ''Occasionally, Jim, just occasionally. And I have always paid you on time.''

''Might I ask why you bugged the phone here?''

''That should be obvious. As a man of finance I always like to know what the tax authorities are up to.'' I heard someone come in through the outside door. Kaizi raised the gun. ''Nothing foolish now. Just turn around and put out your arms.''

I did. The handcuffs snapped shut on my wrists. The grinning thug was very familiar.

"Igor!" It was the truck driver who had taken us to the porcuswine farm.

"Igor, indeed," Kaizi said. "I like to keep track of my employees. Now, if you please, take a chair while we have a little picture show."

He put the holoplay on the desk and actuated it. A holographic image appeared in the air above it.

Angelina! Then she spoke.

"When you see this, Jim, don't do anything sudden or foolish," the image said, then grew smaller as the camera drew back. A masked man stood pointing a gun at her. I could now see that her hands were tied. The image flickered and moved and Gloriana appeared, slavering and angry; she was securely tied by her hind legs and immobile. Another shift and Angelina appeared again. She was coldly angry, snapping out her words.

"It is Kaizi. He is probably there with you now. Here is what he told me to say. Obey his orders. Do what he says. If you don't he promises to kill Gloriana at once."

She was livid with rage and could barely speak the words.

"If that doesn't convince you—he said that I would be next."

CHAPTER 13

THIS IS THE SORT OF situation that I really do not like to be in.

All right; I admit that I have been here before. But no matter how many times you get a gun pointed at you, with a quavering finger on the trigger, you don't really get used to it. And usually I had been alone when threatened. Now my family was involved and in danger. About the only tiny ray of hope in this situation was the fact that Kaizi didn't know Bolivar was in the other room. I looked at Paka and he looked back in silence; he wasn't going to mention Bolivar's presence. The tiny photon of light in the current pall of gloom. I was certainly less than happy with this last turn of events. But losing my temper wasn't going to help in any way. That's it Jim, under control, speak quietly but firmly.

"You are calling the shots, Kaizi. But let us get one thing straight at the very beginning. If my wife suffers even the slightest injury, it will mean that you have signed your death certificate."

"You are in no position to give orders to me!"

"That's not an order, Kaizi, it is a statement of fact. If I am not around to put an end to your miserable existence, then someone else will. Now that we have an understanding—what is it that you want me to do?"

He thought about what I had said, then decided to ignore it. He had an ego as big as dwarf star. He smiled in a most friendly way.

"See. Wasn't that easy?"

He slipped the gun into a shoulder holster and looked at the cowering Paka. Pointed a stern finger at him. "I assume correctly that you want to go on living?"

Paka's skin blanched. He was beyond words and could only nod.

"Good. I could ask you to keep events of what has occurred here to yourself. But I have no assurances that you would." Kaizi looked over at me. "My careful study of your MO revealed the fact that you use knockout gas with an amnesia element to subdue your enemies. Am I correct in assuming you are so equipped now?"

I gave my most surly nod.

"Excellent. Would you be see so kind as to administer a dose to Paka?" He looked on approvingly as the accountant dropped, unconscious. Prodded him with a toe and got only a snore in response. "It is for your protection, as well as mine, to keep our little relationship from being revealed. I want you to take command of the financial procurement operations of my bank."

"I know nothing about banking."

"I am talking about *robbing* banks—and I know for a fact that you have more than a little experience in that line. Up until now Igor here has been in charge of the operation. But he has no imagination or skill and is good only in carrying out orders."

Igor scowled at this description but did not protest.

"I have had to do all the planning myself and I *do* have other matters to think about. You will take over his team of robots. Robbery robots, specially designed for this single purpose."

"It won't work. Robots must obey the Laws of Robotics. They cannot harm man, lie, steal, commit sexual or immoral acts . . ."

"Try not to be so tiresome, Jim. I am not talking about intelligent robots. I am talking about brainless machines that have been carefully programmed. Go with Igor. He has the plans and instructions for your first assignment. The first thing that you will do is to complete the operation where my own bank was broken into."

Things were beginning to fall into place. "You robbed your own bank?"

"Of course. By that simple act I removed myself from the list of suspects from any future bank robberies."

A lot more mental pieces slid into their sockets. "Then, let me guess, you had Bolivar framed for the theft?" He nodded happily. "Which led you even closer to me until—pow!—you pointed me out as the criminal—record and all! You didn't get me to this planet to stop robbing banks—I'm here to do the direct opposite!"

I jumped for him and he touched the holoscreen and Angelina's image appeared before me. I lowered my clutching hands and tried not to froth too much. And the more I thought about it—the more I realized how I had been conned. He nodded cheerful agreement to my sudden realizations.

"It was your avarice that was your undoing," he said, rolling Paka aside with his foot and seating himself in the unconscious man's chair. "As I planned, you could see only the four million a day. That golden dazzle overcame every suspicion you had, led you by the nose into my trap. Any reasonable man would have got out before the trap closed. But no, not you. Not the Stainless Steel Rat who walks alone! I counted upon your monstrous ego to keep you going to the bitter end. Am I not correct?"

Well, deep down, I suppose he was. Though I did not like

that Monstrous Ego crapola. But I wasn't going to give him the satisfaction of having me agree with him. I pulled over a metal folding chair and sat down. Relaxed. Buffed my fingernails on my shirt and admired their shine.

"Kaizi, old thief, did it ever occur to you that I was on to you, and just leading you down the path?"

He shook his head. "No, that is not possible. You are now on the run, sought by all of the various kinds of police on this over-policed planet. You know that I have a hostage that will ensure your complete cooperation. And—" He smiled widely as he inserted one final knife into my deflated ego, gave it a twist as well. "And I have been keeping careful track of your pathetic monetary maneuvers. Thinking that you were outwitting the man who is the master of money laundering and interbank transfers. The only element of originality in the entire process was starting your own bank to conceal my millions. And even that wasn't your own idea, was it? Bolivar came up with it. I was happy to employ such an original thinker in my own bank here. Even happier to turn him over to the police for his foolishness in trying to outdo me."

"I haven't the slightest idea what you are talking about," I said bravely. To disguise the sinking feeling that I knew very well what he was talking about. That smirk again, my fists closed, what a pleasure it would be to wipe it off his face! Relax Jim, I opened my fists and leaned back. If I lost my temper he would win.

"Those millions I paid you, the golden goad that kept you going. They are gone from your bank and returned to mine once more. What do you think of that?"

"I think we had better change the subject before you get yourself overexcited and burst a blood vessel. We were talking about lies. I respect you for that, if nothing else, for you are a master liar. The more I think about it the more I begin to think that probably everything you have told me since we met was a lie. You only wanted me on Fetorr as a cover for *your* robberies. To be the one and only suspect in what I am sure is to be a spectacular series of future bank thefts. The profits of which will go to *you*!''

He smiled and took a small bow. ''One must have a certain imagination to get rich in this competitive galaxy. And Fetorr is the perfect place for this particular operation. Corrupt police, greedy capitalists, nonexistent income-tax laws. It is positively a license to print money.''

I fought even harder now to control my anger: if ever a cool head was needed it was at this moment. There had to be an end to the approaching series of bank robberies—then what? ''So I run the operation for you. What then? After the last robbery—what happens?''

''That is completely up to you, my dear friend. If you are captured there is a great deal that you could reveal about my operations. The Fetorr police are well versed in techniques for extracting information from even the most reluctant witness. You probably would not be believed, but it could be an embarrassment to me if you were. So you must not allow yourself to be captured. I have carefully examined your criminal record—which is why I decided to employ you. You are very good at this sort of thing. I suppose that with a great deal of effort you might be able to escape, flee this planet, go into hiding when your employment is finished. In fact that that is just what I suggest you do. Out of sheer generosity I will help you escape to a very distant planet. Where your wife will join you. I am sure that there will be no temptations for you to ever return to Fetorr.''

''And what do I get out of all this?''

''Isn't your freedom enough?'' The humor was suddenly gone and I had a quick glimpse of the creature that Kaizi really was. ''Freedom, restored to the bosom of your family once again. I would say that that would be a fair trade in exchange for your services rendered.''

That was it. And there was nothing I could do about it. Now. But other ears than mine had heard us talking. The wall was thin, the inside doors flimsy. Bolivar must have heard every word spoken here. He would know that I could take care of myself, know at the same that he had to follow Kaizi, run him to ground—and find out where Angelina was being kept. If her freedom were secured then Kaizi's plans were instantly worthless. Which meant that all I could do was mark time, do as I was told. And find a way to open some lines of communication with Bolivar.

Really, I had no choice.

"When do I start?" I asked quietly, keeping all my true feelings under lock and key. For the moment.

"Excellent!" Kaizi said, rubbing his hands together with pecuniary pleasure. "Igor will supply transportation, and will pass my orders on to you." He looked out of the window at the darkening sky. "The banks are closed. My employees gone, the premises empty. Go now to the coffers of the Widows and Orphans and restore that which was temporarily taken from me."

We went. Kaizi in his luxurious limousine. Igor and I in the same springless and filthy vehicle. I climbed up into the cab beside him.

"One of these days, Igor, I am going to maim and kill you. Or worse." He emitted a sound somewhere halfway between a laugh and a grunt.

"No way. Boss got you by the short and curlies. We work now."

We trundled steadily into Fetorrscoria, with the rush-hour traffic going in the opposite direction. No one took heed of our inconspicuous truck. Even the police turned glassy eyes away when we went by. Off the payway into the main streets, then passing the Widows and Orphans 1st Interstellar Bank, we turned into the alleyway behind it. Igor put on the brakes and we juddered to a stop. He dug into the clutter on the seat between us and produced a small recorder; hung it by a lanyard around his neck before he pressed the button that turned it on.

"Deactivate alarms by placing your hand on the plate beside the rear entrance to the bank. Do it now."

Igor grunted an understanding grunt, opened the cab door and climbed down. I saw him place his knuckles against the plate. Heard the tiny voice speak again. *"The palm of your hand."* Was there a note of exasperation in the recorded voice?

The hidden machinery whirred and the massive entrance portal slid slowly into the ground. Igor climbed back into the cab and thumbed the machine again.

"Drive into the bank," the computer-generated voice said. Wonderful! This cretin probably couldn't even read. We trundled into the bank, and still following the recorded instructions, he closed the garage door and waved me after him. *"Activate robots,"* was the next command.

We went around to the rear and let down a ramp, climbed inside. In the semidarkness I could make out the metallic clutter of a number of small, low-slung robots. Igor bent over and, one by one, switched them on. Green lights glowed, wheels and tracks shifted slightly then stopped. Igor pressed the button for more information.

"Everyone and every thing into the bank."

Igor turned back to me. "Bring robots. Follow me."

"Let's go, guys," I said. Nothing happened. All of the robots I have used were voice operated. These weren't. I bent and looked at the nearest one and saw a lever between the rear treads. I kicked the lever and the thing beeped and started forward. I kicked madly at all the others until they were trundling about in circles, then followed me when I went down the ramp and into the bank after Igor. I wondered what sadomasochistic mind had designed the robotic controls.

We proceeded at a snail's pace; I hoped we would be out by dawn. Pausing often for instructions, we made our way into the bank's innards. Alarms were switched off, lights turned on, grilles and gates open. Until we finally stood before the massive door of the vault.

"Enter six, six, six, six times," the robotic voice ordered.

Igor did as ordered and the tumblers fell: a green light blinked. While he was waiting for orders to turn the locking wheel I turned the locking wheel. The bars did from their sockets and I tugged the door open.

The last time I had looked into the vault with Bolivar it had been a scene of cruel theft. Safety-deposit boxes torn from their niches and thrown, empty, to the floor. Most of them were back in place, though there were gaps where those too battered to fit had been removed. Now what?

''Go to box three two five and open it.'' I beat him to it; it wasn't locked and slid soundlessly out. *''Activate device.''* The box was empty save for a plastic container with a button labeled PUSH ME on top of it. I pushed it—then began to slide and fall.

The entire floor of the vault, hinged at the doorway, was dropping down. Lights came on below revealing a chamber that occupied the area beneath the vault.

Which was filled from wall to wall with transparent plastic bundles stuffed with credits of all denominations. And jewelry and works of art. Obviously the contents of all the safety-deposit boxes.

''A great scenario,'' I said. ''I tip my hat to Kaizi, a true criminal genius. As well as being a brain-twisted swine.''

This was the perfect way to rob your own bank. Slip into the vault after closing time and open the chamber under it; undoubtedly installed by crooked offworld builders. Then clean out all of the valuables and raise the lid. Grand theft, shock, horror—and undoubtedly, writhing and complaining, the insurance companies paid out for the losses. Now, doubly rewarded, this crooked banker still had the theoretically stolen loot.

A few more kicks put the programmed robots to work. Handbots grabbed up the credits and loaded up the cartbots, which trundled away with the loot. Igor and I stood by and watched this industrious scene until the hidden chamber was empty, save a few bits of torn plastic. We followed our helpers back as Igor, ever so slowly, received recorded instructions to close and seal the vault and the bank. Obviously lacking the intelligence to reverse the commands for entry.

It was midnight, and I was tired, before we were done. I almost dozed off as we trundled down the dark streets, barely illuminated by the far-spaced streetlights. We finally stopped before the looming bulk of a large warehouse. He had obviously done this before because—without instructions!—he keyed the transmitter hanging next to the soft dice above the dashboard. Hidden motors whined and the large garage door ground open. We drove in.

"Where do we sleep?" I asked hopefully. "And, possibly, eat?"

"Unload first."

The inner room was thick-walled and well-sealed. I sat on a box and dozed while the scurrying robots carried the ill-gotten gains from the truck into the vault. Only when this had been done, and the robots kicked in the direction of their recharging outlets, did Igor yawn loudly and lead the way to what might laughingly be called living quarters. If you lived like a porcuswine in a wallow.

Igor drank his dinner directly from an amber bottle, muttered something completely unintelligible, then dropped onto one of the ragged bunks and fell asleep. I resisted the urge to kick him in the head and went exploring.

There was a desk with a telephone on it which I completely ignored. That one would be hooked directly to Kaizi's control center. The plumbing facilities looked as grim as the sleeping accommodations. But there was a freeze-n-fry unit that seemed to be operating. All of the storage compartments seemed to be empty other than the one labeled Octopus Nuggets 'n-Chips. I threw the frozen contents of the box into the hopper to the fryer, and a few minutes later it discharged a solid lump of what purported to be food.

I chewed down as much as I could of it, threw the rest of

it out and found the bunk farthest from the loudly snoring Igor.

And so to sleep.

My last thought as I corked off was yes, I certainly had seen better days.

CHAPTER 14

TWO HOUR PASSED BEFORE THE alarm in my watch went off, and vibrated silently against my wrist. Igor was still snoring away, and surely would for quite some time yet, considering all of the booze he had drunk. It was time to open some lines of communication—if possible. I slipped out of this dismal gent's dormitory, stepped over the charging robots, and found a small door close to the garage entrance. It was of course alarmed and locked, but even in my tired state I opened it easily enough. I looked out: the street was empty. Filthy and shabby. A run-down district that was perfect for Kaizi's needs. There was a good chance that no one would be out and about this time of night. I hoped that it would stay that way since I made a memorable sight in my ruined tuxedo. The rain had stopped but the streets were still wet; I turned up my coat collar and went looking for a phone.

I found two in the space of half an hour; both vandalized. I was bone-weary—but I had to go on. This might be the only chance I had to be on my own for some time—and it was imperative that I make contact with my son. I kept going. I was the only pedestrian about at this time of night, although the occasional car or truck whistled by. Another vandalized phone and I was about to give up hope—when I saw the cluster of colored lights ahead.

A mechomart! Which was exactly what I wanted. This was an all-day and all-night shopping mall, completely automated, with never another human being in sight—if you didn't count the customers. There were a few of them and I stayed out of their way. Which was easy enough to do since they pointedly ignored each other as they loaded up on beer and groceries. I bypassed them and probed the inner shopping walkways, which were now completely silent and deserted. But as I approached, motion detectors sensed my approach and switched on their amplified appeals. I ignored the shouted appeals to buy shoes, furniture, dildoes, books, vibrators and weight-reduction pills; all the necessities of our modern society.

"Buy my suit!" a mannequin in a window shouted as I walked.

"Buy me . . ." a sexbot whispered seductively from the depths of a pink bed.

"Win credits on the lottery!"

"Get drunk quicker and stay drunk longer than you ever imagined with SkunkDrunk, the intravenous alcohol drip!"

"Talk as you go—" That was it!

The holodisplay swirled with color and phone shapes. I punched my way through the commands until I found a portable phone small enough to fit in my shirt pocket. I poked coins into the money slot, then more credit notes for a lot of connection time in advance. Finally the screen lit up with a rainbow of light, a brass band played a short fanfare and a smarmy voice said, "Thanks good buddy—you've been a great customer!"

The phone finally rattled into the basket; I grabbed it up and left. To find a dark doorway to make my calls. I worked the directory until I got the right number, punched it in.

"Welcome to the galaxy-famous Colosseo. Now featuring

the incredible Bolshoi's Big Top. If you wish to contact the box office for advance ticket sales press one. If you wish . . . "

I pressed until my thumb was sore, working my way through menu after menu until I finally got the number I wanted. The phone rang a long time until a sleepy voice answered.

"*Do you know what time of the night it is?*"

"I do, Gar—and wouldn't do this if it wasn't an emergency. Your great-aunt Matilda is ill and at death's door. For more information would you please call this number . . ." The silence stretched out—then he spoke.

"*Wait a second, I have to find a stylo.*"

Done! Gar Goyle was no longer in the Special Corps—but he hadn't forgotten the Matilda code. And had responded with the Stylo countersign. It was simplicity itself. If an agent thought that a phone number had been compromised, tapped into or no longer safe, he would use a sentence with Matilda in it. After that the phone number would be given—with the last four numbers being one digit too high. If they were four, seven, zero, nine, the transcriber would write them down as five, eight, one, zero. Simple and foolproof. I rung off and started walking back to the warehouse.

Gar must have had as much trouble finding an unvandalized phone as I had had. I was almost back to the warehouse before the phone bleeped.

"Is that you, Marvell?"

"Yes. I am sure that a certain illegal party has bugged all the phones at the Colosseo—keep that in mind. Is Megalith Man back yet?"

"No. Should he be?"

"I'm not sure. He was safe when I left him, but we were out in the boonies and he had no transportation." I looked at my watch. "Tell him to call me from a safe phone at noon. If he doesn't return until after that, tell him to try again at midnight. And keep doing that until we make contact. Do you read?"

"*I read,*" he said and hung up.

That was all that I could do. Bolivar in his Megalith Man outfit might find it more than a little difficult to get back to the circus. But as long as Kaizi or the police hadn't found him I knew that he could do it.

I hoped. "No—know he is safe and will get back!" I shouted out loud to build my morale a bit. Went and let myself back into the building. Igor was still out and still snoring. I pulled the blanket over my head and tried to emulate his good example.

I awoke cursing. My dimwit companion was kicking at the bed. Then he moved fast enough so my swinging fist missed him.

"Got orders. We gotta go. North, that's good. Boss came by. This for you. Go north." He almost smiled. I did not question him: I would find out soon enough why north was good. I picked up the package and read the label on the side.

MASK-A-RAID on one side. On the other, FOOL YOUR FRIENDS. I opened it and looked at the face inside. It was no one I knew. Which, I imagine, was the whole idea. A mask of pseudoflesh with operating instructions. How to stick it to my face. How to keep it in working order. How to feed it. Apparently it lived on chicken soup rich with nutrients. A can of soup and a funnel were included in the package.

It worked a wonder. A different me stared back out of the cracked mirror. Well, at least I did not have to worry about the police anymore. Kaizi was enough to keep my worrier going full time.

I had a bit of an appetite, but when I watched Igor chomp down two greasy servings of octopus nuggets, all thoughts of food vanished. And I wished, not for the first time, that I could do with a less disgusting roommate. I skipped breakfast.

We kicked our crew of robots to electronic life and rolled them aboard the truck. Then Igor added one item that I found very interesting. A portable battery charger that he plugged into the truck's electrical system. Which meant that we would not be returning this night. I wondered just where in the north we would be.

We trundled through the morning traffic until we reached the tollway. This was fully automated and switched the truck over to autocontrol as soon as we left the slipway. We speeded up until we were exactly ten meters behind another truck. We stayed there with machinelike precision. With the tollway doing all the driving, Igor fell instantly asleep. I watched the dismal industrial landscape slide by—and timed the service areas. One appeared every half an hour. Very organized.

It was just ten minutes to noon when I killed the road control and turned off the tollway. A loud siren sounded; Igor woke in a panic and wrested back control of the truck. Pulled over and braked to a juddering stop.

"You try kill us!"

"No. I just wanted to stop."

"Stop? Why stop?"

"Rest stop stop. Little boys' room."

"What little boy?"

"Pee, you moron."

"Yeh, pee." His eyes rolled up as he took a bladder-pressure test. "Yeah." We went inside.

I kept an eye on my watch, finished and exited the rest room before he did.

"Where you going?"

"Food. See you back at the truck."

He was suspicious but there was nothing he could do about it. I waited until I saw him head for the parking area. Ten minutes to noon. Just enough time to punch in the vending machine for a kafinkola—I was still tired from the night before—and a high-energy beanwich. I sat in a booth in back, eating and slurping and watching the door.

My phone rang exactly at noon.

"Bolivar?"

"None other."

"Tell me—no don't!" Igor had suddenly appeared and was

coming in the door. "Give me your number, be ready to take a call at midnight."

I crouched down in the booth, put my finger in my drink and wrote his phone number out in wet figures of kafinkola on the tabletop. Had the phone back in my pocket an instant before my companion in crookery popped into sight.

"No time. Gotta go."

"Go, go, here I come." Memorizing the number as I stood up.

Things got better the farther north we went. The mills, mines and factories gave way to automated farms. It was nice to see a bit of greenery. Then trees, more and more of them until the road was cutting a wide swath through virgin forest. A tunnel ahead dived under rolling hills—to emerge above a coastal plain bordered by a blue sea. I was beginning to see why Igor thought the north was good.

The first of the homes appeared, most of them sprawling mansions. Even the verges of the payway were landscaped now.

"Bosses live here?" I asked.

The answering grunt sounded positive. Top and bottom in this polarized society—with very little in the middle I was sure. We took the first exit, found a high-tech industrial estate hidden by trees from view of the road. Igor had obviously been here before. He worked his way through the numbered drives to the rear of an isolated unit. The sun shone warmly on a patch of grass and an umbrella-shaded table. And shone as well on Kaizi, who was sipping from a frosted glass.

"You look disgusting," he said when I swung down from the truck. He was right. My unshaven face was beginning to itch under the living mask. My eyes were gritty and an interesting shade of red. After being soaked with rain my once-fancy dress was not fancy at all.

"About Angelina—"

"I shall tell you nothing," he snarled. Under that that flint-like exterior beat an even more flintlike heart. "You are my employee and will do exactly what I order you to do. Events need speeding up.'' He threw a cashcard on the table before me. ''There is a mechomart in rollway fourteen. Get some clothes, smart dressy clothes, dipshave, soap, you know what. This is not Fettorscoria. I want you looking exactly like everyone else here so the police don't get curious. This is the finest residential site on the entire planet. When you buy the clothes, think rich. And try not let anyone see you dressed like that. You are completely out of place here. The police routinely stop and search anyone who looks out of place. Let us not forget that the police are still looking for you. If they catch you—remember that you are not the only one who will be in jeopardy.''

Was there any point in arguing?

Flower-bordered walkways cut between the various commercial units. I noted the numbers and made my way to rollway fourteen. A few vehicles hummed down the roads between the units and I made sure that they didn't see me. A couple were in the mechomart buying wine. I slipped by them and made it to the clothing section, where I bought a lightweight sports jacket which I put on. I started to discard my tuxedo jacket, thought better of it. It was the kind of clue the police would just love to find. I finished the rest of my purchases, bought a hold-all to hold everything, and retraced my steps.

When I returned with my purchases the truck was gone and, blissfully, so was Igor. I started to talk, but Kaizi waved me to silence. ''Clean yourself up first. I find your present presence as revolting as that of Igor.'' I was in total agreement. ''In there.'' He pointed to a doorway of an office, at the end of the building. The legend on the door read CHAFUKA INVESTMENT SERVICES. Another of Kaizi's enterprises?

There was a residential suite behind the office with a single bed. I took my face off, had a relaxing hot shower, followed by an invigorating cold one. Washed clean, shaved close, and dressed sportily I felt eminently better. I rinsed the dust off of my new face and put it back on. On my way out I passed a small and well-stocked bar that tempted me sorely. I did not resist. I strolled out with a tinkling glass to find my employer, joined him at the table. He looked me up and down and nodded approval.

"Any more banks you want me to rob?" I said sourly.

"No. Something bigger than that. What do you know about the atomic generation of electricity?"

"I can trustfully say very, very little. I turn the switch on the wall and the lights come on."

He threw some blueprints across the table to me. "Keep these. I will have more material for you soon. This particular problem is still in an early stage. We will talk about it later. Meanwhile you have a more pressing assignment. Not a single bank—but a single source of supply to a number of banks. You are going to take the armored van that distributes the cash to all the banks in this city. You have two days' time to work out exactly how it is to be done. The next day after that is deposit day, when the van will be fully loaded with credits to distribute to the local banks."

"And what exactly is your plan?"

There was not an iota of humor in his smile. "I told you, work it out for yourself. I have absolutely no idea how it can be done. You are the expert, so you devise the robbery." He took a projector from his pocket and slid it across the table to me. "Here are all details of pickup and delivery times, route, vehicle, drivers, everything you might want to know. I personally think that it is impossible to do. With all that information I have never been able to work out a plan for a successful robbery. I will be very interested in your solution to the problem."

"And if I can't find a way to do it?"

He pointed to the black watchlike object on his wrist, at the silver button set into its center. "I have only to touch this twice and you will never see your wife again. You will not know if she is dead or alive, taken to another planet, imprisoned here or just what. You will never know. She will just be gone.

I think you had better get to work. I have things to take care of, and won't be back until tomorrow. You will sleep here."

"There's only the one bed. Do I have to share it with Igor?" That was a singularly repulsive thought.

"No. He sleeps in the truck. He prefers it that way."

"So do I."

He finished his drink, put it down and started to leave. Turned back. "Don't do anything that you—and your wife—will regret."

I sipped my drink and I am pretty sure that my expression did not change. Particularly since I was wearing a new face. But at that moment I knew that I not only had to get Angelina out of this predicament—but I had to stop Kaizi's clock as well. I must put him out of business, bring him down, ruin him or worse. I promised myself that.

"Hungry . . ." the thin voice said. Just at the edge of audibility. I looked around, but I was still alone. Then I heard it again—and realized what it was. Before I did anything else I was going to have to feed my face. Literally. I put it into the bathroom sink and got out the funnel. Then opened the can of chicken soup.

With this task out of the way I could get down to work and plan the robbery. "A piece of cake," I said, reaching for the projector.

An hour later I was beginning to regret the rashness of my promise. The van was armed and armored, sealed, gas proofed. With a two-way radio. All of its many alarms automatically radioed in to the police if they were set off. The driver and the two other men were all heavily armed. The thing even had radiation proofing in case someone tried to nuke it. Kaizi was gone, I was on my own. He would return in the morning and expect some answers. It was getting late, the sun was setting, I was feeling thick-headed and stupid. I ran through the data just one more time. The crime was impossible.

"Impossible!" I shouted and went to the bar for another Silurian Slivovitz. "Not even magic could get into that thing."

Some blurred minutes passed until I blinked and realized that I had poured the entire bottle into my glass, poured it out and over my hand and it was soaking into the rug. I put the bottle and glass down. Because I was nibbling at the very periphery of an idea.

No guns, bombs, blasts, violence. Magic!

CHAPTER 15

OH DEAR MAESTRO, GOOD GREAT Grissini, blessed be thy name, peaceful and alcoholic may your retirement years be. For you taught me your skills—and, more important, taught me to look at the world with a magical eye. To turn reality on its head. To question everything, to misdirect and deceive. Make an armored car vanish? Why not? Size did not matter. But illusion did. If it could be done with a porcuswine—why not with a vehicle? The illusion supports and enriches the trick. When it is done properly, magic is the most effective persuader of all since it is they, the audience, who are actually persuading themselves.

I raided the office for paper and began drawing up the illusion to end all illusions. A few hours later I had most of the details roughed out—but I kept waking up with my face lying on the desk, snoring. Enough! I knew what had to be done, the overall concept was clear. I could work out all of the details in the morning after a good night's sleep. I set my alarm, stumbled towards the bed and crashed.

In my dreams a large insect had alighted on my arm, sat there buzzing and sinister. Opened its jaws wide and buzzed even louder—

I awoke, yawning broadly, and turned off the alarm. Ten

minutes to midnight. I splashed cold water on my face then slipped out into the street away from the buildings. There were too many bugs and detectors on this planet to take chances. I knew that my employer had already made good use of them. This place was probably thickly bugged. I stood in the middle of the road and phoned Bolivar.

And let the phone ring twenty times before I gave up.

"Don't worry, Jim," I reassured myself. "Something came up, he couldn't get to the phone. He's a tough lad—he's all right. Try again in twelve hours." Despite all this, still exhausted, I had trouble getting back to sleep.

By the time Kaizi arrived in the morning I had worked all of the details out. I had made a diagram of the construction, as well as printing out a list of all the materials that I would need. I slid the printout sheets across the table to him.

"Here is a list of everything that I will need to set the trap. The sooner I get all of it the sooner you will get your armored truck."

He flipped through the pages, growing more perplexed all the time.

"What is all this? Seven hundred and fifty square meters of microwave-oven screening? Four multi-megawatt holo projectors—a light truck—plywood—aluminum powder—iron filings—what are you going to do with all this?"

"Perform the heist of the century. Now you can get it for me—or we can sit here talking about it. In which case we won't be able to finish in time. Over to you."

His eyes did a good job of boring holes into my skull. I blew on my fingernails, then buffed them on my shirt. I won the waiting game.

"If you are just playing games with me, diGriz . . ."

"I assure you that I am not. Get me all of these items and I will get you the money. Now one important question—is this part of the world, this city—what do you call it?"

"Sunkist-by-the-Sea."

"Charming. Is this city and the surrounding countryside under satellite observation?"

"*All* of this world is under satellite observation. Whatever you do will be seen, every moment traced and recorded."

"Good. That is just the way I want it. I want them to see what they believe happened. I want their attention misdirected. So by the time they discover the truth we will be long gone. Where is Igor?"

"Sleeping in the truck."

"Wake him. Send him back to Fetorrscoria. Have him get everything I need and bring it back here. I am sure you know how to scatter the purchases about so no one supplier gets suspicious. I'll buy the van here. Don't worry—it will never be traced."

After one more head-drilling look he picked up his phone and called Igor.

"He is on the way. Before he gets here you have enough time to explain just what you have in mind."

"Of course," I said, sliding the diagram over to him. "Like all good magic it is simple when you have it explained to you."

Kaizi was actually smiling when Igor arrived. "Yes, I do believe that it will work." The smile vanished. "But this is going to have to work, isn't it, Jim? You have too much riding on this to make any mistakes." I turned away; it wasn't worth bothering to respond to his endless threats. I waited until Igor had departed before I went in and poured myself the first drink of the day.

"A little early in the day for the hooch," Kaizi said.

"Perhaps. And it is not going to be the last. I intend to make an easy day of it, because the hard work won't begin until Igor returns with the supplies. What about the van that I will need?"

"There are dealers in the city. Use the card I gave you. If there problems getting instant delivery, use cash." He passed over a thick wad of bills. "Finish that drink when you return. I have better things to do than watch you imbibe."

Kaizi dropped me off in the center of the town near a Wings and Wheels dealer. I watched him drive away. I had a half an hour before I had to make my call to Bolivar. There was a restaurant and bar nearby, empty at this time of day. I had a drink in the patio and phoned at noon. The phone answered on the second ring.

"Bolivar!"

There was a buzz and a crackle, then his voice.

"I'm not here at the present. But everything is fine. I can't go into details on an open line. Please call again at this time, two days from now. Over and out."

Something was happening—and I had no idea what. So I was not going to worry about it. Put it from my mind and concentrate on the job at hand. I finished my drink and walked back to Wings and Wheels.

This really was a rich little part of Fetorr. Instead of a robot salesman, there was actually a human being doing this smarmy job.

"Good morning, *sir*! My name is Jumanne and I am completely at your service. We've just had a delivery of personalized copters, two-seaters, just perfect for you and your beloved. Each vehicle comes with your name in gold covering all the surfaces, fitted at no extra charge."

"Emm . . ." I said, which filled him with enthusiasm.

"A wonderful choice! Of course you might have your beloved's name instead of your own. Still without any extra charge whatsoever. Her, his or its cherished name surrounding you with fond memories as you fly . . ."

"I need a light van."

He shifted gears smoothly. "Long-running, no maintenance, no unsprung weight, lifetime guarantee, on sale for today only, our Loaded-Meyster-Shyster is *exactly* what you want . . ."

"What colors you got?"

Kaizi's cashcard worked fine. As did the driving record and license of one of his employees that was held in the central computer's records. No other queries were made. My clothes, money, cash tip and mere presence in this habitat of the good and golden was passport enough. I drove out into the sunlit brightness of the day.

I spent the next few hours apparently driving around at random through the city and suburbs of Sunkist-by-the-Sea. Which really did live up to its name. The houses were mansions, their swimming pools were lakes. The women strolling in and out of the expensive shops were gorgeous and glamorous beyond belief. When I nodded serenely to a traffic policeman he gave me a snappy salute in return. This sun-scrubbed paradise reflected a direct contrast to the grit and grime of Fetorrscoria. It was as though all of the money and life had been squeezed out of the one city and lavished on the other—which was probably true. I could readily understand why the galactic tax men and union organizers were zeroing in on the planet. In a way I wished that I could have helped them. Instead of crime and havoc I should be digging out all the dirty deals that the plutocratic financial barons had devised. Jim diGriz—Warrior of the People! A not very likely scenario. I rode on.

But I was doing more than sightseeing. Not all at once, but in little chunks, I managed to drive the route that the armored car would take. I had to smile. I could pull it off.

"Congratulations, Jim," I congratulated myself. "You really are the best. When they made you they broke the mold. This little bank heist will go down in the annals of perfect crimes."

Then depression hit because not only would I not be making a profit for all my efforts, at the risk of a lifetime in some sordid jail, but I was doing it under duress and blackmail. Even if it worked perfectly I would still be rooted in the same black spot. The bullseye in the middle of the target. And Angelina—what of her?

But worry only gives one ulcers. Back at the rendezvous I poured myself a heroically large drink, stretched out on the bed and watched the sports channel on the gogglebox. It was a clickett, or crikket, match, I could not tell which from the adenoidal accents of the announcer. A recently revived sport that should have remained blissfully dead. Balls, bats, stumps, people in white uniforms running about; I was asleep within seconds.

The grate of wheels in the drive outside woke me from a most pleasant sleep. The endless clickett game was still in progress and I received great pleasure by killing it. It was after dark and Igor had returned with his purchases. Two days to go. I yawned and stretched. It was going to be a long night.

And an even longer day after that. I was chewing uppers like candy and knew that my abused system would pay for all this later. Igor wasn't much help so I told him to retire. I would use the workbots to assist me. They not only did a better job than he could but they seemed to be a lot brighter.

I was bleary-eyed and staggering when Kaizi came in the afternoon of the next day.

"Tomorrow is R day," he said.

"R for robbery. Don't worry about it. The equipment is ready and I'll get it into place after dark tonight."

"What about the truck?"

"The same."

"Let me see it."

We went out to the garage and called out to Igor to turn off the lights before we opened the door. I didn't want any chance passersby to see what was going on inside. I closed it behind me before I turned the lights back on.

"Great isn't it," I said, proud of my construction.

"It wouldn't fool a three-year-old," Kaizi grouched. Igor went back to work spreading silver paint on the plywood body. I was tired; anger flared.

"Put your brains into gear, Kaizi. It is not supposed to fool anything other than a camera in space. The paint has the same albedo as the paint on the armored truck. It also has the same shape and size. If it casts a shadow it will be the same shadow as the truck. If you both follow my careful and precise instructions it will work.''

''I don't like driving this thing,'' Igor said, echoing the doubts of his employer. ''Not with all that stuff packed in around me.''

''Shut up!'' I suggested. ''Follow orders and try not to think. It is wasted effort.'' I looked at my watch and tried to cool down. ''You have an hour to finish painting the thing. Then you have to paint your own truck—and it has to be done exactly as I told you. Success or failure depend upon it. Now—work!''

I had mixed the timer catalyst in the paint myself. If this were not done correctly it could jeopardize the entire operation. And end us all in jail.

Kaizi left then, being personally opposed to hard labor of any kind. Other than making money, that is. He had memorized my instructions on where and when he was to be and managed to get it word perfect without any effort. I had some rest then, waiting until the dark hours after midnight to get our gear into place. It was a pleasure to kick Igor awake, then push him, groggy with sleep, to our dummy armored van. I led the way, driving his truck with all our gear.

Dawn was just breaking when we got back. R day was here.

It was also T day or telephone day. I called again at noon but heard only the same recorded message. Concerned as I was, I knew that events of the day would soon drive any ongoing fears from my mind.

Kaizi came out of the office and looked at me just as I was putting the phone back into my pocket. Had he seen it? Attack was the best defense.

''You are supposed to be in lovely Sunkist-by-the-Sea—not here.''

''There is no rush. And I didn't want to be seen spending too much time there, staying in the same place. People might remember. Is your installation finished?''

''All in place. We leave in ten minutes.''

"Don't make any mistakes. You know the penalty."

Then he went out. Luckily for him. I was bone-tired and really not myself. My fingers had a life of their own as they tried to reach out and snap his neck. I kicked a few robots and cursed Igor out and felt a little bit better.

We drove Igor's now yellow-painted truck out to the site of the operation and backed it under the shelter of the trees. I then led him back along the road to the spot where I had painted a red X on the grass. I pointed.

"Stand there. Do not move." I looked again at my watch. "In a few minutes the armored van will come over the top of the hill there. That's it, use the binoculars, sight along the arrow painted on the ground. Good. And what do you do when you see the van?"

"Press button like this!" He squeezed the toggle as I was sure he would. And nothing happened because I hadn't connected it yet.

"Nothing happened!" he said with amazement.

"Nothing was supposed to happen since you haven't seen the target yet." I was right—the brainless robots were smarter. "Stand. Wait. Look. See. Press. Run."

I hurried back to my position. Checked that all the controls were to hand. Checked my watch one more time. If the armored car were on time—and Kaizi had assured me that it always was—it should be within sight in two minutes. I took a chance and armed Igor's button. Rolled my eyes heavenward in a silent prayer that he could get this simple job right.

Then reality shifted as the holoprojectors came on. I jumped because my arm seemed embedded in a large tree. I pulled it out of the image and admired my handiwork. Lovely! I heard running footsteps go by me. At least Igor had remembered his second instruction. After pressing the button, drop it. And get to the fake armored van hidden under the trees nearby.

The real armored van would have been seen briefly through a gap in the trees. Before it went around a bend in the road. One of the many bends in this picturesque winding road that led from one garden suburb to another. A road the van always took.

But what driver ever remembers every single bend in every single road? I was counting upon the fact that most drivers drove familiar bits of road on autopilot. This driver would now be rounding the bend. Normally proceeding on a bit farther, before turning round the bend to the right.

Only not now. The holoprojectors had created a different image for him, where the road appeared to turn slowly to the left. He would drive that way.

Or would he catch on and brake? My heart did the old hammering-loudly bit until I heard the sound of an engine—growing louder. Then it appeared right beside me trundling along happily. Until the brakes slammed on hard, the wheels locked and it skidded by me.

Any driver would have done the same. One moment he would be driving down the tree-shaded rural road. The next instant a rock wall would appear just in front of the van. No time to think—just hit the brakes by reflex.

I thumbed the actuator and two things happened. The holo-projectors changed their images. The road now ran through the trees as it had always done before. Anyone driving by now would only see trees and forest on both sides. That there were extra trees mixed in among the real ones, masking our truck and the armored van, would not be noticed.

At the same moment that the projectors changed images, the hinged screen dropped down from the trees above and slammed into position. The other walls of the radiation-proof cage were already there, boxing in the armored vehicle. Hidden from sight by the holo projections. As the gate closed the gauss bomb exploded below the money van. I shivered as the magnetic wave surged through me, plucking at the hemoglobin in my blood no doubt. A magnetic surge, even one this strong, wouldn't hurt a human being.

But, oh what it would do to any electric or electronic circuitry!

Sizzle them, melt them, short them out and wipe them. The van's engine would be dead. As well as all the electronic and communication equipment that they had in there with them. The lights would have blown and the electric door locks would have been fused shut; the three men inside were trapped in the darkness. Even if they had tried to get out a radio message before the bomb went off, the metal screening of the cage would have stopped it.

The trapped men would be frightened—but not for long. There were loud explosions as my makeshift mortars—just lengths of pipe buried in the ground—blasted shaped charges up into the belly of the van, punching holes in it. But jetting in sleepgas rather than explosives or flying metal.

I pulled on the gas mask with the darkened lenses. Turned on the brilliant flame of the thermal lance and began to burn a circle in the bottom of the van. But I was listening as well, and smiled when I heard the disguised van engine start, then move away.

In outer space, thousands of miles above our heads, the never-sleeping eye of the observation satellite would be recording events below. It would see the armored van drive down the road and under the trees. Then see it emerge again and peacefully trundle towards its destination at the next bank.

Which unhappily it would never reach.

I rolled aside as the glowing disk of metal dropped to the ground. Just to make sure I would not be disturbed I threw some more sleepgas charges up into the van. I took off the gas mask with its dark lenses, put filter plugs in my nostrils before I climbed in myself. Spun about at the strange grating sound. Saw in the light of my torch a snoring policeman. Asleep and uninjured as were the other two.

I used my diamond saw to cut off the fused lock on the rear door. Kicked it open to let in fresh air and birdsong. Dragged over the first of the money-filled lockboxes and threw it onto the ground outside.

This was the hard part and it had worked perfectly. But had

Igor done his far more straightforward job correctly? It was really very simple. All he had to do was drive the dummy van down through the hills and into the village beyond. But not to the bank, oh dear no.

To the loading bay of the market in the mall nearby. Empty of personnel at this time of day. Do it, Igor! Park. Open the door. Press the actuator. Don't run! It is a twenty-second fuse, you have all the time in the world. Into the mall and stroll out the other side. Into Kaizi's waiting car—

I could almost see the flaring blaze that blotted out the sunshine. Aluminum and iron. Thermite. A timeless recipe for the hottest of flames. Flame that incinerated everything that it touched, melted the metals it could not burn. A fire that ran its incendiary course until nothing of the fake armored van was left behind other than a white-hot ruin. Let them analyze that when it cooled. Nothing could be identified after a flame like that.

I was throwing out the last box when I heard a vehicle brake to a stop on the road. A stranger! No. It had to be Kaizi. Because a door slammed and heavy footsteps approached. The engine gunned as the car pulled away.

"Start getting these into the truck," I told Igor. "This is the final step in the greatest bank heist of all time."

CHAPTER 16

IT WAS DONE. FINISHED. OR was it? Had I made any mistakes? Had I covered all the planned points and details of the robbery? The armored car had been tricked by the holos and had driven off the road. Right. It had braked neatly in place inside the screened enclosure as planned. I had dropped the last screen while they were still braking—so there had been no time for them to radio a warning, had they even thought of doing so. The truck had braked to an emergency stop, then the gauss charge had fried everything electrical. Then the sleepgas mortar shells. Its crew had been rendered unconscious, none of them injured. I had checked that myself. While this was happening the fake van had driven out from under the trees and had taken the real van's place on the road. Where it would be watched by the never-sleeping eye of the satellite. Then it had driven to that distant mall—where it had burned spectacularly. Igor must have made his way safely to Kaizi in the waiting car, because he was here now throwing the money boxes into his truck.

What would the emergency services be doing at this time? Running in circles I hoped. The firemen would be dousing the steaming wreckage. Police investigators would soon be poking rods into the congealed mess. Eyewitness reports might identify it as an armored van. More confusion, more phone calls. Yes, the money van had left the last bank. No, it had not arrived at the next bank. More calls. Satellite images sent for and analyzed. More authorities getting into the act. More time wasted. The entire thing had gone exactly as I had planned. And there was Igor struggling with the last of the money boxes. It was time to leave.

Leave. The mnemonic triggered my memory and I slapped the pouch hanging from my belt.

Two things. The pillbox opened to my touch as I climbed back into the money van. I put a time-release capsule under the tongue of each of the sleeping guards. They would dissolve in four hours and release the antidote to the sleepgas. I didn't want anyone dying on me. They would wake up and then, if they had not yet been discovered, they would raise the alarm. I needed only an hour's time to make my getaway, so we had plenty of leeway. Slipping the guards the capsules had been the first thing that I had to do.

I was not too charmed by the second thing.

I took out the metal image of a rat cut from the finest stainless steel. Clutched it a moment, cursing, then threw it to the floor. Kaizi had warned me what would happen if it wasn't found at the scene of the crime.

I climbed wearily to the ground, climbed even more wearily up into the cab of Igor's now-yellow truck. He was just sealing the back. "Drive on." I husked when he joined me. "To the payway and Fetorrscoria. If I should fall asleep you are ordered, under penalty of death, not to wake me."

I dozed on and off until we reached the payway, then yawned myself back to life and fumbled out the catalytic activator. The mouth of the tunnel through the hills appeared ahead. As soon as we entered it I pressed the switch on the activator.

The long, strong burst of radio energy, at exactly the 46.8-meter wavelength, would trip the catalytic molecules in the yellow paint that now made the truck so visible. This would reduce their adhesion factor to zero; the paint would then blow away in a cloud of fine dust. Returning the vehicle to its normal filthy and stained pink. The empty armored van would be found. Satellite pictures of that bit of road would eventually reveal a yellow truck driving away from the scene of the crime. If they managed to track it as far as the tollway it would appear to have vanished in the tunnel. The perfect crime. Hugging this thought to myself I eventually settled down and slept the better for all of this.

And woke just long enough when we pulled into the Fetorrscoria warehouse to put my face in the sink and give it a drink of water. Myself as well. Then to stumble to my cot. I had a slight smile on my lips as sleep overwhelmed me. It really had been a perfect crime.

"The crime of the century, that's what they are calling it!"

I opened gritty eyes to see the loathsome form of Kaizi standing over me, hands filled with printouts from the news channel. He threw them onto my chest. I plucked at them feebly.

The top one was a photo of a meaty official hand holding the metal stainless steel rat. All of the headlines were hysterical.

RAT CRIMINAL STRIKES IN WEALTHY HEARTLAND
MILLIONS MISSING!!
PANIC IN MONEY MARKETS
INSURANCE RATES TO RISE

I bet they would! There would be cold shivers throughout the boardrooms. Not my problem. I scanned through the rest of the news, found an obscure item at the very end.

UNION STRIKE LOCKOUT AT STEEL PLANT

It looked like Gar Goyle was doing his union organizing bit now, when he wasn't putting on his freak act. Which made me think of Bolivar, who was still hidden in the act in his role of Megalith Man. Which in turn made me look at my watch. I had to phone him again at noon. I dropped the printouts and, with some effort, managed to climb to my feet. All of this activity had not disturbed Igor, who was still snoring on his bed.

"You look terrible," Kaizi said.

"I feel worse."

"If you are seen in the street in those filthy sports clothes you will be under suspicion at once."

"So what do I do?"

"Put this on." He handed me an anonymous dark-green work suit. "Go out and get some workmen's clothes. Heavy boots. Then get back here and wait. I will have another assignment for you soon. Give me the card."

"What?" My head was still fuzzy; no more pep pills for a while.

"The cashcard that you used to buy the van. I don't want it traced to any purchases here." He passed over a bundle of bills. "Use cash from now on."

"Where do I go? I don't know anything about this city."

"There is a mechomart not far from here."

"You'll drive me there?"

A look of quick distaste came and went. "Not very likely. Turn right outside the door. And don't take too long."

"Yeah, yeah. But isn't the door locked?"

"Of course. From the outside. Igor will let you back in."

I tore off my tired sports clothes, at the same time palming my telephone, which I slipped into the prole outfit I had been given. Then washed up, as well as I could, with cold water in the chipped and filthy sink. Dried off my face and gave it a quick feed of chicken soup, emptying the can. I would have to buy more. The work suit was well worn but clean. Kaizi was gone when I came out, nor was there any sign of his car in the street outside. There was a bit more traffic now than there had been at night. All of it passing through, since there seemed to be little to stop for in this run-down neighborhood. The traffic light at the next corner was red, with a few pedestrians waiting for it to change. When I joined them a young man turned and put a card into my hand. Advertising? A panhandler? I glanced at it.

DON'T TALK! it read. Followed by PTO.

I did, and the message on the other side was quite specific.

GIVE ME YOUR TELEPHONE.

A street robbery? For the first time I looked closely at the man who had given me the card. Well dressed. Tanned brown skin. Dark beard and mustache. Deep blue eyes that I had seen before.

I shaped the word *Bolivar* with my mouth. He nodded and held out his hand. I gave him the phone and watched with great interest as he slapped an adhesive pad onto it. The traffic light changed, the cars began to move: he pressed the phone against the rear fender of the nearest one. We watched as it trundled out of sight. I turned to speak and faced the DON'T TALK card again. Then following his beckoning hand into a nearby alleyway. He pulled out a detector and scanned me. Removed a wired five-credit coin from my pocket, then cut a button off my jacket and placed them carefully into a radiation-proof bag. He did not speak until he had sealed it.

"Hi, Dad," he finally said. "I wasn't sure it was you at first—nice new face you have there. But I recognized you from the back when you walked out. It is really great to see you."

"And you as well!"

"When you called last time I zapped back a detector signal and found out that your phone was bugged. That's why you got the recorded message."

"Kaizi! I thought he might have seen me using it."

"He undoubtedly did. The tracer spotted you moving all over—then ending up here. I have been watching the warehouse all morning. That was a classic heist."

"Thank you, it was. But completely without profit I want you to know. I am but an employee and Kaizi gets all the profit. Any word on your mother?" I tried not to sound as disturbed as I was.

"None. But not for want of trying. With James here now I can double the effort."

"James! You were supposed to stop him."

"He is unstoppable. But he has a new identity. He came as a bank examiner with the Banco Cuerpo Especial."

"Which is a front for the Special Corps! In here." We had reached the mechomart; thirst and hunger struck lightning into my midriff. "Food first!" I said as I led the way to Eat-fast Pay-less. He did not join me in a bearburger with fried grasshoppers, which appeared to be the least-loathsome item on the dispenser's menu. But he added another blue beer to the order. He sipped and spoke.

"James brought me new ID and this new personality as his assistant. So I have retired from the freak-show business. It was fun while it lasted. But wasn't too great for dating girls. Of course, as a married man I have abandoned that practice. We have done a lot digging in the records here, with some great help from the Special Corps, and we're getting a better fix on your employer."

"Kaizi. Is he really the richest man in the galaxy?" I chewed hard, then picked a grasshopper leg from between my front teeth.

"Far from it. It took a little time to track down his trail. He doesn't own most of the banks he is supposed to."

"Smart. I'll bet that they were just there to con me into taking the job with the circus." I punched for two more beers. I had to slow down the grasshoppers that were now leaping about in my stomach.

"The circus was a plant as well. I hired private investigators on three different planets who accessed the databases directly. The data they found was all planted and easy enough to see on the spot."

"But not on a search from another planet. But why did Kaizi go to all this trouble?"

He slurped his beer and frowned. "He wanted you on this planet. Just why we are not sure yet. A first guess would be that he needed some crimes committed and wanted a pro like you to do them for him. And he also worked very hard to see that you joined Bolshoi's Big Top. We think he wants you there as a spy for him. As you know, a good number of the acts are fronts for various interstellar organizations. Perhaps he needed you there to keep an eye on them."

My brain was churning and seething—as was my stomach. Rusty's Robot Bar was nearby. I pointed to it. "Let's move the party over there. Get something to drink that will kill the bear and drown the grasshoppers."

"Welcome, welcome," the rusty voice said as I pushed open the swinging door. "Welcome, that is, if you are over eighteen."

"I'm over eighteen," I said. "But at times I have the brains of a five-year-old. It is really depressing how easily I fell for Kaizi's con. I am afraid that I must agree with you. The entire thing, the money, the supposed bank robberies, were nothing but a ploy to get me to this dismal planet, then blackmail me into doing his dirty work for him."

Bolivar looked as depressed as I did as he nodded agreement. We went and sat at the bar.

"Rusty says Hi gents—and what will it be?

"Got every drink from Ale to Zygodactyl pee."

Rusty really was rusty, an ancient iron robot studded with rivet heads. I looked at the racked bottles.

"A digestive I said. Something to settle the tum . . ."

"Minced Rotifer Bitter," it grated, shooting out an extensible arm. The dark liquid smoked when it hit the glass. I sipped and belched a dragon's belch. It helped. But I was still depressed.

"I am but a stainless steel slave to this criminal puppet master."

"Slightly over the top—but basically true. But there is one fact about your puppet master that is most interesting. Although he has some interstellar holdings his core business is here on Fetorr. The private bank, the Widows and Orphans 1st Interstellar Bank. We know a good deal about that. I think he made me manager there to keep a close eye on me. Then framed me for the robbery.''

''So do I—since I helped him clean it out afterwards. The apparently stolen loot was there under the floor of the vault all the time.''

''What is more interesting than the bank is the fact that he also controls a very large brokerage office.''

I understood the words but not the meaning. The Rotifer Bitter was getting to me. I wiped it off my tongue and threw it on the floor.

''Do again,'' I said, enunciating very clearly.

''This appears to be circular trade with a vengeance. First he robs his own bank. When the insurance company pays him off he has essentially doubled his money. Next he cleans out another bank and blames you for it. Then he blackmails you into working for him in order to steal the armored car credits. Which he next launders through his bank to make more investments and more credits.''

''Give him credit for that,'' I said and laughed with a strange cackle.

Bolivar lifted an eyebrow and looked worried. ''Let's sit down for a bit. Before that bar stool throws you.''

''Let's.'' I stumbled over and dropped heavily into the booth. ''Sorry. I've been on pep pills for a couple of days while I was arranging the heist. I don't think they mix well with the detestable drinks in this place. I had better get back now. How do I get in touch with you?''

He took out a notepad of attractive green paper and wrote a number on it.

''Call at any time. James or I will answer. And be careful to check for bugs first.''

I memorized the number and ate the paper. It tasted of peppermint and it helped. Then the unavoidable subject could not be avoided anymore.

''And you keep looking. The most important thing that you

have to do is to find out where your mother is being held.''

His face fell. ''I know. We only have negative information so far. His bank and brokerage office are both clean. No hidden rooms—other than the one under the vault in the bank that you just mentioned. Could she possibly be there?''

''A long chance. I'll drop by with some testing equipment.''

''Do that.''

''We also discovered that Kaizi has a bachelor pad here in the city. I broke in, did the burglar act. Pinched his television. And had a good chance to search the place before the alarm tripped. We have been watching his movements closely and have no other premises or places that are suspicious. What about Sunkist-by-the-Sea?''

''A possibility. He has an office and garage there, but no sealed rooms that I saw.''

''Let me have the address. I can make a more detailed search.''

''Right.''

I scribbled directions on his green pad, handed it back. Depressed. There was nothing else to say. I took all the eavesdropping bugs out of the shielded bag and put them in my pocket. And waved a silent good-by.

CHAPTER 17

I PICKED UP SOME NONDESCRIPT clothes at the mechomart—along with some clean sheets and blankets. Since I was doomed to spend more time in Igor's dank den, I would like to spend it in relative comfort. My stomach was feeling a little better, but I was bone-tired still. I picked up some more chicken soup for my face, some cans of beer for myself. By the time I reached the warehouse my feet were dragging. Since I had not been trusted with a key I hammered on the door until Igor reluctantly answered it.

"Igor sleep," he grumbled.

"How can you tell? Igor brain-dead."

It was the fatigue and the worry speaking. Normally I would have known better and not gone out of my way by looking for trouble. Or I would not have made fun of somebody because of a physical handicap. I just wasn't thinking. He snarled something incomprehensible.

And when I passed by him he hit me in the side of the head with his fist.

It wasn't the kind of blow designed to kill or maim. Probably just the reflex physical response of someone who was frustratingly limited by verbal skills. Still—it knocked me to the floor, sent my purchases flying.

But it also triggered all the pent-up rage generated by the impossible situation that I was in. Trained reflexes took over. He was above me—a kick to the knee brought him down to my level. As he went by my elbow hit his solar plexus knocking the wind out of him. He was out of the fight and I should have left it there: the strength of my anger almost ended the matter in tragedy.

Without conscious volition my left arm was around his neck while I clutched the wrist with my right hand. The killer headlock. Steady pressure crushes the windpipe and stops the flow of blood in the carotid artery. First unconsciousness, then death. Or if you wanted to finish the affair quickly, sudden levered pressure could break the spine and death would then be instantaneous.

The red haze that obscured my vision faded. Just inches away was his face, eyes bulging, tongue protruding. Seconds away from the end.

It took a great effort of will for me to break the grip. I dropped him and stood up, breathing hoarsely, His eyes were still closed, but at least he was gasping in air. I waited until his eyes opened, then tapped my toe against his ribs to get his attention. With my thumb and forefinger I framed the tiniest space, held them before him.

"*That* is how close you were to death. If you ever touch me again it will be all the way."

I stumbled as I picked up my scattered purchases and walked away. Tired as I had been before, this burst of adrenaline-fired activity had pushed me closer to exhaustion: the upper pills were still taking their toll. I dropped everything onto the bed and fought not to drop myself as well. I did not fancy being asleep when Igor recovered—and the thought of revenge began to trickle through his sluggish synapses. I fed my face, then looked around.

For the first time I explored the depths of the warehouse. There was clutter and filth—and far to the rear there was a door half-shielded by empty metal drums. I rolled them aside to reveal an armored motorcycle as well. Used in the other bank heist, no doubt. I pushed this away too and pulled the door open to reveal a small office, ill-lit by a barred and cobwebbed window. It all looked most attractive. Fighting the depths of fatigue I pushed the scarred desk against the wall, then went to get my cot. Igor was not in sight and I did not miss him. Dragging the cot across the floor diminished my small reserves of energy. Pushing it into the office seemed to take hours. The door opened inwards. There was no lock. Nothing I could wedge under the handle. I leaned against it and looked around. The desk. It was heavy enough to slow someone down if he tried to get in. Give me enough time to wake up. Pushing it across the room depleted my reserves completely. It slammed into place and I slammed down onto the cot, my bundles under me. I crashed.

The light was fading from the window when I woke up. My mouth was bone dry and my lips smacked with thirst. The beer was packed in chillo cans: I cracked the lid on one of them. It bubbled with released refrigerants and water began to condense on the outside. I slugged it down and felt infinitely better. I opened a second can and drank only a little bit of it when fatigue got the better of me again. Sleep called.

The hammering didn't wake me up. I worked it into an elaborate dream and I slept on. Only when I heard the grating sound of the desk being pushed along the floor did I snap awake.

"Stop that!" I shouted and instantly regretted it as the steel band clamped hard around my head. Eased as the grating stopped.

"Boss want you."

"Tell him I'm coming . . ." In a hoarse whisper.

I felt a slight measure better after I put my head under the running water. Toweled myself dry, put on my face back on and went out to meet my master.

He looked at my rumpled state and said nothing. Merely curled his lip as he went to the table that was still cluttered with the greasy remains of Igor's last meal. He swept everything to the floor.

"Igor—clean this mess up."

He sat in a chair and waited until the muttering Igor had kicked the scraps to one side. A slight improvement. Then Igor went and lay on his bunk and turned on his gogglebox. Kaizi waved me over. I moved the chair so I would not have my back facing the room, sat down.

"What do you know about bearer bonds?" he asked.

"Something to do with whips, leather straps?"

"Either you are being facetious—or you are as much of an imbecile as Igor. Not bondage but *bonds*. A financial entity."

"Ohh. I didn't know." Although I did. But I could see he was ready for a lecture so I let him have his fun.

"Bonds, of which you seem to be ignorant, are certificates of ownership of a specified portion of a debt due by government, or some business organization, perhaps an airline, or other corporation, to individual holders, and usually bearing a fixed rate of interest. These are duly registered in the purchaser's name and records are kept. If they are later sold there is a record of the sale and purchase. But bearer bonds are quite different. There are no names involved. They can be bought and sold easily and are as good as cash to the owner. Do you have any idea what I am talking about?"

"A piece of paper worth a lot of cash to whoever has their hands on it."

"Generally speaking, yes."

"And I'll bet that you know where there is a bunch of these bonds and you want me to grab them for you?"

"Speaking crudely—again, yes."

"Good. But before we talk about that I want you to tell me about Angelina."

"She is fine and sends you her love." Kaizi was perfectly repellent when he smirked.

"Don't patronize me, you kidnapping crook. I want hard evidence, not generalities." I looked around, then saw in the rubbish on the floor the printouts he had brought, with the headlines about the armored-car theft. I seized them, dusted off the top sheet and handed it to him.

"Take this. And bring me back a video of you handing it to my wife. Let her read the news, then hold it up to the camera. Then I want her to say something that will positively identify her. Tell her that. She will think of something."

He chewed his lip in thought, then shook his head. "That will be difficult and time-consuming. Impossible."

"Make it possible. Because I am not planning and executing any more crimes for you until I have seen her alive and well."

He thought deeply about this, then realized that I meant what I said. I had no intention of continuing to aid him without some reassurances. "All right. I will do it. But in return you must study a certain building in great detail. Become so familiar with it that you can find your way around it in the dark."

Why not? I had nothing to lose and everything to gain.

"All right. What do you have?"

He took a palmtop computer from his case and put it on the table between us. "I have a mole, a very deep mole, who was planted in this particular building some years ago. He has been taking photographs of this building all of that time." He typed in a command and a holopic of an immense white structure appeared before us. Mighty pillars supported a great plinth. Stairs led up the entrance behind the pillars and, as the point of view moved forwards, I could read the words incised in the marble above.

PLANETARY CENTRAL DEPOSITORY

"Let me guess," I said. "Somewhere in this monetary mausoleum is a room or rooms stuffed with bearer bonds."

"Correct," he said.

"Front entrance," the computer said in a deep masculine voice.

"You will tour this building while I am away," he said. "You can walk through it with the virtual reality program, study it closely. Open and close doors, remember everything. By the time I return I expect you to be completely familiar with it. When you have done that—why, then I will tell you what you have to do."

I considered this briefly—then nodded. "Do it. I'm not going anyplace."

He started to stand. I stopped him. "Will Igor be in on this next job?"

"I imagine so. Yes, he will probably be needed."

"Then put the frighteners on him. He hit me—so I hit him back. Very hard. Can you convince him that if he touches me again, that I will kill him?"

"Igor!" his master shouted. Our loutish companion looked up from the gogglebox. Stood and shambled over.

"I believe that you and Jim here have had a difference of opinion."

"Don't like him."

"Neither do I. But we must work together. You will look after him and guard him well. Because if anything happens to him—the same thing will happen to you. And if you try to escape I will surely find you. Remember the last time?"

Igor was looking very unhappy. Clutching at his trousers, looking around the room, finally speaking in a low voice.

"Remember . . ."

"Good. Than I shall not have to do that kind of thing a second time." He turned to me before he left. "You are safe. I'll give you one day. When I return you will be an authority on this building."

"I will—as long as you bring the video I asked for. And another thing. I want a key to the front door. I can't eat the swill this creature does."

He made a quick decision. Dropped the key on the table and left. I turned to the computer.

I was interested in the building—why shouldn't I be?—

considering the assets that should be stored there. When I had visited most of the structure and could find my way around easily, I started looking into some of the more interesting vaults. Banknotes, freshly minted coins, stores of specie and bullion. It was so restful.

After a couple of hours I knew everything that I would need to know to satisfy my employer. I yawned and stretched. It was time for a beer. Or breakfast. Or both. And more than time to talk to the twins.

Igor looked up when I started for the door. Cringed and looked quickly back at the screen. I almost felt sorry for him. Thin screams and moans came from the set and I kept my eyes averted when I passed, not caring to examine his viewing taste too closely.

I entered the precincts of the mechomart and probed a little deeper into its bowels, until I found an upmarket restaurant that actually had a human headwaiter. Or a well-disguised robot.

"Good day, sire. Luncheon is about to be served. Today's special is steak. Genetically restored, genuine Jurassic Brontosaurus steak. Very lean, grilled to your choice. The normal order is one kilo, but for the really hungry we can serve any size portion. Ten, twenty, thirty kilos—" I raised my hand, almost losing my appetite at the thought.

But the robot kitchen was good, the robot service fast, the drinks tasty and cold. Well-refreshed I left and went to the telephone dispenser I had used before. But this time I bought the cheapest model, then found a quiet spot in an alleyway to make my call. But only after I had put the eavesdropping bugs on the ground and walked away from them.

"Dad! Good to hear from you. We spotted Kaizi leaving the warehouse, but lost track of him on the payway."

"Going north?"

"You got it."

"I thought he might." I explained about my need to see recent evidence of Angelina's safety, as well as the preparation for the new crime. "I thought he might go to Sunkist-by-the-

Sea. He is sure to have a residence there. When he said it would take some time to make the video I was pretty sure he did not have her here in the city.''

''So what to we do?''

''Just what you are doing now. Hold fast and keep an eye on Kaizi whenever you can without alerting him to the surveillance.''

''We'll do better than that. I will, me, Bolivar, will keep an eye on this superswine. That frees James with his computer know-how to do a little snooping around in the public records of Sunkist-by-the-Sea. See if we can't track down his property holdings.''

''Brilliant. I'll phone back tomorrow when I know more about the next job in my new crime career.'' I dropped the phone into a rubbish bin and retrieved all the little eavesdroppers. Put them back into my pocket.

I was cheered by the sorely needed help the boys were supplying. Depressed by thoughts of Angelina still in jeopardy. Refreshed by my meal and the animal proteins now coursing through my bloodstream. Downcast at the thought of returning to the warehouse and Igor's imbecilic presence. Reluctant to go indoors on this warm and sunny day. A patio bar caught my eye—just the thing. A few beers in the boozer would do me no harm.

There was a newspaper vending machine by the entrance. Normally a rarity in our technology-driven galaxy. I tried to imagine someone too poor to have a computer with news-service printouts and I could not. Yet they must exist here on Fetorr for I popped in a coin and held the irrefutable evidence in my hands.

Flipped through it as I sipped my beer. More hysteria about my one-man crime wave, along with a completely fictionalized biography of the Stainless Steel Rat. They held me responsible for every major crime of the past forty years. In the inner pages I found the item ''STRIKE IN SEVENTH DAY,'' which showed that Gar Goyle was still hard at work. Puissanto as well: ''TAX SCANDAL HITS PROMINENT BANKER.'' Unhappily, they weren't talking about Kaizi.

With banking on my mind I turned to the financial page.

BANK DEPOSITS HIT NEW LOW
FETORR CREDIT RATE SHAKEN
MUNICIPAL BOND SALES SPURRED

I yawned, very glad that James was the banker, not I. This sort of thing made very dull reading. I turned to the 3D crossword puzzle and dug out my stylo.

CHAPTER 13

IT WAS ALMOST LIKE A day off—something I had not enjoyed since our disastrous picnic attempt, the day when Kaizi had forced his obnoxious presence into our lives. I could not relax completely, not with my Angelina still in jeopardy. But I could make the attempt.

I dallied as long as I could over the newspaper. Then threw it away and, most reluctantly, returned to the warehouse. I carried Kaizi's computer into my monastic cell, where I ran the virtual reality program a few more times to hone my skills in finding my way about the depository. Then I hooked through to the television function of the computer and found I could access over a thousand stations. A plethora of crap I quickly discovered. Who was it who said that there were a lot more garbagemen than college professors in this universe? It didn't take a genius to figure out who most of the programs were made for. Igor's peer group. Finally, by paying extra—Kaizi's account could bear it—I found a historical channel. All about planetary settlements and the destruction of indigenous life-forms. I watched it with enthusiastic participation since there were a few other life-forms I could name that could do with a little destruction.

Kaizi arrived late the next morning carrying a small suitcase. "There has been a change of plan . . ."

"There certainly has. We don't talk about that or anything else until I have seen your home video. Give."

He produced the memory card and I slipped it into the computer. The screen lit up and I smiled, relaxed, not realizing how uptight I had been.

"Hello, Jim," she said. "As you can see I am doing fine, as is Gloriana." I heard the echo of a little grunt when her name was mentioned. "Though I think I am putting on weight without any exercise."

"You are gorgeous!" I shouted.

"Here is the headline you wanted to see, about the successful crime of the century, as they call it. I will not congratulate you since I imagine all of the profit will go to the loathsome presence holding the camera. Turn that back on!" she added as the picture faded. She appeared again suddenly.

"Sorry about that pause. But I had to convince a certain party that, in these days of technological wonders, the previous bit of this interview could have been electronically faked. What cannot be faked is a fact known only to you and me. So cast your mind back down the long light-years to the time when we first met. I always wore a locket around my neck. Do you remember what was in it?"

How could I ever forget? A photograph I had only glimpsed for an instant as she destroyed it. Of her in what might be called an earlier existence. Not beautiful—not even pretty. It was easy to understand how her embittered early self could get involved in crime. To get the large sums needed for plastic surgery. Until this moment we had never talked about that picture again. Her mentioning it now was a message of some kind. Trapped in her cell I could easily imagine how she felt.

"My photograph. Take care of yourself, darling."

Then she was gone. "Let's get to work," I said, sadly.

"There has been a change in strategy, as I said. The bearer bonds have waited a long time in their vault. They can wait a bit longer. You will have a different assignment first—''

''Wait just a moment. Where is this going to end? How many of these assignments are you going to send me on before we end our enforced relationship?''

Kaizi rubbed his jaw. ''That's a fair question. I must not let your morale lag by thinking that your work, and your wife's captivity, will stretch out into the endless future. My business ventures will reach a satisfactory conclusion soon. If you follow my orders, I guarantee that the bearer-bond retrieval will be our last job together. You will be free to leave. In fact I very much want you off this planet.''

''Alone?''

''Of course not. You and your wife will leave on the spacer together.''

I didn't believe a word of what he was saying. But I had very few options open. I had to get on with it.

''All right. What's next?''

''Atomic energy and the generation of electricity. It keeps our technological society running. What do you know about it?''

''Nothing. Or rather the knowledge, or faith, that when I press a button the lights come on.''

''Look at these.'' He opened his bag and took out a set of blueprints and a map. ''This is the atomic generator on Sikuzote Island. Here, you can see it on this map. It is just off the southern coast and separated from the mainland by the channel of the same name. You will go there—''

''How?''

''By maglev train. There is a direct service from the central station here. You will have a new identification to go with your new face. You will go as a tourist. The south coast is known for its pebble beaches, simple amusements. As well as the gambling casino in Swartzlegen. It is much favored by the workers on their holidays.''

''Don't they go north to the sunny joys of Sunkist-by-the-Sea?''

"No. They are not welcome there." Irony did not penetrate his sense of superiority. "Since it rains a good deal in the south the beaches are not much frequented. The indoor entertainments are much favored, as you can imagine. One of them is the guided tour of the atomic facility. Quite popular, and also free. You will go on that tour."

"Look, Kaizi, can you give me some slight idea what this is all about? There is nothing to steal down there, is there?"

He sat back and thought about that. "You are right. There is nothing financial about your role in this matter. I will take care of that. You will be involved in a simple bit of industrial sabotage."

"Like what? Blowing up—or melting down—the nuclear reactor?"

"Yes. That is what I had in mind."

"No way!" I jumped to my feet and paced the room. "This is not down my alley. If I go anywhere near that place I'll probably end up glowing in the dark."

He was not impressed. "Shut up. Sit down. Look at this."

This was the floor plan and elevations of the nuclear plant. Filled with highly unattractive labels like radioactive waste, coolant rod storage, reactor room.

"What you must do is interrupt the electrical supplies from this generator."

"For how long?"

"Weeks at least. Preferably months. This nuclear generator supplies nearly a third of the electrical capacity of Fetorr. There will be financial repercussions."

I was beginning to see what he had in mind. "It's money again, isn't it Kaizi? We are going through troublesome economic times here on good old Fetorr, if you can believe what you read in the news. Bank robberies, currency robberies, disruption among the working classes. And next—an electrical crisis. Why if someone knew this was going to happen he might snap up a lot of stock in nonnuclear electrical generation plants.

Then that person might make an awful lot of money. Don't you think?''

"I think you are getting very out of line, diGriz. You stick to what you do best—and let me worry about finances and profits. So—how can you cut off the electrical supply?''

"I haven't the slightest idea.'' I held the plans up to the light, but no inspired thoughts flowed. "Shutting down the nuclear reactor would certainly do the trick. But that has to be the last option. It would mean penetrating the plant, avoiding guards and alarms. And then what? I have no technical knowledge about this kind of thing.'' I folded the plans. "I suggest that I get down there as a tourist and look things over. Then call you. I don't know anything about buying the material that I will need when I am there. Can you send any supplies I require by truck?''

"Too long, too slow. The levtrain has a most efficient freight service.'' He thought about this a bit, then dug into his bag and took out a plastic cylinder.

"What is it?''

"Playtexx. Completely sealed so it can't be detected.''

He passed it over and I took it with some hesitation. It was the most concentrated and most powerful explosive known. I knew that it existed but I had never used it. Since I don't usually go around blowing up things.

"How stable is it?'' I asked.

"As inert as clay. Shoot it, light it, jump on it—and nothing will happen. This is the only thing that will set it off.'' He passed over a timer disc with a sharp skewer projecting from it. "Set the timer. Push the spike through the plastic container. Then get out of there. Now—put everything into this bag, along with some clothes. You leave at once. I'll expect a report by tomorrow in the very latest.''

I opened my mouth to protest. Shut it again when I realized the futility. A holiday in friendly Swartzlegen seemed to be very much in order. Kaizi drove me to the station himself. Gave me anther bundle of money and a telephone. And issued more orders to which I nodded, but didn't listen. I knew what had to be done. Something dangerous, possibly deadly, in the sunny south.

It started to rain as soon as the train reached the southern plain. The landscape became darker and more dismal, black wet rock piled on more black wet rock, with black clouds scudding across the dismal landscape. Quite depressing—but only to me. Everyone else on the train seemed to be working hard at getting drunk. The men at least. Not the women. There were very few of them, even fewer children. There was a bar at the end of every car, and they were doing very good business indeed. Not much of a family outing. Just a way for the lads to let off steam and spend what credits they had before returning to the joys of industry.

A few hour later we reached the worker's paradise.

The end of Swartzlegen Station opened right onto the sea. An elevated promenade ran along the seafront, stretching out to the horizon in both directions. I leaned on the railing in the driving rain and watched the waves rush high up on the black-pebbled beach. When the waves ran back again they carried some of the stones along with them, grating and grumbling like underwater thunder. There was a good bit of that in the sky too. Sudden flares of lightning followed by earsplitting claps of thunder.

Lightning flared again out to sea. Giving me a quick glimpse of pale land against the black clouds. And the forms of low, clustered buildings. Sikuzote Island and the atomic generator. I turned my back to the ocean and scanned the row of buildings that lined the other side of the promenade. Amusement arcades, bars, restaurants, bars, squalid-looking hotels, bars, electronics, bars, souvenirs, bars, telephones, bars. I got the message. I had not drunk anything on the train. I would head for the nearest bar and get a beer. But not before I contacted Bolivar.

The automated electronic shop was having a sale on detectors. I pushed in enough money for one. Turned it on and swept it over my body. It bleeped like an electronic pinball machine. Kaizi sure didn't trust me. I dug out the coins, buttons, discs—even a nail in my new shoes. And of course the new phone he had given me. I was getting very tired of this constant attention. I went and threw the whole lot into the ocean before buying a new phone. I put this into my bag and headed for the adjacent bar. Where I bought a beer and found an empty booth. Easy enough to do since the place was deserted. Took out the phone and tapped the buttons. Bolivar answered on the third ring.

"Good to hear from you. No luck yet on finding Kaizi's place in Sunkist-by-the-Sea, but James is beavering away at it. How are you doing?"

"Traveling on a new assignment." I told him about the planned sabotage and my starring role.

"Sounds dangerous. Could you use a little help?"

"Not really—but thanks for offering. If I can't do it alone it probably can't be done. What you can do is take this phone number and call me if there are any developments."

"Got you. Stay safe."

Safe. I appreciated the thought but doubted very much of it could be done. I turned the phone off. Changed it from ring to vibrate. Drank the rest of the beer, picked up my bag and went to get more.

"Pretty rainy today," I said to the head barman. He was polishing a glass and keeping a keen eye on his staff of robot bartenders.

"It's always rainy today." A real cheery soul.

"Not too full.'

"Not this time of day. The rain drives them in after dark."

"I hear that there's a tour of the electricity works."

"Volt City. Boring stuff. But at least it's dry." He put down the well-burnished glass, took up another one. Pointed his thumb. "Down there. Next to the pier. Tours every half an hour all day. By ferry."

"Sounds like a winner," I said with little enthusiasm.

"Or stay here and drink. Your choice."

"Can I leave my bag here?"

"Ten credits," he said. I took the telephone out of the bag before I passed it over. He stowed it behind the bar. "We never close."

Cheered on by this hearty interplay I went out into the rain again. Was it stopping? Hard to say with the wind blowing water in all directions.

Tied up by the pier, bobbing ominously, the small ferry *Miss Kilowatt* did not actually inspire confidence. At least the rain was letting up, though not the wind.

"Welcome aboard *Miss Kilowatt* for your grand electrical tour," a very bored girl in an electric blue uniform said. She handed me a booklet. "We cast off in ten minutes and thus will begin the tour of your lifetime." Her nasal and uninflected tone made it sound like the end of a lifetime. I went to the bow and sat down on a wet bench. I was soaked through already and this would make no difference. I leafed through the booklet, then sat on it. I was still wet. A little while later there was a rumble in *Miss Kilowatt*'s bowels and she moved slowly away from the pier.

As the rain let up I could make out our destination more clearly. A low island with the waves breaking into white foam on its rocky shore. A long cluster of white buildings attached to a larger and more formidable building. A very tall chimney rose up from this, thin smoke blowing inland from its top. No doubt spreading atomic debris over the town. From the farthest end of the buildings thick black wires emerged and stretched out to a massive tower. Swung long catenary loops across the water to another tower on the mainland. Marched away on more towers, vanishing inland, transporting all those amperes and joules to the industry of Fetorrscoria. Inspiring.

The passage was rough and blissfully short. I was happy to join the small crowd at the exit. Followed them down the pier towards the building complex. A wide entrance flashed a dazzling array of lights and emitted scratchy music.

"Welcome." The canned voice said. "Welcome to your grand electrical tour. Your guide is waiting inside to tell you just how AtomGen is making your world a finer place to live in."

We had to go single file through the narrow entrance. Past a uniformed guard with a counter in his hand, clicking it for every visitor. No, not every one. A mother and the little girl with her did not merit a click. Just the male visitors, I noticed idly. I paid more attention when I passed him. He clicked and looked at the readout.

"Number fifty," he said aloud, and smiled. "This is your lucky day and you have won a valuable prize worth two hundred credits. Please follow me to that room over there where it is waiting for you."

He handed me a golden disk with a lightning bolt inscribed on it. Pointed to the door with the same symbol.

I did not like being singled out. But did not dare protest. I meekly took the disk and followed him through the door. It locked behind us with an all too solid sound.

"Last one for the day, Geuka," he called out to another guard. Who unlocked a barred door. Through the bars I could see into the room beyond, could see some dejected-looking men lolling miserably in chairs.

"What's going on?" I protested. "I'm not going in there."

As I spoke I felt what could be a gun grind into the small of my back. Geuka unclipped an electric prod from his belt. "In," he said very firmly. "You and these other gentlemen have volunteered for only an hour's work on the night shift. For which you will be paid two hundred credits."

"Work? What kind of work?" Should I make a grab for the gun?

One of the incarcerated men was now standing at the gate holding onto the bars, enjoying the show.

"Simple labor, you'll see," the guard behind me said. He had moved aside, out of reach now. With the gun still leveled.

The man clutching the bars laughed what could only have been called a dirty laugh.

"Believe that and you'll believe anything. It's cleaning up radioactive waste. You're gonna get a lifetime's worth of radiation in that hour."

CHAPTER 19

"JUST SHUT YOUR MOUTH OVER there—or you're in big trouble," the guard said, waving the electric prod in his direction.

The man laughed. "How much bigger trouble is there than getting nuked?"

He shook the gate angrily but it was solid.

Distraction.

I turned my head just a fraction so I could see the guard beside me out of the corner of my eye. There was more shouting now from the other men locked in the room. The gun was steady—but I saw him look at the other guard.

The edge of my hand sliced down hard on his wrist.

He yiped in pain and the gun dropped to the floor. He dropped after it as I continued the turn so my rigid hand next caught him in the neck.

I had turned completely about and was facing the door we had just come through. Seized the handle and tore it open, went through it and pulled it shut behind me. This had taken only a few seconds.

The entrance hall was almost empty because the tour was leaving. The last of the people on the tour were filing out into the hallway. No one was looking my way. I walked fast, not running, towards the exit from the building. There was safety outside, the dock, the ferry. No, that was not a very good idea. Any moment now armed thugs would be coming out of the room. Heading towards the exit door. There had to be a better way to avoid them. I turned and joined the tour as it left the room.

If I went outside I was sure to be caught. There would be no way to escape on the ferry, even less running around on the island. This was the only other option. It would take them awhile to discover that I had not fled the building but had continued deeper inside it.

I walked behind the other visitors. The hall widened into a chamber, the lights dimmed and the wall before us glowed with golden light. The tour guide produced a weary monologue.

"The first thing you will notice about this fascinating display is just how much the nuclear generator dominates the life of our little electric generating family here, dedicated to bringing you your electricity at the lowest possible price. Clean power and how very efficient this is will be seen . . ."

Our guide droned on through her monotonous speech while the tour members gaped at the models and flickering lights. I looked over my shoulder after I had moved along the back of the tour, putting bodies between me and the entrance hall. Someone was running towards the outside door; there were loud shouts. Some heads turned to look as I worked my way farther into the room.

There—on the far wall—was the exit the tour would be taking soon. I moved slowly in that direction. Turned as though I were looking at the display. And shuffled backwards at the same time. Until I was in the hallway. No one was looking in my direction, and the crowd hid me from sight of the entrance hall. I turned and walked calmly around a bend and out of sight.

"Think fast, Jim," I muttered as I walked. The hallway was empty—but how long would it stay that way? Anyone I met would be an employee and they would know that I did not belong here. If I were seen, stopped, found—that would be the end of this little escape.

No doors. Just backlit panoramas set into the wall visualizing the glories of nuclear power. Mighty machines, stalwart builders, sizzling electrons. I hurried past them. The hall ended in an escalator that was grinding silently upwards into the depths of the building. Should I take it? Hide behind it? A stupid action—I would be easily found. I had to keep moving. I got onto the escalator—then ran back down it as quickly as I could. From above I had seen that there was a door at the very end of the hallway.

With a discreet sign on it saying EMPLOYEES ONLY.

The tour group was still in the first hall. No one had seen me yet. I was about to become an employee. A quick twist of the picklock did the trick. I was looking into musty darkness: I hesitated.

"Now if you will all follow me . . ."

I slipped inside and closed the door behind me. Heard the lock click. Let out a deep and shuddering breath that I hadn't realized I was holding.

I was safe for moment. The hunted animal gone to ground. And I had been like a fleeing animal up until this moment. Fleeing, not thinking, just escaping.

"Well done, Jim," I told myself in a hoarse whisper, a little spirit bolstering being very much in order. But it was time to put the brain into gear now. I tried to visualize what was happening outside.

No alarms had gone off yet so it looked as though this was going to be a silent chase. After the first shouting someone with intelligence would take charge. They did not want to disturb the visitors who had not been drafted for radioactive duty. Someone in authority had realized that if the ferry were stopped from leaving, I would also be stopped from leaving the island. They would take care of the ferry first. After it had been searched and I wasn't found, then someone would remember about the guided tour. That would take some time because the only person who had seen me clearly was the guard I had knocked down. He would have to be revived, sent after the tour to identify me. And I wouldn't be there. The search would widen to the island. And more sinister, would extend through this building. What next?

Get away from the door for openers, dummy. Anyone who comes through it will spot you at once.

I was right. And by this time my eyes were getting used to the semidarkness. I looked around. Light spilled in through a series of holes and strangely shaped openings. I blinked at this—then realized I was looking at the rear of the dioramas I had passed in the hallway. This space was used to work on them, change them perhaps, dust them. I walked slowly back the way I had come, but this just ended in a dead-end wall. The other direction had better offer something far better or it was back to the hallway for me. I would be easily found if and when they decided to search in here. The workspace dead-ended again. But at least there was another door here. I opened it a crack and put my eye to the slit.

There was a cavernous hall beyond, well lit. With people moving about. It had to be a workshop of some kind; I could even smell paint. There was scaffolding as well. Cables and ladders. And the distant clanging of a bell.

''What's up?'' a man's voice said a few feet from my head.

I stood, frozen, clutching the edge of the door. He was just inside the door. He moved forward inside the room, almost close enough to touch. He was not looking my way.

''Alarm of some kind,'' another voice said. ''They want us all out of the building.''

''Not another one of their idiotic fire alarms? We are never going to get this display finished by Founder's Day if they keep playing these kind of games.''

He must have become aware of the partly open door because he grabbed the handle and slammed it shut. Moved off, still complaining.

And he had not seen me!

I waited what I thought was a respectable amount of time. Then waited a little bit more. Opened the door again ever so carefully. The workshop beyond was silent and empty. I went in slowly, listening. There was the sound of some voices in the distance, a door closed, then silence. I didn't know how much time I had before they returned. Before that happened I had to have a plan, an escape, a hiding place. Something.

The panorama they were building was life-size. A laboratory of some kind, hulking machines with dangling wires. A nude window-dressing dummy was working incongruously at a desk. Others dummies were stacked nearby, some partly clothed. In the rear was a white-coated figure wearing breathing apparatus. Blazoned on its chest was the tripartite red warning signal for radiation. Was there danger?! I jumped back.

"Don't be a dummy," I scolded myself. "Like the rest of these dummies. They wouldn't have real radiation sources in a display. Everything is a mockup."

I went behind the rear of the display and found cabinets, a paint locker, shelves of parts and models. Plenty of places to hide. Plenty of places that would be well searched. I had to move on.

Or did I. Look. Think. Think like a magician. Always misdirection. People look for secrets, complications. They never notice the obvious.

And the obvious was staring me in the face.

I lifted off the breathing apparatus carefully and stared into the painted eyes of the dummy inside.

"You have been demoted," I said.

I noted its position carefully before I undressed it. Once it was naked I carried it over to the piled up dummies on the floor. There were seven of them there. By careful digging and rearranging they became eight, with the newcomer concealed at the bottom. They were dusty, had been there awhile. Hopefully the additional plastic corpse would not be noted. I pulled on the white clothing and leaned against the bench just as the original had. Put the breathing apparatus on and instantly began to suffocate. Took it off and found that all of the valves were closed. I opened them and tried again. Musty but bearable.

I took it off and placed it down on the bench before me. Then I wriggled around to find a position where I could stand without moving, in some degree of comfort. When I had done that, I sat down on the nearby chair and waited.

I had plenty of warning. Closing doors and loud voices. When they came back into the room I was immobile at the bench and looking at them through the dusty eyepieces.

''Where are we on this plan?'' the guard asked as he came into view. The same one that I had knocked down. He had a large and much-folded chart in his hand.

''Right here,'' one of the technicians said. ''Right off the central hall.'' There were a half-dozen more men with the guard.

''Is there a door down this way?''

''Just one to the workspace behind the hall displays.''

''We'll search there first.''

They did. I had been right to get out of there. When they came back they began to methodically search the rest of the area. Opening and banging shut the cabinets and storerooms. When they returned, one by one, they walked behind me. I stood, rigid, my back tingling.

There was a loud sneeze and the guard reappeared.

''Don't you care how dusty it is in there?''

''We work in here. Never go near that hall. What difference does it make to you?''

''Not healthy.'' The guard rubbed his nose on the back of his hand. One of nature's gentlemen. ''Maybe he's hiding in here.'' He kicked the pile of dummies.

''Stop that! You break anything and you are in trouble.'' The speaker pushed the guard's shoe aside, straightened the limb he had assaulted.

Would he notice the extra figure?

Surely they could hear my heart hammering. The blood thudding in my ears.

''Or maybe he is in here,'' the guard said. Pointing at me. Looking me square in the face. The others looked. I looked back and wondered what I should do when they found me.

"I made that thing myself," one of the technicians said. "Can we get on with this search? We'll be working after quitting time if we don't start moving."

"Yeah, yeah," the guard said. "Now show me again on the map."

I began to shiver with released tension when the door closed behind them at last. Although it was not hot at all I was soaked with sweat. I tremored over to the chair and dropped into it.

"Jim," I confided to myself, "you are getting too old for this kind of crap."

I laid the breathing apparatus next to the chair and kept the white clothing on. When they came back I was ready to do the dummy act again.

But they didn't return. Perhaps it was past their work time. Or, more likely, everyone was involved in the search. So what did I do next? I had eluded my pursuers for the moment—but I was still trapped on the island. They would have searched the ferry by now. If I could make it to the ferry after dark, hide there. Then maybe I could get off the island when it left. A slim reed to lean on. That was the only way off the island and they knew it. It would be searched again before it pulled out.

What then? The answer was very simple. I needed help. Although I was the rat that walked alone, I could see where a little aid and succor might very well be in order. Should I stay in this room? The lights stayed on, but the skylight in the ceiling above darkened. I was probably as safe here until morning as I would be anyplace else. And a good deal might be accomplished before the sun came up.

I took out the phone and dialed the number.

"Bolivar," I said when he answered. "I wonder if you would be kind enough to do me a little favor."

CHAPTER 20

THE SEARCH FOR ANGELINA WAS still on; he told me about that first. And I'll give him credit. He did not laugh when I told him where I was and why I was here. He listened while I explained, in great detail, what had happened. Then he asked a few cogent questions.

"It is going to be alright," he finally said.

"I'm glad to hear you say that, but things here look plenty black at this time."

"After darkness comes the sunshine. I'm going to call James and see if the new computer can help. And I have a few ideas of my own."

"I'm glad of that, because that is a few more than I have."

"Stay put. Don't get caught. I'll get back to you. Get some rest."

Rest! Trapped inside a diorama, inside a nuclear power plant on an island with no exit. Yet it wasn't a bad idea. I arranged some of the drop cloths into a nest behind a partition where I couldn't be seen easily if anyone should come in. I lay tense for some time, waiting for the sound of approaching footsteps. Then I must have fallen asleep because the next thing that I was aware of was vibration of the phone waking me up.

"We have the germ of an idea but we need a few more facts. Were the guards in uniform?"

"Blue with gold buttons."

"Did they wear badges?"

I tried to remember. "No. Just name tags."

Bolivar had some more questions, then wished me a good night. I thanked him and this time I was too tired to stay worried. When I opened my eyes again the skylight was getting light. Just to make the day complete the rain was thrumming down on it again. I felt absolutely rotten. Sore, bleary-eyed, depressed. I took off my face and rubbed the stubble on my face. I heard a tiny voice speaking. I looked around, the room was empty, then I heard it again. I held my face close to my ear.

"Chicken soup . . . " it said plaintively.

"You'll get fed when I get fed—and not an instant before. But I'll get you a drink of water though, I need one myself."

I found a big sink, with paint brushes soaking in it, well to the rear of the workshop. I splashed water on both my faces, then drank from my cupped hands. Carefully poured water into the tiny funnel to slake the face's thirst. The phone vibrated in my pocket. I switched it on.

"Are you alright?" Bolivar asked.

"Tired and miserable—but still free."

"Try and stay that way for a little while longer. I have found out that there are night watchmen on the island. They are the only ones who overnight on the island. The rest of the staff commute by ferry. I'll be on the first ferry trip of the day."

"I hope you know what you are doing."

"I do. I am an officer in the Health and Security Police and you are one of our agents."

"I am? I've never heard of the organization."

"Neither has anyone else. James created it and planted it in the government memory banks. There are so many kinds of

police on Fetorr that one more won't be noticed. How do we get together?"

"If they see me they'll grab me!"

"Not if you are with me."

I thought for a moment. "Come in the front entrance with the others," I told him. "Then turn left, through a large room and down the hall. You'll come to an escalator—but don't take it. Phone me and I'll join you."

"Agreed! Over and out."

I put the face back on—ignoring its whimpered plea for chicken soup—and went back to the display that was under construction. I couldn't possibly hide there as I had hidden myself the night before, not for any length of time. I put the clothes and breathing apparatus on the dummy and restored it to its original position. Then went out the door I had originally entered by and back along the hall behind the dioramas. To the far end where I wouldn't be seen—unless another deliberate search was taking place. I sat down with my back to the wall and even managed to doze off again.

I was awake the moment the phone vibrated.

"Where are you?"

"By the escalator you mentioned."

"Stay there—I'm on my way."

A feeling of great relief passed over me. I didn't know what Bolivar had in mind, but I knew that he would get me out of this particular mess. I opened the door to the hall and there he was in a very smart and official uniform.

Standing next to him were the two guards who had tried to grab me. And a clutch of business types in white lab coats. I started to draw back, but Bolivar stepped forward and put his arm around my shoulder.

"You did a magnificent job, Inspector Kidogo. The department is proud of you." He thrust his right hand out and I shook it. And palmed something metallic that was in his hand.

"Now tell me inspector—do you recognize anyone here?"

"I certainly do. These two men here."

Instead of seizing me the two guards trembled with fear.

"Is it true that they threatened you with violence and tried to force you into certain undesirable actions?" I nodded agreement. "Good. One last thing then. What is it that they wanted you to do?"

"They wanted me—against my will—to work with radioactive material!"

"That's it!" Bolivar shouted and stabbed an accusatory finger at the group of men behind the guards. Who now looked as terrified as the guards. "Show these men your identification, inspector."

I reached into my pocket and produced the palmed badge. A very official-looking one in gold with blue lettering that spelled out Health and Security Police. They stared at it as though it were a poisonous snake and trembled with fear. Bolivar punched a number into his phone; there was only dumb silence among the electrical employees as he spoke.

"Yes, general, we have the evidence. The security on the island was easily penetrated, just as you feared. Inspector Kidogo easily eluded the so-called guards here. He actually entered the nuclear enclosure and photographed everything. And there is more than that, sir. The rumor that we heard, about the scientists here using forced labor for nuclear cleanup is true. They won't be able to hide that spill any longer. We have the evidence! Yes, sir, thank you, sir. They are all under arrest? Of course. They have no place to run to." He hung up and glared a very impressive glare.

"The Security Police choppers on their way. If you attempt to leave this building you will be shot at once. Now—clear out your desks because none of you will *ever* be coming back here!"

They turned and staggered off, their careers in ruins and only prison awaiting them. It was very nice to see. When the last trembling back had disappeared, Bolivar and I went out the front door and walked towards the waiting ferry.

"Congratulations," I said. "That was very neatly done."

"You can thank James. It was his idea—and he fed it all into the computerized files. The psychology was perfect because they knew that they were all guilty of breaking a number of laws. Now, while they are waiting for the ax to fall we will make our getaway. And I think that I *will* phone the authorities as soon as we are clear, to report this lot. They are criminals and deserve what they will get. I'm afraid that the only copter here is the one I came in, so they will have a long wait. We'll take the copter and be clear of this place as soon as possible."

"We can't." I dropped into a chair in the empty cabin as the ferry got under way. "I still have to pull off the demolition job for Kaizi. And that will be impossible now with everyone in this place stirred up and waiting for the police."

"Don't worry about it. We'll do the job before we leave."

I gaped, openmouthed, shook my head in disbelief. Said, "What, what?"

"Just a matter of putting two and two together. You told me that Kaizi had given you the explosive. Which, I assume, you have left in a safe spot."

"Bar. On shore."

"Good. As I flew in I had that explosive in my mind. As I dropped down for a landing I saw how easy it would be to do."

"Easy? Excuse me if you think that I am acting like a moron this morning. That is only because I feel like one. What did you see when you were landing this morning?"

He grinned mightily—and pointed up into the sky. I followed his finger—and my face broke into an echoing grin even bigger than his.

There was the answer in the sky.

The great cables that carried the electricity from the island!

"The only vessel that uses this channel is the ferry. The tower is sited on the rocky headland just above the shore. There are no roads or buildings near it or below it. If the tower is dropped correctly it—and the cables—will fall into the sea without injuring a soul."

"And it will hit the water with an immense sizzling that will be heard all the way to the stock exchange. All the lights will go out and all the maglev trains will be stopped in their tracks. I'm glad that we are flying!"

Once ashore we headed directly to the bar. We enjoyed a beer and a bearburger before I retrieved my bag. And a cup of chicken soup as well, for my face, so it wouldn't fall off from fatigue. Bolivar was driving a rental runabout from the copter field. There was little traffic on the road out of town. We waited until there was none before we took the service road that led to the electricity tower. We parked halfway there behind a jumble of large rocks, then went the rest of the way on foot.

I looked up at the great steel mass of the tower and shook my head. "I am forced to admit that I know nothing at all about demolition."

Bolivar gently took the explosive from my hands. "I never heard you say that before. I grew up believing that you could do anything."

"Well, I am forced to admit, *almost* anything."

"Demolition is the first thing I learned when I started lunar exploration. This baby is going to make some mark when it comes down."

A fence topped with razor wire ringed the base of the tower. Now this was something I did know about. I unlocked the gate while Bolivar measured the steel structure with his eyes.

"See how the four legs are embedded in the rock? Solid and just about immovable. But as they rise up higher they thin down so that eventually the four legs form a single lattice that supports the cross bar and the cables."

I leaned back, looking up, farther and farther, until I almost fell over backwards.

"That is one awfully high tower."

"Nice, isn't it? Almost as good as rock climbing. See you in a bit."

The explosive was slung in the bag over his shoulder, and

he was off before I could say another word. Warn him to be careful? Wish him luck?

He was a good and experienced climber. I would have stopped for breath by this time. He just went at it hand over hand at a steady pace. Reached the junction of the four legs. That should be it. But no, he went on until he appeared to be as high as the cables pendant from their immense insulators. Then he stopped. A dark smudge against the bright metal of the tower.

And seemed to remain there for an awfully long time.

I don't know much clock time passed before he started back down. Subjective time seemed to last and last. And then I could see that he was moving back down, surely and steadily. He jumped the last few meters, smiling and wiping the grit from his hands.

"A piece of cake. Timed to blow in two hours."

"We'll have a front seat for the show."

"We will indeed."

He drove the rental runabout back to the heliport. Which had a neat little robobar that did a fine line in hooch. I washed away some of the fatigue with internal lubrication. Bolivar had a mineral water and looked at his watch. "After you finish knocking that one back, Dad, we are up and away."

The sun was behind us we flew over the dark beaches. Everything on the ground had been washed clear by the night's rain. Our copter passed low over the thick cables, turned in a lazy circle.

"Ferry is still tied up," I said. "No one below—no traffic on the road either."

"Just about time—" Bolivar said when the ball of flame flared out. Changed to dark billows of smoke.

For long moments nothing happened. The copter bumped a bit when the sound of the explosion reached us.

"Now," Bolivar said.

And it was going. The top of the tower was bending, falling almost gracefully. Then the giant insulators began to turn and twist, the immense cables stirring and writhing. Falling.

I could see lightning spear out as the falling cables broke, twisting as though in pain. Twisted and fell, faster and faster, followed by the ruined tower. Splashing down into the sea in great furrows of waves that stretched across the width of the channel.

"That will give those criminals back on the island something to think about," Bolivar said with great satisfaction. "Normally I wouldn't enjoy doing something like this. But anyone who drafts holidaymakers into clearing up atomic debris deserves no less."

I am pleased to say that I was in complete agreement.

CHAPTER 21

BEFORE WE PARTED AT THE heliport we called James one last time. Still no news, still no luck in finding Kaizi's elusive living quarters. It had been easier to crack into the government records than it was now to get past the privacy barriers of that exclusive city. When Bolivar was gone I picked up my bag and trudged wearily back into Fetorrscoria. I was too tired to go very far. When I came to a liquor store, with a bench out in front of it for the alcoholics, I knew I had reached journey's end. Popping a cold beer I settled back in the sun and called Kaizi.

"Pretty good job if I say so myself."

"Where are you?"

I told him and hung up. By the time I had finished the beer his car rolled up. The door opened and I climbed in. I threw the fake ID he had supplied me with onto the back seat. Took off my face and heard one last plaintive *"chicken soup?"* as I threw it back there as well.

"Plenty of people saw me in Swartzlegen. And I had to use the face and ID to rent a copter. Since the maglev train pretty obviously wasn't running. Did you like the job I did?"

"I would be more pleased if you hadn't seen fit to cut off all communication."

"If you mean all the bugs you planted on me—of course I got rid of them. I do value my privacy."

"You will be going to the depository tonight."

"No thanks? No day off? No pat on the back?"

"Don't be tiresome, diGriz. This will be your last assignment, as I promised. I should think that you would be very pleased that our relationship will soon be over."

I would be pleased when it really was over. I did not trust him in the slightest. Once back at the warehouse he got right down to business.

"Igor. Bring the large box from the car and then go away."

Igor scuffled back with it, dropped it onto the table and went out. Kaizi took a photograph from the box and passed it over to me.

"This man is known as Iba Ibada, nicknamed Iba-ill-favored for obvious reasons."

Too true! A man of average height and schlumpy build. He wouldn't have looked that bad had it not been for the jagged scar that ran down from his forehead, across his nose—leaving a deep dent—and down his cheek. It had been coarsely stitched up, so roughly that the scars of the sutures still showed.

"Industrial accident," Kaizi said. "Machine caught him. He was sewn up by the first-aid assistant, who obviously had little experience. Then Iba was fired from the job for taking the rest of the day off from work. He was very grateful to me when I found him employment on the cleaning squad at the depository. In addition to his salary I pay him very well, to enable him to indulge in his repulsive vices. He is appreciative and does me favors. You will take his place tonight."

"Won't anyone notice?"

"No. I have planned this down to the last detail."

And so he had. The artificial scar that he brought out was identical to the original. Waterproof as well, and could only be removed by a special solvent. Shaped wedges went inside my cheeks and puffed them out to match Iba's photograph. His work clothes were baggy and ugly enough to cover any differences in build. The heavy boots suitably scuffed.

"How about ID?" I asked, scowling in disgust at my image in the mirror. Kaizi passed over a small case. "A contact lens, right eye. Do not lose it. It is expensive and irreplaceable. It has his retinal patterns. And four sets of plastic gloves with his palm pattern on them. That should be enough, since you will only be in the repository twice. Once to see for yourself the layout and the alarms, particularly those on the bearer-bond vault, in order to plot out the theft. Then the theft on the next night. I have a specialized security-trapper kit that is also expensive and irreplaceable. Do you know how to operate it?"

I took it, opened it—and sneered. "I was making better kits than this before I learned to shave. And what makes you think that I will be able to do to the job on the second night?"

"You have to. There will not be a second chance. A ticket has been bought for Iba and he has been paid a large bonus. He will be going offplanet today. And don't forget—remember the video you looked at—that you are what might be called a hostage to fortune."

And I was, surely enough.

"Look at this," Kaizi said, breaking into my thoughts, passing over another memory card. I plugged it into the computer. "This is Iba on his nightly round. The route he takes, the cleaning he does. You will note that he is not a very fast worker. So you can do his job—and still have time to complete yours."

"How do I get to work?"

"Igor will drive you there and will leave you close by. He will pick you up at the same spot when your shift is over. Do you have any questions before I go?"

"None that I can think of now."

"There will be no opportunity later. I will not see you again until after you have returned here."

If there is anything more boring than mopping floors and emptying out shredding machines—it is watching someone else doing it. Including an extraordinary amount of standing about, nose and bum scratching, since the workbots did most of the cleaning. I had some fun when I speeded the film up, but even that grew tiresome. I memorized everything I needed then, since I would not be leaving until close to midnight, I lay on my cot and dozed off in front of the television.

"Time go," was my chauffeur's shouted suggestion.

We went. Trundling through the dark and empty streets. The contact lens in my eye itched and I had to strongly resist the temptation to scratch it. My palm print gloves were pulled on and the trapper kit was in my pocket. Igor stopped the truck finally and pointed ahead. "Around corner."

To work. A few other night workers, also in uniform, were climbing the steps to the depository. I ignored them—just as Iba had done in my training film.

"How's your girlfriend?" one of them shouted, a question that promoted great glee among the other mental giants. I answered, as did Iba in the film.

"Bowb off."

These were the only words I ever heard him speak. Quite often. A bored guard held open an outer door: I walked slower in order to make sure that I would be last one in. If my fake identification did not work I wanted to get out of this place just as quickly as I could. As I walked towards the glowing eye of the retinal pattern detector I blinked inadvertently, my eye irritated by the contact lens. Which slid out of position.

I cursed, walked even slower, trying to push it back into position, watched the last man before me walk away from the detector.

"Move it, big-butt," the guard helpfully suggested. "I ain't got all night."

Thus encouraged I pressed the contact lens hard, hoping it was in the right place, bent and looked into the opening. There was a brief flash of light.

I stood up, holding my breath, waiting for the alarm bells.

The entry light flashed green. I walked slowly towards the locked door. Pressed my palm on the plate next to it.

The door clicked open and I walked in.

The other night workers fanned out and disappeared in the dark and silent building. I pushed open the door to the service steps and went down two flights. The lights came on when I entered the battery room, illuminating the peaceful ranks of silent robots.

"Bowb off," I said, as my double always did. Hanging by the door was my lightning prod, fully charged. I unplugged it and jabbed the nearest robot. "Bowb off."

A great spark snapped into the thing's receiver plate, closing a relay and bringing it to robotic life. Its charging cable disconnected and slid back into its container. The robot turned and exited the room as I danced about my charges, goosing them electrically, until they were all under way.

Through office after office. The rattle and thud of shredders being emptied, clatter of ashtrays. Behind us was the swish of mops cleaning the floor as we went. Occasionally one of the brainless robots would freeze in a feedback cycle, picking up and emptying a container over and over. A quick spark in the right place would jolt it back to work. I imagined doing this job for the rest of my life and shuddered. I had been at it for a little over an hour and was bored to stupidity. I stuck with it. Sparking and cursing monotonously until we reached the vault level.

"All stop. Take a ten-minute break."

They kept going and I cursed again. What was the correct order?

"Stop. Stop. Stop. Stop." On the fourth repetition they did. I leaned my lightning prod against the wall and trotted down the dimly lit hall. Counting the entrances as I went past them, rewalking in reality the virtual reality that I had walked through so many times before. There it was.

The outer door had an uncomplicated lock and no alarms; I opened it easily. The inner, metal-barred gate, would not be that simple. Thank goodness all of the alarms were antiques. More suitable for a museum than their guardian function.

First a length of wire to short the alarm on the electronic lock. There were supposed to be millions of combinations possible on this ancient mechanism, making it impossible to open without hours of computer time. My machine broke the code in less than three minutes. I punched the numbers into the thing's memory and relocked the gate.

The alarms built into the door frame would not be a problem; I had passed through their type often in the past. However, when I put on infrared goggles the room beyond lit up with a pattern of interlaced beams. Break one beam and all the alarms would sound.

But if I put a beam generator of the correct frequency in front of the receiver lens I would be able walk around the room undetected, no matter how many beams I cut.

That was it. I could get into the room. I could remove the bonds from their shelves. Load the robots down and take the bonds away. To where? And, even more important, how could I get them out of the building?

"Bowb off!" I said, with some feeling this time, as I sparked my robots back to life. I had until the end of my shift to figure out a way.

Time dragged. Time crawled its sluggish track. Robots mopped, dumped, clattered, sparked and, eventually, my mid-shift break came. I zapped my horde into frozen silence and looked for a pleasant place to dine. The office of some major executive seemed fine. Seated in his leather chair, gazing across many square meters of glistening desktop, I looked out through his crystal window at the light-sparkled bulk of a bank building. And tried not to taste what I was eating. For some perverse reason Iba had a passion for pickled and smoked porcuswine tails, and always brought a container to work. For verities' sake I had to do the same. I chewed and gagged on the gristly bits, pulled a quill from a piece of attached skin, used it to dig horrible fragments from between my teeth.

But, even as I suffered through my grisly repast, my subconscious was at work. Analyzing, plotting, scheming, working.

I finished quickly, threw the porcine remains into the contraterrene disposal unit—where they flared into cosmic rays—and stood to leave.

Then sat down again as the solution to my problems surfaced in my brain and bobbed about in my cerebral cortex.

Yes, it could be done. Not easily, and there were some very risky factors involved. I was probably the only person in the known galaxy, I thought humbly, who could even imagine a crime like this, much less pull it off.

And all for no profit. There *must* be a way to get out of Kaizi's clutching grasp.

CHAPTER 22

DAWN WAS LIGHTENING THE WESTERN sky when I exited the repository. I shuffled off to our meeting place where Igor was already waiting. We rode in silence back to the warehouse where I saw, as the door swung open, that Kaizi's car was there already. He strode out and stopped the truck with the upraised palm of his hand. I climbed wearily down.

"Igor," he commanded. "Machine empty. Go buy beer."

"No money."

"Here money. Go."

I was sure that it was privacy he wanted, not beer.

"How did it go?" he asked as soon as the door was closed.

"A piece of cake. I can get into that vault and have those bearer bonds out of there within ten minutes. Most of that time will be spent in carrying them away."

"Splendid."

"It is, isn't it? However there is one slight problem in this otherwise most successful robbery plan."

"Problem? What do you mean?"

He looked worried. I turned the knife in the wound.

"Although I can get the bonds out of the vault—there is no way to get them out of the building the same night."

"I don't know what you are taking about." He spoke the words slowly through tight-clamped teeth.

"It is really so simple that Igor could understand it. Take bonds out room, no out building."

He was flushed with rage; I was making a big mistake in taunting him at this stage. I hurried to make amends.

"It can be done, I can get the bonds out of the vault, and eventually out of the building, that I can assure you. It is just that it will take more time. You'll have your bonds, do not fear. But not on the morning after the theft. I toured that building and checked every entrance. They are all locked from the outside. So I would need an accomplice outside to open the door. And there would have to be a truck waiting there as well to carry away the loot."

"There is a possibility that could be arranged."

"But not easily. The street gates for vehicles are locked at night as well. There is no nighttime traffic. The truck would be too easy to see, the risk too great. But there is another way the job can be done with no risk at all. And I can do it alone, so no one else will need to be involved. And I must give you all credit for the plan. It is a variation of the scam you used to rob your own bank. You have a genius for this sort of thing."

He preened a bit; there is a rule that no egotist can recognize false flattery.

"If I were not a genius I would not be the richest man in the galaxy. Go on."

"Follow closely. *Before* I empty the bond vault I go to storeroom number eight zero three. This is where the stationery supplies are kept. Bureaucracies thrive on paperwork so, as you can well imagine, this is a very large room. I will go to the rear of the stacks, which won't be touched for months—if not years—and remove a volume of paper equal in size to the bonds to be stolen."

"Why?"

"Stay with me for a bit longer. After opening the bond vault I stack the paper in the middle of floor, then I remove the bonds. Next I put a time-fused thermite bomb—I *do* love thermite—on the piles of paper. Next I place, a stroke of genius if I may say so, some of the stolen bonds, half-burned and scorched, about the room. As though the heat of the flame blew them there . . .''

''Let me finish!'' Kaizi shouted enthusiastically. ''You take the stolen bonds to the *stationery storage room!* Where you bury them in the back, in the empty space were you took the paper earlier! Then you leave the building at the usual time in the morning—and the thermite goes off after you are gone. You leave the bond room locked?''

''Of course.''

''Then there is a mystery. Did the bonds light spontaneously? Who piled them up? What happened? A sealed-room mystery? Investigation and suspicion. Theft not considered at the time. Certainly not a theft that leaves the bonds still in the building.''

''May I add a few facts to your masterful reconstruction?'' I smarmed. He nodded condescendingly. ''Orders for stationery are forwarded from the various departments to the central ordering room. Which sends it to the supplier. Who brings the supplies once a week.'' He leaned forward expectantly as I played out my story for all it was worth.

''The next delivery will be in three day's time. The driver, accompanied by one of the building guards, takes it directly to the storage room. But this time I will be the driver. After delivering the stationery the guard will fall asleep. The bonds will be loaded onto the handcar, the sleeping guard left in their place. Exit the building. The crime of the century.''

He sighed and leaned back in his chair, smiling, contemplating this perfect crime. Igor came in and Kaizi grabbed one of the beers, opened it and took an immense swig. Then looked at me speculatively. ''You can do this?''

''I can. But I'll need some more equipment.''

''Give me the list. You will have it before you leave tonight.''

"Fine. Now I am going to get something to eat, then get me some sleep."

He did not try to stop me. Knowing that he had absolute power over me as long as Angelina was his prisoner. I slowly strolled the streets among the wage slaves hurrying to work. Entered the now familiar environs of the mechomart and buried myself in its depths. If I were being followed I wanted to lose my tail. I entered the first office building I came to. Up the elevator alone. Down the stairs and out the rear door—did this sort of thing a number of times until I was sure I wasn't being followed. Only then did I go and buy a cheap telephone. After I first threw mine away. Kaizi had had the entire night to bug this phone—and to plant more of his bugs on me.

"Waiter. Come here," I said as soon as Bolivar answered it. "Let me remember what I ate the last time I was here. Yes, a bearburger and some beer."

I hung up and strolled away. And dropped the phone in the nearest waste receptacle. Hoping that Bolivar would catch on that I was still probably bugged, and letting him know I would be at the restaurant we had met in before. I knew I had not been followed. But I also knew that I was undoubtedly still bugged.

I moved about, never staying in one place very long—in case there was a tracker on one of my bugs. It was on my third pass that I saw Bolivar sitting in a corner booth. I made a wide circle, then went back and moved as quickly as I could to the restaurant. I came up behind him and held up a card when he turned. Which read:

SEARCH ME FOR BUGS

Which he instantly did—after one shocked look at my face. Whipping out the detector and passing it down my body. Three coins, the usual, but one of my metal fly buttons turned on the red light as well. Kaizi was getting trickier all the time. I tore off the button and handed it to Bolivar along with the coins. He took the insulated pouch from his pocket and tipped all the miniature transmitters into it, then sealed it shut.

"They're shielded now and can't transmit," Bolivar said. "I barely recognized you—great makeup. And I have some good news. Bolivar has found Kaizi's house."

"But you are Bolivar!"

"James, Dad. You'll never get it right."

"Is she there?"

"We don't know. But it is a very big place, and there is a prime-class robot in the house."

Prime class. Intelligent and expensive. We would have to be very careful before we tackled it.

"While you and Bolivar were holidaying in Swartzlegen I finally cracked into the local government files in Sunkist-by-the-Sea. I had to do it physically."

"You've lost me."

"I mean that their anti-hacking programs were unbeatable without leaving signs of forced entry. So I did a little burglary one night and stole some office machines as a cover. Since I had planted a transceiver inside their main computer bank. The computer is now wide open. I left Bolivar tracking down the construction details in the government files. Planning permission and such should tell us everything about the house that we need to know."

"I've had a long night," I said and punched for the drinks menu. I ordered double eye-openers for both of us. "Let me tell you all about it."

"Wow!" he said when I had finished, took too big a slug of his drink and started coughing. I slapped him on the back, which worked. "That is the most ambitious caper I have ever heard of," he wheezed.

"Thank you. I am proud of it. But I am afraid that I was a little untruthful to my employer about one detail."

"Which is? . . . "

"The stationery delivery will be in two day's time—not three."

He instantly assessed the importance of this fact. And smiled broadly.

"You plan to get the bonds out—and keep them!"

"Exactly. But before we even consider doing that we have to be absolutely sure that your mother is safe. And I have another assignment for you. This is not a casual disguise that I am wearing—I look like an employee of the depository named Iba. I'm worried about him. Kaizi says that he left on a spacer yesterday, got paid off."

"And you think differently? That is not Kaizi's way."

"Exactly. Find out who did leave the planet yesterday. And look at all the news reports as well."

"Good as done. Any way that I can report to you?"

"I doubt it. I think it is best if we stay away from each other. If Kaizi gets any hint that I am seeing you we are in deep doodoo. I'll phone you again, early, about this time tomorrow. After the bond operation."

"Take care of yourself," he said. He looked worried.

"I always do," I said, putting more enthusiasm than I felt into my words. I was more than a little stressed out.

He passed me the shielded bag and I shook out the bugs and put them into my pocket. He took back the bag and we waved good-by in silence. I made my way back to the warehouse and a bit of a rest.

I thought. Igor looked at me when I came in, then turned away. Kaizi glared at me and had other ideas. "I don't like you wandering around the city alone."

"What harm can I get into?"

"I don't trust you, diGriz. You are too smooth." He pointed to the parcels on the table. "Here are all the items you will need for tonight's operation."

"Good."

He reached into his bag and took out his handgun. "I want you to sit very still while Igor puts the handcuffs on you."

There was absolutely nothing that I could do. The big thug came from behind me: the gun pointed unwaveringly. The cuffs clicked into place. And if this wasn't bad enough he locked my ankles together with another pair. Kaizi put the gun away and smiled.

"Get some sleep," he ordered. "You have a big night ahead of you."

They both looked on as I struggled to my feet, then turned and hopped to my cot, fell heavily onto it. Struggled about until I was lying on my back. Looked down at the handcuffs and knew why Kaizi had smiled. I couldn't use a picklock on these. They had a combination lock inset so deeply that I couldn't have turned it, even if I could have reached it by twisting my fingers around. I tried. It couldn't be done.

I was tired enough to sleep deeply despite the cramped position. I woke a bit when I heard voices, fell asleep again almost instantly. It wasn't until I felt Igor's hot breath on my cheek—smelled it as well—that I awoke fully. He was bent over and trying to work the combination lock. I opened my hands ready to throttle him, when I saw Kaizi in the doorway, gun pointed.

"Bring him in here where you can see better."

Igor grabbed me by the ankles and dragged me off the bed. I threw myself sideways so I landed on my shoulder instead of my head. He hauled me, bumping and cursing into the other room. Then sat on me while he opened both pairs of cuffs.

"Is this the way you treat a loyal employee?" I said as I pushed myself up from the floor and sat down in the chair.

"Igor will take you to the depository now," he said. "I will be right behind you in my car. All of the way. I will also be close by when you come out in the morning. If I have any suspicion at all that you have not done exactly what you described, you can be perfectly sure that you will never see your wife again."

I couldn't trust myself to answer him. He took my silence as assent. He looked at his watch. "Time to go. Take your lunch box. All the equipment you will need is inside it, under that repulsive food."

The same drive to the same corner. The same walk to the

front door of the repository. The only difference was the black car that drove silently behind me, waited across the street from the entrance.

I was happy to leave it behind. My contact lens stayed in place this time. My palm unlocked the door and I walked in.

"Hey you. Iba, I'm talking to you."

"Bowb off," I said sullenly, not looking at the speaker. What had gone wrong?

"Come here. Got something for you." I had to stop and look at him. At the newspaper he was holding out to me. "Some guy gave me this for you. Gave me five credits too, can you believe that? Nothing special, I looked at, just today's paper. Almost threw it away." He dropped it to the floor and walked off.

Newspaper? Who? Certainly not Kaizi. It could only have been James. But why?

I could not look at it now. The inside guard was staring at me suspiciously as it was. "Bowb off," I called after the retreating back. Scooped up the paper and hurried to my waiting charges.

As they surged into pseudolife I opened the newspaper. Quickly looked through it. I didn't have the time to read it now—no, wait. On the last page a tiny semicircle had been torn off the edge of the paper. Next to advertisement for a Do-it-Yourself hernia repair kit. That couldn't be it. I looked at the other side, at the small news item there.

DROWNING SUICIDE IN CENTRAL PARK LAKE

I felt suddenly very cold. Scanned the report quickly.

Person unknown . . . ragged clothing . . . water in lungs . . . no identification.

And then the last line.

Disfiguring scar on face.

There would no need to check the passenger lists now. Iba had missed his connection. He had known too much about Kaizi's business.

So I knew exactly what was in store for me as well.

CHAPTER 23

FOR THE FIRST TIME I was glad that this job was so brainless. My thoughts trudged in endless circles looking for a way out, but not finding it. I could steal the bonds, that was the easiest part. But after I had committed the theft, I would then be handcuffed again. Locked up for two days before the supposed delivery to bring out the bonds. Yet the delivery would be a day earlier. Should I admit that? If I did I would be forced to get the bonds and bring them to him. After that I would quickly join Iba in the lake. Or worse.

The robots chuntered along their appointed courses and I was barely aware of them. Only if one of them stalled in a feedback cycle did I remember what I was supposed to be doing and shock it back into action. Then I would sink back into the insolvable circle of my thoughts.

Enough! I was driving myself slightly around the bend with my brain also locked an endless feedback cycle. It was time to do something. Time for the robbery. I turned off all the robots, except for the one I needed, to keep them from wandering. Then I manhandled the bins off the largest wheelbot and jolted it into following me. To the stationery supply room, where the door wasn't even locked. Only the dim night-lights lit my way through this mausoleum of bureaucracy. Printed forms stacked almost to the ceiling, envelopes and reams of paper. We passed it all by and moved deeper into the cavernous room. There was dust on the floor here, dry and musty darkness. The very last access way just at the back wall was my goal. The air was dusty as well, the forms dry and brown-edged. They would burn fine. I loaded the robot high with them, stopping only to sneeze a few times. Finally done, and one last sneeze, and I was out of the paper room with my faithful robot grinding along after me. It then waited with metallic patience while I burgled the bond room.

I shorted out the electronic door lock, then accessed the door frame alarms and neutralized them as well. Then came the only tricky part; sliding the infrared generator in front of the receiving lens without breaking the beam. Slowly forward, angled square on, only too aware of the sweat that was trickling down my face. There!

And no alarms.

After that it was just a lot of physical work that I had to do myself. I piled the paper forms in the center of the room, spreading them out so they would burn all the better. By the time I got around to loading the bearer bonds onto the wheelbot I was breathing hard. One last task. I grabbed up a handful of the bonds—worth over a million altogether—what a waste! And took them far down the hall away from any fire detectors. I lit them, one by one, with my lighter. Let them singe a bit before I put them out. When they were satisfactorily charred I went back and sprinkled them tastefully about the room. Then, the very last thing, I twisted the dial and set the thermite bomb. It would go off an hour after I left the building, a few minutes before the day workers arrived. They were going to have a far livelier time today than they expected.

Then I stopped to take a break. Cooled down and rubbed my hands together to supple my fingers. Only then, and with infinite patience, did I trust myself to withdraw the infrared projector. Slowly, slowly—done! The rest was child's play.

Relocking the door and then restoring all the alarms to working order.

One last trip back in the storeroom, where I carefully hid the bonds among the stationery. I slid some ancient forms in front of them, then I was done. The bonds would be safe there until I came to retrieve them. Or, depressingly gloomy thought, they would remain concealed forever if I made any mistakes.

The next hours dragged slowly by: I worked hard not to think about the thermite bomb. If the thing went off before it should? Don't even think about thinking about it. Then the last ashtray and the last shredder. Down to their underground lair where my metallic aides were tucked away and sucking happily on their electrical teats. I washed the traces of soot off my hands. When the shift ended I left with the others.

There was more than a little tension as I exited the building. If I had not set the thermite timer correctly—I would have to make a run for it. My stomach stayed in a knot until I was safely in the street outside. I walked slowly to the appointed corner. The van was not there.

Was something wrong? Before my thoughts ran away with themselves Kaizi's black car pulled up beside me.

"Get in," he said.

"Where's Igor?"

"That is no business of yours," he said as we drove away. "Everything go as planned?"

"Yes."

He smiled and licked his lips. Then drove with one hand as he pushed a notebook with a stylo attached over to me. "Write down all the details about the storeroom. Where the bonds are. The name of the stationery company and driver . . ."

"I don't think that I should do that."

"Don't play games with me diGriz. And you know very well why are going to give me that information."

"I know. But my wife comes first. And your threats against her life. That is what I want to talk about. What happens to her after I bring you the bearer bonds?"

"Why she joins you, of course."

Joins me. In the grave.

"And what guarantees do I have that that is what will happen?"

"My word, of course."

"Not good enough. You are too much of a liar, Kaizi."

He gave me a quick, cold look, but did not respond.

"Look—let us make a deal. I'll get the bonds for you—if you release her first."

He was quiet as he drove. Then shook his head. "No, I can't do that."

"Then I can't give you the information that you will need if you attempt to get the bonds yourself."

Nothing more was said after that. The warehouse door opened as we approached, swung shut behind us. Igor and his truck were not there. Kaizi got out first, opened the rear door of the car and reached inside.

"Look at this," he said.

I looked—and desperately tried to leap aside. He was faster. The two metal prongs of the electric stunner slammed into my side. The high voltage washed pain through my body. My muscles spasmed uncontrollably as I fell to the floor.

I was conscious but could not move. He dragged me through all the ancient filth and litter on the floor, then rolled me onto the cot. I still could not resist as he locked one pair of handcuffs on my wrists, then secured my leg to the metal bed frame with the other. The numbness was beginning to wear off as he dragged the bed with my limp body across the room and slammed it against the wall.

He went into the other room and came back with another pair of cuffs. I saw what he had in mind and struggled to roll away, kick out, kick him. My free leg barely twitched as he pulled it out. Then cuffed my ankle to a metal pipe that ran along the wall. He was breathing hard, his face twisted with anger. The sophisticated multimillionaire had vanished; he punched me in the face again and again. Stopped only when he hurt his knuckles on my jaw.

"No one goes against my will, no one." He rubbed his hand over his bruised knuckles. "You, a common criminal, seek to dictate terms to me. I will have none of this." The cruel smile was back, his heavy breathing slowed. The painful kick into my ribs was not done in anger, but was carefully calculated to drive his convincing argument home.

"You are helpless. So I can do what I want with you. What I want to do now is to leave you here for a few days without food or water. I am sure that when I return you will be eager to tell me how I can obtain those bonds. If you talk, why then I might let you live."

This was the real Kaizi, unmasked.

"You will let me live just the way you let Iba live? In the lake in the park."

He was turning away when I shouted this after him. Turned back, his face livid. Why had I let my own anger carry me away? I realized that I had signed my own death certificate.

"You are lying in your grave," he said. Then he went out, slamming the door behind him. I heard the car start and the squeaking of the garage door as it opened. It closed again and I was alone.

"Someday, Jim, you will have to learn to keep your big mouth shut," I said aloud. This was sage advice. I wish I had given it to myself earlier. Now—how could I get myself out of this mess?

Not easily, I realized, after a good deal of tugging and twisting and rasp of hard metal against soft skin. I could reach the cuffs on my legs and rotate the dials on their locks. But I was never going to find the combinations by random twisting. And the pipe along the wall was securely in place. I lay back, panting with the effort. With that, and the night's stressful events, despite my perilous position, I fell sound asleep.

Something woke me up. How long had I been asleep? It was still morning by the light in the window. My face hurt where it had been battered. As did my ribs. A sound outside the door, a thin scratching. Someone there. I shuffled about as best I could, saw the door handle. Saw it slowly turn.

Kaizi? Igor? Nothing good I was sure. At this instant I felt just about as low as I had ever felt. Or lower. The door slowly opened. A dark figure slipped through. I started to shout, thought better of it. Waited until he had finished the traditional bug search and sealed away his trophies in the radiation-proof bag. Then I let my breath out in a rush.

"Bolivar!"

"No, James. Bolivar is still checking the planning permission and building records."

"Get me out of here!"

He pulled at the cuffs and shook his head. "Easier said than done."

"Are you driving?"

"Yes."

"Tool kit. Pliers, hammer."

"You got it!"

The pliers were wrecked cutting the cuffs that held me to the pipe. But the bed frame wasn't that strong and Bolivar hammered it apart to free me. Helped me to my feet.

"You don't look so great, Dad," he said. "What with the fake scar and the real bruising, handcuffs and all." He shook his head unhappily.

"Get me to the car and your first-aid kit. Then to a shop that sells cutting tools. I guarantee that I will feel better then." I hobbled from the room, cuffs rattling and clattering. "And thanks for the sudden appearance."

"I thought it was about time. You never phoned when you said you would. I decided to stake this place out. And that big thug who was driving the truck should be getting to Sunkist-by-the-Sea by now. I followed him until he drove onto the payway headed in that direction."

"And Kaizi?"

"He is probably still at his bank. His car is still parked in its slot there. I checked that out before I came back here. I figured that I could at least look in, find out what was going down.''

''Everything . . .''

His phone rang and he answered it. ''On the way, both of us,'' he said, and closed the phone. ''James has the plans to the house. He wants us there as soon as possible.''

''Is there a chopper rental in this town?''

''Absolutely. Cutting tool first—then the sunny suburbs.''

Bolivar stopped just along enough in front of Tools-R-Us to dive through the front door. He was back moments later with a molecular debinder. Threw it to me then jumped the car forward. I turned it on, pressed it against the cuffs. A thin plane of energy loosened the atomic bonds in the metal and a tiny shower of molecules ran down my arm. By the time we got to the copter field I was rubbing cream into the cuts and abrasions. I was about to throw the debinder into the back of the car with the remains of the cuffs. Then thought better of it and stuffed it into my pocket.

An interstellar flying license, along with wads of cash and a credit card, worked wonders. I stayed inside the car until I saw the copter taxi out. Walked over quickly and jumped in.

''Just talked to James,'' he said as we shot into the air. ''He says that Igor's truck is outside the house. He wants to go in—but I told him to wait until we got there.''

I nodded agreement. ''Three are better than one. Is this thing going as fast as it can?''

''Needle against the peg. I told him to find a place where we can set the copter down and to meet us there.''

We were going fast, but I kept feeling that it wasn't fast enough. My brain was whizzing as fast as the copter. Why had Igor gone to the house? If Angelina were there, she might very well be the reason for the trip. He wouldn't harm her, not without Kaizi's orders. But what had been his orders? My thoughts sizzled in circles, my stomach grumbled and complained. My side hurt. I dug deeper into the first-aid kit from the car and discovered a flask of medicinal brandy.

"Not me, I'm driving," Bolivar said. "But you look like you need it."

"Looks don't lie." The ardent spirits hurt the cuts in my mouth, but did wonders when it hit my stomach. Was I getting too old for this kind of thing? I certainly felt that way. At this moment I was well aware that I was really getting very much around the bend.

"We're coming in over the grid reference now—and I see the field," Bolivar said into the phone. "James, is that you waving? Great—I'm setting her down."

We ran to the car before the copter's blades stopped turning. James gave my face and all the bandages one long stare, but said nothing. We dived in and the wheels spun.

"Bring us up to speed," I said.

"The truck you told me about is beside the building. As far as I know Igor is alone in the house—along with the robot of course. The plans of the building are on the seat next to you."

Large, very large. I counted ten, twelve rooms. A single story, with a penthouse arrangement on the top at one end. The side projection showed the house had been built on a slab with no basement below. I looked at this suspiciously, then tapped the plans.

"All of these rooms have windows," I said.

"Most rooms do," Bolivar said.

"Kaizi made a video at my insistence, to prove that Angelina was safe. The room she was in was artificially lit. And there were no windows in the shot."

"Was it done at night?"

"No. He left in the morning. If he came here he should have returned before dark."

Bolivar looked at the plans. "If any room has sealed windows that's where we look first. We can examine the rooms easily enough from the outside."

"And if the curtains are all open and we can see in?" I asked, then answered myself. "Remember the bank? How

Kaizi concealed the money that was supposed to have been stolen?''

''Of course!'' Bolivar said. ''A secret room under the vault. If he could have that done while the bank was being built right in the heart of the city—it would be infinitely easier to do out here in the suburbs.''

James pulled the car to a stop and pointed. ''The building is located just around the corner, behind that grove of trees.''

CHAPTER 24

WE GOT OUT OF THE car and James was just locking it when we heard the grind of a starter, followed by the sound of a heavy engine turning over.

"That's Igor's truck," James said. "It was parked beside the house. What do we do—let it go and follow it?"

"No," I said. "Stop it. There is a good chance that Angelina is either in the truck or in the house. Igor will know one way or the other."

"But it might be dangerous . . ." Bolivar said, worried.

"My decision," I said. I heard the truck start forward and turn into the road. I stepped off the curb and held up my hand when it appeared.

I was so worried about Angelina that, for the moment, I had completely forgotten what I looked like. I was literally not myself. The scar still cut across the bruised and battered face of Iba. That was what Igor saw standing in the street before him. The effect was very dramatic.

I saw his mouth drop open, his face twisted in a mask of terror.

Then he dropped forward over the steering wheel and the truck continued, coming directly at me.

I dived and rolled, landing on the pavement at the boys' feet.

"Stop the truck!" I shouted. Wincing at the feel of new bruises on top of the old ones.

The out-of-control machine ground forward, driving right across the road and up the curb. Then it drove straight into the grove of trees beyond. Thick trunks splintered and bent—but did not break. They were immovable objects all right. But the truck was no irresistible force. The wheels spun, locked, the whole thing juddered until the engine gave out a large grating sound and died.

James reached it first, pulled the door open. Igor's limp body slid out, would have hit the ground headfirst if James hadn't grabbed him and broken his fall. I climbed over them and into the truck.

Angelina wasn't there. I looked through the window into the body of the truck. Empty.

"Get him on his side, tongue out of the way," Bolivar said. "That's it. Any pulse?"

"Yes. But very weak, rapid and irregular."

"Heart attack?" I asked.

James nodded and looked around. The few houses here were set back from the road. We were the only ones who had seen the accident.

"It looks pretty bad," I said. Igor had never done very well by me. But we just could not stand by and let him die. James said it just before I did.

"I don't want him to die on us. We better call an ambulance." He took out his phone.

"Do that," I said. "Then I think that you should either go with him to the hospital, or follow in the car. While you are doing that Bolivar and I will check out the house. If we don't find anything you will be with him when he regains consciousness. See if you can ask him a few pertinent questions then."

James was talking into the phone, then closed it. "On its way. I'm pretty sure that they will let me go with him. I'll claim to be a relative. I'll keep you informed of what is happening."

"Let's think about that," Bolivar said. "Maybe it would be better if I called you. If we are doing any breaking and entering it would not be that wise to have a phone ringing at the same time. I don't want the phone sounding off while we are snooping around and possibly getting into the building."

"We'll do it that way. Go through the house—and call me the instant you find out anything."

I could hear sirens in the distance as we went into the grove of trees that bordered the house on two sides. We kept under their cover as we worked around to the back. As we went we could see inside the building, through all of the windows; none of them were covered. The penthouse was almost completely made of glass and we could look right through that as well.

"I'll check the other side of the house," Bolivar said. "Best for you to wait here for me."

He was gone before I could answer. Slipping around the large swimming pool. I stayed under the trees, watching the house. Nothing moved inside. There was a large two-car garage to the rear of the property. Locked, but that did not slow me down. But the only form of transport inside was an ancient moped with a flat tire. The floor was a solid slab of oil-stained cement. It sounded quite solid when I kicked it. I went back outside and within a minute Bolivar had returned, shaking his head. "None of the windows are covered. I think that your theory of a concealed underground room is very much in order. Do we go in?"

"Call James first. They should be in the hospital by now. If they are not, surely the paramedic will have sent all the vital signals of the patient to the hospital. So by now he will know what has happened."

Bolivar turned on the external speaker and phoned. "Uncle Tom here. We are all so worried."

"With good reason, Tom. Igor collapsed and had a massive heart attack. He has had an acute posterior myocardial

infarction, a major one. It knocked out a good deal of the right ventricle. He is responding to the emergency treatment and the consultants are talking about bypass surgery as soon as we reach the hospital. How is your house hunting going?''

''It's a fine house with a fine view from every window. We're going inside now.''

''We must keep in touch.''

''We shall indeed.''

''Poor Igor,'' I said. ''I know I don't look great, but not enough to give someone a coronary.''

''Unless they had a guilty conscience—and had something to do with the disappearance of the original Iba.''

''That's a thought. And a particularly nasty one. If Igor was involved with that he must have thought that he was seeing a ghost—or his victim roused from the dead. Now—any idea how we should proceed?''

''How about ringing the bell? If there is no answer we let ourselves in.''

''Good thinking, my son. That's just what we shall do. There is nothing more to be seen outside.''

We could hear the chimes go bing-bong somewhere deep in the house. The lens of a security camera projected from the door frame: I stood to one side, hopefully out of its range. I had caused one heart attack today. That was enough. I heard the door open.

''How may I serve you?'' a refined and cultured voice said.

''I am here to see Imperetrix Von Kaiser-Czarski,'' Bolivar said.

''I deeply regret to inform you that my master is not at home. Might I take a message?''

''I'll give you a message,'' I said, stepping into view.

It surely was a fine-looking robot. Taller than I was and made of highly burnished steel. Its eye facets appeared to be large and beautifully cut diamonds. And it was wearing white gloves. It looked me up and down with a most superior robotic air.

"And what, if I may be so bold to ask, is your message, sir?"

"It is a very simple one. Step aside. We are coming into the house." I started forward and was stopped firmly by a steel hand in a white glove.

"I have strict orders not to permit that. You will leave now."

"I will not leave and you cannot stop me."

I stepped forward and the robot removed its hand. Made a hard fist and hit me in the jaw with a right cross.

"The Laws of Robotics!" I shouted, holding on to my sore jaw. "A robot cannot harm a human being."

"You are not human. You're a disguised alien life-form." It said. Bolivar put his foot between the door and the frame so it could not be closed. The robot stamped hard on his foot. Then slammed the door shut when he jumped back.

"Ouch!" he cried, hopping about on his uninjured foot.

"Ouch indeed," I agreed, rubbing my aching jaw. "I'm not sure that I like that robot."

With this I pulled out the molecular debinder. Turned it on and cut a quick circle around the lock. Which dropped out and fell onto the welcome mat. We went in. The robot, which had been walking away, turned back.

"Entrance is prohibited. And you have caused an injury to this dwelling. I shall communicate with the police."

"We are the police," I shouted. "Officer, show this thing your badge."

Bolivar flashed the brilliant, but fake, ruby-set golden badge that he always carried.

"We had reports of a rogue robot at this address. We're taking you in."

"I am forbidden to leave these premises. Depart at once."

"The law takes precedence. You struck me and you must be aware that it is a terrible crime to strike a human being. You are under arrest."

"I am aware of the law. But you are not a human being."

"You can see that I am! Just as you can also see that you are a construct—which indicates a constructor. You were made by humans—and you can also see that I am a human. Therefore I am a member of the human race who constructed you. And a construct must always obey the orders of the constructor." I shook my head. Not really believing that I was having a teleological argument with a robot.

"I can see that you are not. My master has instructed me that all the humans on this planet are imposters. Aliens in disguise. He has also told me and identified who the few real humans are in this city. You are not listed among their number. Therefore you must leave. If you do not leave I have orders to demolish all alien life-forms."

It started forward and Bolivar moved quickly aside so we were equidistant from the thing. The robot hesitated, caught in a feedback loop, unable to figure out which of us to tackle first. "You must leave. Entrance forbidden to nonhuman humans. Death will follow quickly."

I walked around it which had the unhappy result of breaking the feedback. "You must both leave." It turned and grabbed at me. "Strangers not permitted to enter the house. You have entered farthest so you will be made to leave first or be deconstructed." It sounded pleased by this piece of specious logic as it seized me in an unbreakable grip.

Bolivar ran past us and shouted, "I am farthest into the house—I must be made to leave first."

"Farthest must be made to leave first," it said creakily. Then it let go of my arm and made a grab for Bolivar. I ran in the opposite direction, shouting. "I'm farthest—you must make me leave first."

It had Bolivar by the arm now, but its head was twisted around to look at me.

"Farthest!" I called back. It made a strange grating sound and I hoped that it had blown its logic circuits. It seemed to have forgotten Bolivar when it came after me—pulling him along by the arm.

"Hey!" Bolivar shouted, trying to shake the thing loose. Then it had me by the arm as well. The time for argument was past. I had no desire to be deconstructed. I took out the molecular debinder and held it up.

"Do you know what this is?" I asked, waving the device before its diamond eyes.

"I do."

"Then you had better remember the rest of the robotic laws. You must prevent injury to yourself. Let go at once or I will cut your arms off. It's hard for an armless robot to get work these days."

It uttered the grating sound again and its hands opened. It stood stock-still as a trickle of smoke rose from its head.

"Great work, Dad. You sure do know how to win a debating contest. Particularly a robotic one. Now let's see what we can find."

Which was very little. We searched the rooms, one by one, but they were all empty. Bolivar checked all the closets, while I climbed the steps to look into the penthouse rooms. Nothing.

"And nothing that looks like a door or an opening anywhere down here. Not even in the wine-cellar room."

"The robot would know."

"It would if it hadn't blown a fuse or something."

I kicked the floor. It felt solid.

"There is one place that we didn't look," Bolivar said. "The enclosure by the pool with the heater and filter."

I was opening the sliding door to the pool before he finished speaking. But other than the pool equipment the enclosure was empty. And built on a solid slab.

"It has to be in the house," I said. "We are missing something I'm sure. I want to go over every square centimeter of the floor."

We did it room by room. Moving furniture, kicking aside rugs, even tried shifting the refrigerator. Still nothing.

"Last room," Bolivar said in a worried voice, looking in the door. "The master bedroom."

We tested the en suite bathroom first. All of the plumbing was solidly fixed into place. All of the units were sealed to the walls and floor. In the bedroom the floor was made of wood, close-fitting and burnished planks. Solid. The bed was centered in the middle of the sizable room. I sat down heavily on it; fatigue and structural damage were taking their toll. I dropped my head on my hands. So weary.

Something. What?

Slight scratches in the wood by the leg of the bed.

"Aha!" I aha-d, dropping to my knees and sighting along the scratches.

"Dad! What's wrong?"

"What's right is the answer. See them, the scratches on the floor by the legs of the bed? As though the bed had been moved aside—like this!"

I pushed hard on the bed in the direction of the scratches.

Nothing happened.

At first.

Then I heard a metallic click and the resistance stopped. I fell forward on my face as the bed moved smoothly across the room. And there, scant inches from my nose, was an inset handle. We both reached for it at the same time. Youth won and Bolivar grabbed it, turned and lifted. It was as thick as a bank vault door, but counterweighted so it opened smoothly.

Light streamed up from the opening in the floor as we looked in.

Angelina looked back and smiled.

"Now that is what I call a beautiful sight," she said.

CHAPTER 25

"WE'RE COMING DOWN," I CRIED out.

"Please do. I would much rather join you up there but I'm sort of tied up. Do you see a button or switch of any kind up there?"

"Yes—here it is, inset into the frame."

"Press it," she said and stepped aside.

I thumbed it hard. There was the whine of a motor and a grind of gears as a metal ladder extended down into the chamber below. I was on it even before it touched the floor, down it in a flash and across the room. And into a tight embrace.

"I'm . . . glad to see you too . . . even looking like that . . . but I would like to breathe as well."

"Sorry!" I broke the death-grip and held her at arm's length. "Are you all right?"

"I am now. But, please, how is Gloriana?"

I followed her pointing finger. There, stretched out and motionless, was the porcuswine.

"He gassed her," Angelina said. "Is she . . . dead?"

Her eyes were closed, her mouth gaping open. I bent over her inert form and smoothed back her quills. There was no way I could get through them to feel for a heartbeat. "There is no way I can tell," I said. Admitting defeat.

Angelina was digging through her purse. She produced a compact and handed it over. ''Try this.''

I opened it, puzzled—but intelligence didn't strike until I had opened it and seen the mirror.

''Of course!'' I bent over the still form and held the mirror before her nostrils.

''Nothing—no! Wait! It's fogging up—she's still alive!''

Bolivar was down the ladder now and rooting through his pockets. ''If Igor used gas it was probably sleepgas. I don't think he would be trusted with any kind of poison gas. Here—the antidote.''

I gave our favorite porcuswine a spray in each nostril. Nothing happened. But after another quick blast her eyelid quivered—and her eyes opened. She squealed weakly and stumbled to her feet. I scratched behind her ears and the world was happy again.

Angelina gave Bolivar a motherly kiss on the cheek. ''It's good to see you both. I really do feel alright. Though I will feel even better when you get this thing off me.'' She rattled the length of chain that was shackled to her wrist. The other end was attached to a thick eyelet set into the floor.

''I didn't notice! I'm sorry.'' The molecular debinder made quick work of it.

''This was Igor's idea. He came down the ladder and that was when Gloriana went for his ankles. Did a nice job until he climbed back out of her reach. He went out again and when he came he was carrying a canister. Then he gassed her. After that he threatened me with the spray so I had to let him put this chain on. This was so I couldn't reach the wall where I had been working with the cutlery.'' She pointed at a long groove that had been hacked into the plaster to disclose an armored cable. ''I was trying to cut into it—to hopefully cause a short circuit. If the electric company came around and tried to find the cause of the trouble they might even have found me.''

For the first time I looked around the prison cell where she had been kept. A single, armor-glassed light shone from the ceiling. "On all of the time," she said, following my gaze. "Makes sleeping a little difficult."

A bed, a sink with a single faucet, a lidless toilet. A food dispenser. Spartan and harsh. My anger chilled into a hard knot of resolve. Kaizi was going to pay for this, pay a great deal. And not in money.

"Let us leave," she said, picking up her purse and turning towards the stairs. "And as soon as we can, I would like a large refreshing drink and some good food. All they left me was that machine full of dehydrated meals. Absolute slop. I was even ashamed to feed it to our sweet Gloriana." Gloriana grunted when she heard her name—her vocabulary grew daily—and then put her attention back to carefully climbing the narrow steps. We followed her out of the underground bunker.

"Daylight!" Angelina said. "How delightful. Now you must tell me what has happened in the outside world, while I have been incarcerated in this dungeon."

Bolivar had been busy on the phone, so that when we emerged from the house James was already pulling up the drive in his car. Another blissful reunion and we were in the car and away. While I brought her up to date, James drove us to a shaded mall. He parked as far as he could from the other vehicles, so children could not see me and get nightmares, then he hoofed it to the nearest take-away. Unhappily it was a MacAlpo outlet. But this did not seem to bother Angelina who wolfed down a Double-Doberman as I talked. Gloriana snuffled as she pigged down her double fried potatoes.

"And that is about it. The bonds are safely hidden until I feel like going for them. I don't think Kaizi even knows I'm gone yet. Now that we have both escaped Kaizi's clutches we must make detailed plans of what we should do next."

"I agree," she agreed. "As long as it involves grievous bodily harm to himself and his surly associate."

"Igor's in the hospital, that's where James was. He saw

my face and had a heart attack. If he had anything to do with Iba's murder you can easily understand why. He must have thought I was the dead man walking. How is he?''

James shrugged. ''He was going into surgery when I left. The doctor said that he is strong, and young, and that should help. I don't think that we will have to worry about him for some time yet. Meanwhile look here—I got these newspapers at the hospital. The mysterious fire is front page news. And they are still investigating the sabotage of the electricity cables in Swartzlegen.'' We read the reports, all except James who was sent back for more food. Between us we had missed an awful lot of meals.

Once sated we gave thought to the future.

''I have a great suggestion,'' James said, licking the last of the juice from his Dachs-burger off his fingers and trying not to bark. ''Dad, even when that fake scar is peeled off your face, it is not going to look too great. It is turning an interesting black-and-blue already. And I think Mom has had the worst of it, locked in that cell not knowing what was happening. Which is why I suggest that you both head back to the holiday world of Elysium and let Bolivar and me pick up the pieces here.''

''Second that,'' Bolivar said, looking up from the newspaper for an instant, before diving back into it.

''Sweet of you to offer,'' Angelina said. ''But I have one or two things to take care of before I leave.''

''Me too. Like picking up those bearer bonds.''

''No,'' Angelina said firmly. ''We are not broke—and it is just not worth the risk. I have the strongest feeling that we should turn our backs and walk away from this one. After fixing Kaizi's clock of course.''

I noticed that Bolivar hadn't joined the conversation. He had obviously found his perusal of the papers more interesting. I was about to ask him about it when he wadded the sheets into a ball and said, with some enthusiasm: ''Got it!''

Which, as you might imagine, drew our instant attention.

"I know what Kaizi is up to and what is behind this entire affair."

Attention squared now.

"My brief but interesting career as a banker has now reached its zenith. And shall be put to a good use before I return to lunar research. The pieces are all falling into place. To understand just what is happening we must go right back to the beginning, when Kaizi made the Stainless Steel Rat an offer he couldn't refuse."

"I could have refused it if I had wanted to."

Angelina raised one quizzical and lovely eyebrow at that. "You? Refuse four million credits a day?"

"Well, you must admit, it had certain attractions."

"Kaizi knew exactly what he was doing—he is an interstellar conman of the first degree. Good conmen always let the suckers talk themselves into doing what the confidence trickster wants them to do. First the money, then the data bank searches, then the discovery that all evidence pointed to Bolshoi's Big Top circus and the strongman Puissanto."

I nodded rueful agreement. "A perfect con job. We discovered all the facts on our own, things that we thought Kaizi could not have known about. We thought that, by ourselves, we had uncovered all the links that pointed to the circus. When in reality he had really planted all these facts himself. He did a rush job and a really detailed search, on the spot, would have revealed that. But of course by the time we discovered that we were being conned I was already on this planet, and skidding down a greasy slope. But why me? What did he have against me, us, the family?"

"Nothing. But you were essential to the fruition of his plans. Which goes back to the time when he discovered that Bolshoi's Big Top was coming to Fetorr. The businessmen on this planet are most provincial. They are happy enough to make their profits here and enjoy the bucolic luxuries of life. But not Kaizi. He really does have interstellar interests and knows what is going on in the big galaxy out there. I'll bet that he had some banks or corporations on another planet when the circus came to town there.''

''Interstellar interests? Planets?'' I asked. I still couldn't understand how the pieces fit together.

''He *knew* that the circus was a cover for interstellar investigators. I have the strong feeling that he has tangled with them once before on another planet. So he knew that Puissanto is a Galactic Inspector of Taxes. And Gar Goyle an organizer for GUU, the Galactic Union Union. I did a little digging and uncovered that Belissima, the dancing acrobat, is with FBI. The Forensic Bureau of Investigation. So Kaizi knew that bad times were on the way for tax evaders, nonunion businesses, profit skimmers, crooks, privileged information investors—in short any company with dodgy bookkeeping, or any individuals who kept double sets of books. Trouble was coming—and he was going to profit by that information. The first thing he had to do was make things worse. That's where the Stainless Steel Rat came in. First you had to be there to be blamed for the crimes that Kaizi did on his own—''

''And then I was forced to go on and commit more crimes myself. A conman conned,'' I said with some bitterness. And blinked. ''But I still don't see how he profited by all this. Yes, he got to keep the money he stole from his own bank. But the rest—''

''Just look at the financial pages,'' Bolivar said, smoothing out the crinkled sheets. ''Read these headlines. 'STOCK FALLS AS UNION LOCKOUT CONTINUES.' And this—'INVESTORS FEAR SHARP DROP IN GILTS'—those are government bonds. 'DERIVATIVE MARKET BOOMING.' And this I particularly like, 'FEARING RUN BANK CLOSES FOR LONG WEEKEND.' And that's Kaizi's own bank. By doing that he started a panic and a run, not stopped it.''

''I used to know what a run on a bank was,'' I admitted. ''But . . .''

''But they don't happen much any more because of galactic interbank controls—which apparently don't exist here. You must remember that banks do not keep all of their assets in cash. Usually only a fixed percentage. The rest is out on loan to earn the interest that keeps banks in business. So if people get feeling insecure and they go to their bank in large numbers to take out their deposits—the bank doesn't have enough cash for them all. If the run continues the bank goes bust."

I still didn't see it. "What can he gain by starting a run on his own bank? What if it goes bust?"

"It won't. I imagine he has transferred all the cash he will need from his other holdings. But panic spreads like the plague. Other banks will have runs on them as well, and won't be able to bail themselves out. Next thing will be that the stock market will start getting worried, investors will begin to get hysterical, and all of that will lead to a single and inescapable event. Read this." He passed me the paper, tapped the headline in question.

" 'WEAKENED FETORR CREDIT HITS NEW LOW.' New low against what?"

"The Interstellar Credit. When we first came to this planet they were at par, that is they were worth exactly the same amount. Now, with all the financial upsets, the Fetorr credit is down seventeen points. Which means you can buy a hundred of the local credits with eighty-three Galactic Credits."

The lightbulb finally lit. "You told me something that meant nothing to me at the time. Not only does he own banks—but he has a brokerage firm as well!"

"I hear the words," Angelina said, "but I am afraid that I don't see the results that you financial geniuses seem to be so excited about."

"It is so simple it is almost too simple," James said. "He watched the economy start on the downhill course—and helped it along by giving it a push. More than once. First the disastrous robberies, then the power failure, which might have been the final straw. Now he will sell short and buy the credits back at a lower price."

"He's buying futures!" Angelina said as we all nodded like crazy, like puppets all strung together. "He is betting all of his money that the Fetorr Credit will fall further still. And when it does, it may wreck the economy—but he will make billions!''

''Exactly so,'' Bolivar our financial genius said, wiping his hands together with glee. ''So now that we know his game—we outplay him. Clean him out. Hit him where it really hurts.''

''In his wallet,'' Angelina said. ''But while we are cleaning out his assets let us not leave sight of some personal grudges.'' She lightly touched my bandaged face. ''You boys get the money. I'll get the man.''

There was a new excitement in the air as we drove back to the copter, took wing to Fetorrscoria. Even Gloriana seemed to be enjoying her first-ever flight. As the others elated, made plans, counted soon-to-be-acquired riches, planned vengeance, I began to be depressed. The boys didn't notice my silence but Angelina did. She look worried.

''Do you want some painkiller? Are those bruises acting up?''

''No—but I could really use some liquid painkiller to dispel depression. I have been tracking down a single convoluted train of thought, and have reluctantly arrived at a single repellent conclusion. Bolivar?'' He turned his head. ''How long will it take you to put together your monetary trap for Kaizi?''

''A day, two days at the most. Why?''

''Because, unhappily, it means that I am going to have to return to my incarceration in the warehouse. If he finds that I have escaped, and can pin him for robbery and murder, there is a good chance he will cut and run.''

No one had a ready answer for this one.

''I can't let you,'' Angelina finally said.

''I am afraid that I must do it. But there will be no danger. I'll eat and drink well before I go there, only put on the cuffs when he comes to the warehouse. In fact I think that I am going to enjoy this. The biter bit, the conman conned. If we do this right he won't have a clue as to what is going down.''

CHAPTER 26

BOLIVAR HAD CALLED KAIZI BEFORE we went to the warehouse, but his secretary said he was too busy to come to the phone. I'll bet he was! It is not every day that one breaks the bank of the national economy. The copterport in Fetorrscoria had a restaurant with a secluded little bar attached. We found a table and placed our orders while Bolivar checked the copter back in. The strictly nonalcoholic MoggyCola at MacAlpo's had left a bad taste in my mouth. Which was quickly washed away by a double Rotgutt on the rocks. For a rare instance Angelina joined me in one as well, before switching to white wine.

"We need a plan and a checklist," I said as I pressed the order button for another round. James laid his palmtop computer on the table and made the entries as I listed them.

"A makeup kit to restore my face to its former bashed self when we take these bandages off. Some new handcuffs—as well as a new cot to replace the one Bolivar destroyed."

"And one of those little eavesdropping bugs," Angelina said. "So when Kaizi shows up we can listen in. James, I want you and your credit card to come shopping with me. I must outfit myself from the skin out."

"And we are going to need an awful lot of money to

invest,'' Bolivar said, joining us at the table. ''I can handle the currency purchases and futures—but only if I have the funds.''

''That's where the Banco Cuerpo Especial comes in,'' I said. ''Which is of course owned outright by the Special Corps.. If you have any trouble squeezing out enough credits, get on to Inskipp to authorize the funds. Feel free to use my name.''

Bolivar took a cab to the bank, while James took our shopping list. Angelina and I stayed in the warm security of the bar to await his return. I ordered another drink.

''After we take Kaizi to the cleaners,'' I said, ''I am looking forward to a good long break in the sunshine.''

''So am I—for starters. But I am looking forward to a far longer one than that.''

''Meaning what?''

''Meaning I think, that at our age, we ought to lead a quieter existence.''

''What! Leave show business?''

''Yes. Leave show business, as well as all the monkey business that has kept us occupied down through the years. I'll hang up my guns if you'll hang up your lockpick.''

I laughed—then saw that she was deadly serious. I contemplated a future in the sun in my rocking chair. Or wheelchair . . . ''It would be, well, you might say, perhaps slightly . . . boring.''

''Nonsense. We could travel, there are plenty of planets we haven't visited, meals we haven't eaten—''

''Drink we haven't drunk!''

''Now you are getting into the spirit of things.'' Her happy smile faded. ''I don't complain, Jim, you know that's not like me. But I had plenty of time to think about the future, locked away by myself in that terrible room. It was, well, an experience I would not like to repeat.''

''Being cuffed to that bed and left to maybe die of thirst made me feel the same way.''

''That is exactly what I mean. We should never place ourselves in this kind of position again. You think about it.''

"I will, I promise. Just as soon as we have taken Kaizi to the cleaners."

"Of course. We'll tie this one up. Then walk away without looking back."

James appeared in the doorway and waved. Gloriana woke up and stretched. We went to join him. Holding hands, which felt very good indeed.

I will admit to feeling some hints of apprehension when we drew up before the warehouse. We waited outside until James had swept up all the bugs inside and put them in his insulated bag. Nor was I wildly enthusiastic when the cuffs clicked back on my wrists. Angelina was not happy either as she applied the makeup to my crunched face. Which looked even more crunched by the time she was through. She admired her handiwork, then frowned.

"James, I've changed my mind about having the shopping trip now. I'll take a cab to the hotel where you and Bolivar are staying. I'll have a long bubble bath and a rest. Let Gloriana have a bath too—we both need one. I want you to stay close by in case anything goes wrong here. I want us to forget Kaizi and the money, revenge, the whole works, if it means putting your father in any kind of danger. Do you understand?"

"Loud and clear. I'll be nearby with my ear glued to the output of our pickup bug, but out of sight of the warehouse. We'll keep in touch with this." He held up what looked like a grain of rice. "Fits inside the ear and cannot be seen. Two-way talking, state of the art." He passed it over and I plugged it in.

Angelina had done a wonder job with the makeup, bringing my face back to the ruined condition it had been in earlier. When they were all done James unwrapped the various bugs and listening devices that Kaizi has planted. Angelina blew me a silent kiss as they left.

Depression hit—but so did all the drinks—and I was asleep in seconds.

After a timeless period of rather repellent dreams I awoke

as a voice whispered in my ear. Where the tiny and invisible communicator was located.

"Looks like Kaizi's car coming towards the warehouse," James said.

"What time is it?" I shaped the words with my mouth, not speaking aloud but breathing in the lightest of whispers. James could make out what I was saying.

"Almost dawn. He sure put in a long day at the bank."

"And we know why. Stay in contact."

"You bet."

In an emergency I could open the handcuffs; I hoped that I would not have to. If I played along, just for a short time more, our counterplot against his plot would surely work. I heard the outer door open and close. Then the footsteps approaching the door. A rattle on the knob as he opened it. I turned to look.

"Getting thirsty, Jim?" Kaizi said. His eyes were surrounded by darkened shadows. Working night and day on his crooked schemes. But he still had enough energy left for some gratuitous sadism. I didn't answer, but tried a dry cough instead.

"You are going to get those bearer bonds for me?"

"Water . . ."

"Of course."

He returned with a mug of water. Held it out to me—then poured it onto the floor. I was all method acting now, gasping and mewling. He liked that.

"The bonds?"

"I'll . . . get them . . ." Cracking and husking of course.

A half a cup of tepid water was my reward. Just enough to keep me alive if I really had gone without. He looked at me coldly.

"I don't believe you," he said. "Jim diGriz does not give in that easily. I am going to be busy the next few days. So I think that we will wait for next week's delivery to pick up the bonds." I fell back and gasped dryly, which made him smile.

"Maybe a little water now and then—but no food. I want you weak but I don't want you to die on me. I think another week will bring you around to my side. If not—why then another week. Then perhaps I can supply some interesting interviews with your wife." I writhed realistically at that. "Even you will break, Jim, I guarantee that."

"Rot—in hell," I managed to gasp out as he left. Oh how much he must be enjoying my sadistic theatricals. I dug out the handful of eavesdropping bugs and sealed them once again in their soundproof bag. Then took them out again and spread them out on the bed. He would get suspicious if they stopped broadcasting for any length of time.

"Come and get me, James," I breathed into earphone. "I think that the stage is now set for the last act!"

James opened the hotel-room door as quietly as he could, but Angelina was already awake. Sitting on the couch, very fetching in a man's bathrobe, looking out at the pollution-tinted dawn.

"There is fresh coffee there on the table."

"Wonderful!" I poured two cups, passed one over to James. "Kaizi has come and gone. He is sadistically going to leave me locked in there to stew in my own juices. Before he gets around to thinking about me again—he is going to discover that he has a lot more to think about than he ever realized." I rubbed at my fake scar, which was beginning to come loose. "I'm going to wash off the makeup, and maybe this scar as well, if enough palisade cells on the skin of my face have sloughed off. Will someone kindly call down for lots of breakfast?"

Gloriana, washed and blow-dried, was snoring away happily in her basket. She did not wake up as I cleansed my wounds and put on a matching bathrobe. I emerged to stare at the table laden with food. I am afraid that after that I talked with my mouth full.

"Mrungle . . ."

"Swallow first, talk later," Angelina wisely advised. I finally came up for air and sighed with satisfaction.

"The only thing missing is a cigar."

"I know all of your filthy habits," James said as he passed over a pocket humidor.

"We've raised them right," Angelina said.

We certainly had. Raised them, or dragged them up, right. Sons to be proud of. Not to say daughters-in-law.

"Is the game afoot?"

"Fleet of foot and galloping towards the finish line. The bottom dropped out of the Fetorr Credit when the market and the exchange opened this morning. Everyone is panicking—other than our lot and Kaizi. By the time everything closes tonight he will be the richest man on the planet."

"He thinks," Angelina said. "What happens then?"

"Bolivar is setting it up now." He looked at his watch. "We have some hours yet before the curtain comes down. Shall I pick you up here?"

"Please do." I scratched at a last remaining shard of scar. "I'll need some clothes."

"I'll take care of that," Angelina said, standing up. "Remember that the police are still looking for the face you are wearing now. I'll shop for you as well as myself. James, are you coming with me?"

"Sorry, but as much as I would like to help you spend money, I have more pressing business. Computer problems at the bank. But I've opened a no-limit account for you at Sharrods departmental store."

"That should be enough." She looked sharply at me. "Don't smoke and drink too much while I'm out."

"Never! A single cigar, a sip of wine. The sweet liquor of success is what we will all quaff together."

"That's more like it," James said and left.

I was grateful for the solitude. I was tired and sore in a number of places. But inordinately happy. An emotion that I was sure I shared with Angelina; shopping, shopping to her heart's content. The boys too, happy in their skilled work. Extracting vast amounts of money from reluctant crooked capitalists. And gently slipping the noose around Kaizi's unsuspecting neck. I turned on some soul-soothing music, then found some even more soul-soothing bottles in the bar.

And thought about our holiday to come. I was looking forward to some lazy months in the sun. And the minimum amount of exercise every day, just enough to work up an appetite for dinner.

But how much of that could I take before I got bored to tears? I was not really one who enjoyed just sitting around. Of course we could go the theater more often, even the opera. Maybe not; I shuddered at the thought of one shrill soprano too many. Would I start getting twitchy for some action? Maybe start sneaking out at night with a lockpick to open a safe or two? I must have dozed off at this point because loud snores woke me up. My own. I refreshed my drink and decided not to think any more about the future at this point. Wait, Jim, wait until the job is done.

Angelina was back by midday, leading a squadron of carrybots. The purchases were piled high, the carrybots dismissed, and very soon discarded wrapping littered the room while she displayed her purchases. Not only clothes for herself, but some cheery sports outfits for me.

We were dressed, eager and waiting when the door opened. James was back at last.

"How is everything going?" I called out.

"Everything is going according to plan," Kaizi said, coming through the door, large gun steady and pointed.

CHAPTER 27

THIS SORT OF THING HAS happened so often to me that my reflexes are completely trained to take action, even while my conscious brain was still taking in the new and thoroughly unhappy situation. These well-conditioned reflexes keyed in the commands—jump for the sofa, dive out of the room, tackle the gun, throw the floor lamp at him, shout ''LOOK BEHIND YOU!'' The usual thing in this kind of situation. But, even as my muscles tensed for action, my conscious brain intervened and put all action on hold. I spasmed into the air, then dropped back into the chair.

Because he was not pointing the gun at me at all. Oh, yes, he was looking at me with that chill smile of his—but at the same time he was pointing the gun at Angelina. He had killed before and would have not a moment's hesitation to kill again.

''Very smart,'' he said. ''It would be a dreadful waste, but I would certainly shoot her if you make any dubious moves. Fire first in order to scar her beauty, then shoot to kill, if you continue to persist in your folly. Now if you both will stand slowly and walk to the couch. That's it. Seat yourselves, good.''

Angelina sat stiffly, her hands folded on her purse. I slumped, hands in my pockets, scratching about for anything to fight with. The trousers were brand new. All I came up with was a slip of paper labeled PACKED BY MOSHI LAINI.

Kaizi stepped forward and closed the door behind him. Eyes and gun never wavering. He circled us, felt for the armchair, then seated himself carefully into it.

"What have you done with Igor? He has failed to contact me."

So he didn't know everything. I had to play for time. The longer I kept him talking the longer I had to find a way out of this impasse.

"We never touched him. He must still be in Sunkist-by-the-Sea as far as I know." Truthful enough. But he didn't like it.

"No games, diGriz. He went there because she was causing a disturbance of some kind. He hasn't reported back. I can maim as well as kill." The gun made a muffled *phutt* and the cushion next to Angelina burst out its stuffing through a large hole. "That is the last warning. Speak!" I spoke, quickly. "I was there and I saw him leave the house. You will remember I was still wearing my Iba disguise. He saw me and reacted badly, even wrecked the truck. Possibly because he had something to do with the disappearance of the real Iba." Kaizi remained impassive and did not rise to the bait. "My sudden appearance was a bit of a shock. So much so that he had a massive heart attack."

"You killed him!" He raised the gun.

"No! He is alive. He has been operated on, a quadruple bypass, and is doing well in intensive care. Call the hospital if you don't believe me."

He didn't believe me. But he did after he made the call. Which was most interesting.

"Yes, admitted today. Doing well. Good. Me? I'm his brother. Give him the best treatment and send the bills to me."

"Brother?" I asked when he hung up.

"Yes. Our mother was an X-ray technician. Got her genes

well zapped on the job. Radiation leakage. Some of the genes made for genius. Others for Igor."

"Shouldn't you be in your bank making money?" Angelina said. "Instead of here playing the hoodlum."

"If you think I am not aware of your machinations at the Banco Cuerpo Especial—you are wrong. If you have done anything, you have succeeded in helping me. You will be quite safe as long as you obey my orders."

"If we obey your orders you will certainly kill us," Angelina said. He nodded.

"Yes, that is possible. But as long as you are still alive you will hope that that possibility will never arise. Now let me think now about the best way to do this. You are a loving couple. But you, Angelina, are of the female persuasion and surely more emotional. You will follow your emotions. Therefore you will keep hoping that you will emerge alive from this dilemma. You will call your son James and give him my instructions. You will use this phone because it cannot be traced." He took it from his pocket and threw it onto the couch. She ignored it.

"Why should I do what you say?"

The shot was her answer. Searing pain tore through my upper arm. I clapped my hand over the wound, watched the blood ooze from between my fingers.

"The phone," he said.

She placed the call, never taking her eyes off me. She was calm and composed although quite pale.

"James diGriz. Yes, I know that he is in a meeting. Tell him that it is his mother calling and it is an emergency. Of course you can interrupt him. What do you mean it is as much as your job is worth? Young lady, if you don't call him now I will personally come down there and tear your eyes out."

She waited. Cold and silent. She had never talked like this to anyone before. Although she was icy calm outside, I knew that she was screaming inside.

"Yes, James, most important . . ."

"Tell him to be ready to make the following transfer of funds to my bank."

"I have some instructions for you. Kaizi is here with a rather large gun and, for reasons I can't go into now, I know that he will use it. He wants you transfer some funds . . ."

It all happened at once. A single loud explosion and there was suddenly a great hole blown in the hall door. Kaizi jumped, the gun muzzle wavered.

I was diving towards him as Angelina threw the phone and her purse at him, at the gun.

He fired just once before I had him by the wrist with my blood-soaked hand. The gun went off, again and again, plaster rained down from the ceiling. Then he screamed in pain as Angelina's sharp shoeheels ground down on his arm. Wakened by the noise Gloriana came hurtling into the room and began chewing on his ankle.

The scream was muffled by James's arm around his neck, pulling him backwards. While his hand twisted the gun from Kaizi's limp fingers.

In scant seconds the scene had changed completely. James had launched himself in through the ruined door. He now held the gun and twisted his foot on the back of the neck of the writhing figure on the floor. Gloriana had had enough chewing, he must have tasted fairly repulsive, and was wiping her snout on the rug. Angelina pulled me gently back onto the sofa and dug her thumb hard into the pressure point on my arm to stop the flow of blood that was dripping from my fingertips. She had the telephone in her other hand and was talking with great calmness. "Everything is fine, Bolivar. James is here and took care of the intruder. We'll call you back in a few minutes."

"How did you know?" I asked James.

"That transceiver in your ear. It's still working fine. I came here the second I heard his voice. I didn't alert you. I thought that surprise was the best option in this emergency."

"It was," Angelina said. "After you hush that thing you

are standing on, would you be so kind as to get me a sheet from the bed?''

The single cry of pain gurgled away into silence.

''Yeah team,'' I said. It came out rather feebly. Angelina touched my face delicately with her free hand.

''Don't worry, darling. Everything is going to be all right now.''

Surprisingly enough she was right. James tore the sheet into strips and Angelina made a tourniquet to stop the flow of blood.

''I'll help you into the bedroom,'' he said. ''It is going to be busy around here pretty soon.''

''Don't need any help,'' I said as I leaned on his strong arm, walked slowly out of the room. Gloriana trotted in after us. The bed was soft. Angelina bandaged the wound which was now beginning to throb and ache. ''You need some antibiotic and a painkiller.''

''There's a bottle of painkiller in the bar outside, which will do until the real stuff comes around.''

Loud voices sounded from the other room. When she went out she opened the door quickly then closed it behind her. She was back in a moment with glass and welcome bottle.

''Not too much,'' she said.

''Never,'' I said, knocking back a quick one. ''What's up?''

''Lots of excitement. The house detective showed up and James told him to alert the police and get the doctor on call. Said that Kaizi had broken in and tried to rob us. All the blood was caused by the wound on the burglar's leg.'' I knew better than to ask how that had happened. ''The people in the room above us sounded the alarm when the shot came through floor. Fortunately missed them. The fire department was here but we sent them away. I'll get some better painkiller from the doctor when he arrives. Meanwhile, be a dear and put Bolivar into the picture.''

''Right, good as done.'' A few more sips while I was waiting for him to come to the phone. He sounded worried.

''Don't be. We had an armed intruder, who is no longer

armed and I am sure very sorry that he intruded. James took him out."

"Who was it?"

"Kaizi, would you believe it? Somehow he followed us here."

"Impossible. We have an undercover agent in his bank. He has been there since yesterday, he has never left."

"But . . ." I was at a loss for words. Luckily Bolivar was still in possession of his wits.

"There must be two Kaizis! That would explain a lot of things. Could be twins, like Bolivar and me. I have to go now. I must get back to destroying the economy. Keep me in touch."

Angelina came in and carefully closed the door behind her, cutting off the sound of even more voices. "Police, an insurance investigator, the doctor—I bribed him to get these—and even Puissanto has shown up."

"Kaizi is still in the bank—yet he is lying on the floor out there."

"Lift your arm." She shook antibiotic onto the wound.

"Bolivar thinks that there are two Kaizis."

"Very possible. That would explain how he put me into that cell while he was working on you back here. I always thought that there was something suspicious about him."

"Suspicious? Like his being twins? You never told me!"

"Just feminine intuition. I was waiting to make sure." She tied the compression bandage around the wound, then held the ultrasound injector against my forearm. It blasted painkiller through my skin; everything became quite rosy quite soon. I frowned as she took the bottle and glass away. I was relaxing in the golden glow when the door opened again and she came back in. Only it wasn't her but the muscle-bound figure of Puissanto instead.

"Got yourself into quite a bit of trouble," he said. Looking at the bandage and the blood on my clothes.

"A flesh wound. You should have seen the other guy."

"I have. A good job. But his career is just about at an end. He and his brother's."

"Twins?"

"No. This one's the older brother. He had a little surgery to make them look alike. It helps them in their interstellar con games. We in GIT have been after them for tax evasion for a long time. I'm glad you finally smoked them out."

"What's going to happen to them?"

"A lot. My department of Galactic Tax Inspection has been working closely with the local tax authorities and the police. Their simple-minded brother in the hospital has already been fingered for assisting in the murder of a worker named Iba. Igor will get medical and psychiatric treatment. But the wounded brother in the next room goes down for murder. No death sentence on Fetorr. But a life sentence here really does mean life."

"Two down and one to go."

"They want the other Kaizi on this planet for bank robbery—Igor's confession will help there. They'll put him in the slammer for a good long time for that crime alone. If he ever gets out they will turn him over to us for sentencing for interstellar tax evasion."

"Well done," I said as he turned to leave. "The good guys seem to have won. But what about that wanted criminal who has been in all the papers? The superthief, the Stainless Steel Rat?"

He turned back. "The feeling among the honest police—and there are very few of them—seems to be that he was pretty well framed by Kaizi. They would like to interview him, and they still have some charges outstanding against him. But, unhappily, it has been reported that he fled the planet and is now in hiding well beyond their jurisdiction." He rooted in his pocket, took something out. "Anyway—they never had much evidence." He threw it onto the bed and left.

I picked it up and ran my fingertips over the burnished surface. A metal cutout of a stainless steel rat. I sighed. And fell asleep holding it.

CHAPTER 23

SOME THINGS I REMEMBER, OTHERS I had to be told about. The mixture of painkillers, booze, fatigue, shock, you name it, kept me out of the picture for a bit. We must have left the hotel safely because the next thing I knew I was in a hospital bed recovering from surgery.

"Went absolutely fine," Angelina said. She was sitting by the bed holding my hand. This was the first thing that I saw when I opened my eyes. And not a bad sight at all.

"Fine?" I muttered.

"The operation on your arm. You had a nasty flesh wound right through your biceps. The medicos cultured a fine new chunk of muscle cells from a couple of cells that you donated. Planted the new muscle, then covered the wound with a skin culture of the same kind. The pain should be gone by now."

"It is!" I flexed my arm. Gloriana put her front trotters up on the bed and snuffled my hand. I managed to give her a good scratch or two. "Oh, the miracles of modern medical science." I looked around. "Where am I?"

"In the medical facilities of the Banco Cuerpo Especial. Which in addition to being the bank of the Special Corps is also an official embassy. It also happens to have its own hospital as well. We are here and safe until the Corps spacer arrives. Soon now."

"We?"

"Bolivar is here as well. The Fetorr police are still looking for him for escaping from their jail. But they are not looking too hard since they have so much else on their hands. James will be here soon. He is finishing the last computerized transfers of all the financial shennanigans. A great profit he says, mostly for the Corps, but a good bit for us for setting the whole thing up."

"How do you feel?"

"Perfectly fine. After all it was you who got shot."

"But it was you who had to sit there and watch it." I thrashed about and managed to sit up in the bed. "I'm getting up."

"Of course. Your clothes are folded on the chair there."

I was a little woozy at first, but that soon passed. Angelina led the way down the hall to a relaxing sort of lounge room with attractive-looking food and drink dispensers against the wall. Bolivar was there drinking a beer and it was reunion time all over again.

"I hear that all of your financial gamesmanship has paid off."

"It certainly has. We have turned a good profit without bankrupting the planet, as Kaizi planned to do. Aside from our money-market profits, I am happy to report that you are also well-off financially."

"Who, me? Kaizi told me that he had cleaned my account out of all the money he had paid to me."

"He did. I was sure from the very beginning that is what he planned to do—and there was no real way to stop him. However, as the money was being transferred from bank to bank I saw to it that over five percent was deducted as bank charges. The total sums transferred were so large that even that amount is really impressive. That money is safely buried."

"Buried? I have the feeling that I am missing something."

"It's very simple. The percentage of the money, that we slipped out as it was being transferred, was taken out as cash. Untraceable. With it we bought chips of nanomemory from James's firm. Those chips hold so many nanobytes of memory that one of them the size of your fingernail is worth hundreds of thousands of credits. I buried them in the garden under the roses."

"Well I never . . ." And I hadn't.

"I'm looking forward to picking some of those roses," was Angelina's practical suggestion.

Our happiness was intense, and our pleasure squared when James came in.

"All done!" he announced. "The Fetorr operation has ended most satisfactory for all concerned."

"Not for all I hope," said I. "Have Kaizi, Kaizi-2, and Igor met their just deserts?"

"Justice is swift here, particularly when you try to pinch all of the planetary assets. The gruesome twosome are tucked away where the sun does not shine, with numbers on their chests and bars on their window. Their younger brother is recovering his health and is singing like a bird. He was mentally—if not physically—abused by his older brothers. He is institutionalized and under treatment. Now that he knows that he is beyond the reach of his brothers he appears to be happy for the first time in his life."

"I was feeling guilty about causing him that heart attack," I said. "I guess I shouldn't be." I smacked my lips dryly. "If Angelina is as thirsty as I am she needs liquid aid."

"Good as done. A wine and a beer in that order?" Bolivar asked as he went to the bar. We nodded agreement. James joined him and poured a beer for himself.

Then we all raised our glasses on high.

"Can anyone think of a toast?" Angelina asked.

There was silence until I coughed. They all looked at me.

"Of course. It is a quite simple one. To my family. To missing wives soon to be joined with their distant husbands.

Then—a long life and a happy one for each and every one of us.''

We drank to that.

''And a year's vacation for your mother and I,'' I added.

''I don't believe it,'' James added.

''Nor do I,'' James added.

''But it is true,'' Angelina said. ''We had a long talk about it. No work and plenty play. All calls from Inskipp go unanswered. The Special Corps can take care of itself. We live off of our savings and resist all schemes, honest or dishonest, to add more credits to our kitty.''

Both boys were dumbfounded. James gurgled and spoke for them both.

''And—at the end of the year . . .''

''Why we start another year of doing exactly the same thing,'' Angelina said, smiling sweetly.

The twins looked at me and I nodded patient agreement. ''Look, boys, I have saved the universe just once too often. I have been elected president, traveled in time, defeated alien races, robbed countless banks. The time has come, I do believe, to rest on my laurels.'' I thought a moment. ''There is of course one bit of work I might do . . .''

''You never!'' Angelina said, quite angrily.

''Don't misunderstand! Not crookery. I meant I might write down my memoirs. No one will believe me of course.''

''Then disguise them as fiction!''

''Of course—what a splendid idea. And I even have a title. The first volume shall be titled—*The Stainless Steel Rat*. With plenty more volumes to come.''

Bolivar rubbed his jaw in thought. ''You know, I have always had a secret ambition. After lunar exploration, that is. My newfound expertise in banking will be of great help. I have always felt, deep down, that—I wanted to be a publisher. Can I start with your book, Dad?''

''Of course. Draw up the contract and make sure that the advance on signing is a big one.''

"Good as done!"

He began to enthusiastically punch contract details into his pocket computer. James collected the empty glasses and went to get another round of drinks. Angelina leaned over and took my hand.

"You do mean it, Jim, about retiring?"

"I certainly do. If I had any doubts before, this mess with Kaizi has washed them away. There are lots of worlds out there. Let us go out and enjoy them."

"Those are the most beautiful words that I think I have ever heard." Then she dug into her purse and took something out and passed it over to me.

"Found that in your pocket. Want to keep it?"

I looked at it and shook my head. "What in the world would I do with a stainless steel rat?"

"Then I'll have it," she said, and put it away. "I'll lock it in a box and keep it handy. Then, whenever I am feeling depressed, or out of sorts, or worried or just anything except just plain happy, I will take it out and look at it. To remind myself of all the fun that we have had." She smiled around at her family, leaned over and gave Gloriana a little scratch between the ears.

"And to also remind myself that we are all so very lucky that we came out of all of our various adventures and escapades without permanent damage."

We drank to that as well.

At peace.

THE END?

A2 3/00